———————— ★ ————————

The daughter had been written off as a runaway, her mother as a suicide. No sign of either one had surfaced. No sign. No crime.

Absent a corpse, it was not easy to prove that a death had occurred, let alone a crime.

Brian wandered back to the poppy poem and read it again, willing himself to go with the flow of his vibes. He stared at the painting. There is violence here, he told himself. Violence has been done. He dimly remembered that a poncho had been found up on a mountainside, in the ashes of an unseasonable brushfire, shortly after a woman had been reported missing by her apparently frantic husband.

No, this can't be, Brian told himself; it's just too weird. Still, he knew it was going to keep bugging him until he checked it out.

———————— ★ ————————

"...a warm, often witty and altogether engaging debut..."

—Denver Post

"There is something for every reader in this book and enjoyment for all."

—Mystery News

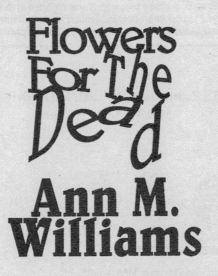

Flowers For The Dead

Ann M. Williams

WORLDWIDE.

TORONTO • NEW YORK • LONDON
AMSTERDAM • PARIS • SYDNEY • HAMBURG
STOCKHOLM • ATHENS • TOKYO • MILAN
MADRID • WARSAW • BUDAPEST • AUCKLAND

To Robert Owen Williams, Jr. (1926-1989)
This one's for you, buddy

FLOWERS FOR THE DEAD

A Worldwide Mystery/March 1995

First published by St. Martin's Press, Incorporated.

ISBN 0-373-28025-4

ACKNOWLEDGMENTS

The author wishes to thank Madelyn Starbuck and Joe Smith, who inadvertently provided the idea for this story, along with all the people who have put up with her over the years—in particular, Michael, Kate, and Karen Lapides, who turned out to be wonderful human beings in spite of having a total wacko for a mother.

ONE

"I'M SORRY, MOM," Brian said, belatedly, into the telephone.

"Listen, sonny, the last time you said those words to me, I scrubbed out your mouth with Ajax cleanser, do you remember that?"

Sigh. "Mom, you never *did* that; you just *threatened* to do it."

"Are you calling your mother a liar?"

"Mom, you probably *believe* that it happened. But it never happened. Take it from me, I'd remember. It's just that you've told the story so many times that you've convinced yourself that it happened."

Silence.

"Mom, I'm sorry."

Silence.

"Mom, listen, I promise. I'll never say 'Oh, shit' to you again. Oh, shit, I just said it, didn't I?"

Silence. Click. Hmmmmm.

Mothers, Brian thought, came with the territory. So far as he knew, it wasn't possible to be born without one. Not that he didn't love the particular one he'd been issued. Well, sure he loved her. Everybody loved their *mother,* for Christ's sake.

"She needs a man," Brian told his cat, Mabel, who had been observing all this with detached interest.

The telephone rang. As always, Brian waited for his answering machine to field the call. Most of the messages were bad news. Lately, his machine had been recording a lot of messages from other machines, a trend that seemed vaguely ominous.

Beep. "I know you're there, Smarty Pants, and I know what you're thinking."

Brian sighed and picked up the phone. A vivid image of his mother—all four feet eleven inches of Sadie Kayne, sea blue eyes snapping, frizz of drop-dead-orange hair standing on end in indignation—flashed into his mind. "Now, Mom..."

"You're thinking, She just needs a man, that's what's wrong with her. She's just a frustrated old lady who needs somebody to fuss over."

"Mom, of course I wasn't thinking that!"

"Well, there never will be another man who can replace your father, God rest him." Sadie's voice began to tremble. "I had your father to fuss over for forty years, and you know what he always told me? 'Sadie, you're going to fuss me right into an early grave.' And maybe he was right."

"Oh, Mom, don't!" Brian felt hideously uncomfortable. "Please don't cry, Mom. Look, do you want me to come down? Maybe I can manage it this weekend; I'll have to check with Lou."

"No, no, don't worry about your mother. You've got your own life, and your lady friend and all. How is she, what's her name, Sheila?"

"Shelley, Mom. And we broke up. Last month. I told you, remember? She's allergic to cats."

"And a cat is more important than a relationship with a nice young woman? You're not getting any younger, you know."

Right, Mom, Brian thought. I'll never see thirty again. Or thirty-one, or thirty-two, or...

"It's time you started thinking about settling down, making a family, giving your mother some grandbabies before she dies."

Brian squeezed his eyes shut. His temples were beginning to throb. The cat had left the room, sensing that this conversation would yield no surprises.

"Look, Mom, I'll be down this weekend. I'll let you know when. Now, go make yourself a nice cup of tea, okay? I love you, Mom. Bye."

Brian gently depressed the button. Why did he feel as if he'd been had?

THE DOUBLE frosted-glass doors bore the following inscription:

NORMAN   BASCOMBE
PALOMA   COUNTY
DISTRICT   ATTORNEY

When one of the doors was propped open, as was usually the case, the suite of offices appeared to house one Norman Paloma District, Bascombe County Attorney. Which made about as much sense as a lot of the stuff that went on inside, Brian thought from the dark perspective of his morning funk.

Marge Hedstrom did not look up from whatever she was furiously typing at her desk. "You're due in court in ten minutes," she said without breaking stroke.

"I know," Brian said, nimbly skirting the man-eating Scheffleria that dominated the reception lobby.

"The Duran case."

"I know." He jogged down the corridor that led to the Investigation Division.

"Courtroom Thirty-four!" Marge hollered after him.

"Thanks!" Brian hollered back, wondering whether he dared take time to stop in the men's room. No, he'd chance doing without—courtroom 34 meant Judge Doherty, who at age seventy-three was sure to call for an early break. He flung his briefcase onto his desk, snapped it open, and began frantically riffling through papers.

"You're wasting your time," Lou Espinoza growled from around his pipe.

"Huh?"

"The Duran file. Isn't that what you're looking for?"

"Yeah?"

"Yeah. Well, you left it on your desk last night."

"Oh, shit, I didn't." Brian felt sick. That meant a stiff fine if building security had spotted it; evidence files were supposed to be locked away when not in active use.

"Well, this time you lucked out." Espinoza slapped the folder down on Brian's desk. "I picked it up and locked it in my drawer."

"Hey, Lou, thanks. Hey, I owe you one."

"Damn right."

"I'll see you at lunch, okay?" Brian slam-dunked the Duran file into his briefcase, buttoned his jacket, and launched himself in the direction of courtroom 34, offering a silent prayer to Bladder Control.

TWO

"DAMN!" JOANNA BARELY repressed an urge to hurl the calculator across the room. Three times she had added up the figures in the "Expenses" column, only to get three different answers. Well, maybe it didn't matter which number was right; all three numbers were dismayingly larger than the total at the bottom of the "Receipts" column. How much longer could this go on?

She closed the ledger and wandered into the kitchen, where Gretchen was embellishing a tray of small iced cakes with candied violets. Gretchen—small but solid, her sketchily graying hair pulled back in a stubby ponytail—created the edibles and potables served at Blue Cottage; Jo's department was supposed to be providing food for the soul—and keeping the books.

"Maybe they were right after all." Joanna sighed, helping herself from the sun-tea jar that permanently occupied the greenhouse window.

"'They' are seldom right," Gretchen pronounced. "You should never believe what 'they' tell you. After all, 'they' told us we wouldn't last a month, and here we still are."

"Yes, here we still are—still in the red. At least I think so. Gretch, I keep trying to tell you that I'm hopeless about numbers. I sure wish we'd start making money, if only so we could hire a part-time bookkeeper."

"Cheer up. You know we expected that it would be at least six months before we started showing a profit." Gretchen deftly slid the tray of cakes into one of the deep cupboards that lined the large, cheerful kitchen. "People don't know we're here yet. There's not much foot traffic on Jasmine Way, no reason for tourists to come down here. Business should pick up when the new chamber of commerce brochure comes out."

"I don't know. I'm beginning to think that the whole idea is just too far out. A bit schizophrenic, even for Southern California. Are we a tearoom or an art gallery? Lots of people seem confused, and I think I'm one of them."

"Piffle." Gretchen removed a basin of grapes from the refrigerator and headed for the sink. "Blue Cottage is just the sort of oddball, quaintsy place that people expect to find in Crystal Cove. The weekenders down from La-La Land will love us. But first they have to find us. Here, slice these lemons while you're standing there brooding."

"Oh Lordy, Gretch, I can't. I've got to go out to the studio and cut some mats." Jo ran her fingers through her pale thatch of hair, reminding herself that she absolutely must Do Something About It before Saturday.

"I thought you had everything ready for the show."

"I thought so, too, but Sam sent three new poems yesterday. I worked most of the night on the paintings. Anyway, I see Jill coming up the driveway, she can cut your lemons." Jill, the bouncy high school girl who worked as their summer waitress, was late again as usual. "Come and holler at me if you get busy, okay?"

Jo slipped out of the screen door before Gretchen could protest, and hurried down the gravel drive that led to what had once been a detached garage at the rear of the lot. By installing an old-fashioned glass-paned skylight—one that could be cranked open to let in the ocean breeze—and a couple of windows, in addition to some rudimentary plumbing, Gretchen's contractor husband had transformed the building into a functional, if not fancy, atelier. Like the main house, it was painted cornflower blue with white trim.

The house, Joanna reflected ruefully, was to blame for this whole mad venture. A neo-Victorian gingerbread confection, built just after the First World War when Crystal Cove was fast becoming a popular retreat for the movie people who had settled on the West Coast and for the writers and artists who followed them, it had always been known as Blue Cottage. For many years, it had been occupied by the widow of a silent-screen star. After her death—she had been well into her nineties, reportedly—the house had sat vacant and forlorn for months until Gretchen and Bill had

fallen in love with its scalloped shingles and intricate woodwork and bought it as a fixer-upper investment. By then,
Joanna had moved back to Crystal Cove, at loose ends and
in need of sorting out, searching for something resembling
roots and stability.

What she found was her old friend Gretchen, also at loose
ends, with two children in college and "the baby" a gan-
gling high school junior. Gretchen, who had been head
cheerleader and champion cookie-baker of Crystal Cove
High School, had married young and produced three children with characteristic efficiency while managing to ac-
quire an English degree and a modest reputation as a
cookbook writer. Gretchen was so different from Joanna in
every way, and yet—amazingly—still and always her clos-
est woman friend.

That crazy picture from their high school yearbook said
it all, Jo thought. How fortunate that she had been dating
the photo editor of the yearbook, and so had wangled the
original print! Framed, it now held pride of place on her
bedside table. There they were, the two of them, side by
side—Jo and Gretch (or "Go and Fetch," as Gretchen's
brother Jack had dubbed them), wearing identical awful
gym suits and self-conscious grins, forever frozen at age
fifteen.

They still argued good-naturedly about which one had
looked worse in her gym suit. "I look like a duck," Gretch
would complain. "Dig those fat knees. And anyone who
didn't know how tall you are would assume I was a midget."
"At least you had boobs," Jo would retort. "I look like a
stork. And my hair!" "Well, I warned you that perm was
going to be a mistake." And so it would go.

Neither of them had conformed to the mold of their generation, Joanna had often reflected. Believing herself to be
apolitical, Jo had had no interest in marching or sitting-in
or getting herself maced. Her indulgent and rather elderly
parents had been willing (and, fortunately, able) to subsi-
dize their only child during her art studies in Paris, her
Shakespearean period (during which she had cultivated what
she hoped was an upper-class English accent), her appren-
ticeship to a Spanish couturier, her brief marriage to a failed

playwright. The years had slipped by as Joanna had flitted from place to place, doing "interesting" things and meeting "interesting" people. Men had come and gone—often the next morning. She had flown back to Crystal Cove to bury first her mother and then, not long afterward, her father. There had been a final, intense affair that ended painfully. One morning, Jo had looked in the mirror to find forty staring her in the face. Forty, in just a few months. Forty with nothing real to show for it. Forty, and alone.

She had packed a suitcase and gotten on a plane, and spent the next two weeks crying in Gretchen's spare room. But somehow she had healed. With funds from the trust established by Jo's parents, Blue Cottage was transformed into a tearoom for Gretchen. Its attic was remodeled into a charming, if small, apartment for Joanna. And so she had begun to create a charming, if small, new life for herself.

Now she looked critically at the three watercolors tacked to the corkboard in the studio. Did it show that she had dashed them off in the middle of the night, half-looped on white zinfandel? Joanna sighed as she riffled through her inventory of mat board. She often thought that she did her best work when she was a tad squiffy—not that she'd ever admit it, of course. She had no intention of ending up in the Betty Ford Clinic. Let's see, pale gray with a black liner would do nicely for the poppy.

"Ouch!" A bit careless there, testing the blade on her X-Acto knife. It wouldn't do to bleed all over the mat board—an expensive accident. Blood and money. Love and death. She looked at the blood-red poppy and thought of Sam's "little works of fantasy." Why was Sam, who seemed the gentlest of men, so obsessed with violent death?

Sam Fox, poet and dreamer—the reason for the show over which she was fretting so mightily. For ten years, she had been illustrating his work, emptying her soul to him in weekly letters, and, yes, fantasizing about him. Would all this end when they finally met face to face? She wondered whether Sam was struggling with the same qualms, up on the ranch in Paloma County. Yet it had been his idea to come down to Crystal Cove for the opening. "It's only a four-hour drive," he had pointed out in his last letter. "If my old truck doesn't make it, I'll hitchhike."

She felt a shiver of excitement and fear. The opening was less than a week away. Would people come? What would they think of the show? And even more important, how would Sam feel about the way she had illustrated his poems and fables?

"Who am I trying to kid?" Joanna said aloud. She put down the mat knife and stared out the window. Of course she wanted Sam to approve of her artwork, but what would he think of *her*? It was strange; she felt so close to this man, felt she knew him intimately after reading all those thousands of words in hundreds of letters over the years, yet she didn't even know what he looked like. She did know his voice, from occasional late-night phone calls when he was feeling depressed or discouraged. Of course she had never dared to call *him*. Even when laid low by the Deep Purples, one doesn't call a married man in the middle of the night.

Jo forced herself back to the job at hand. If she was lucky, she'd have an hour or so to work before Jill needed help with the midafternoon tea ladies. Maybe one would actually buy a painting today, or one of her tide-pool sketches. The collages seemed to be selling well; she really ought to turn out a few more of them this week. And today was Dancercize class; she was due at Sunset Vista at five o'clock. Had she remembered to wash her leotard? So many things to worry about. Maybe if she let her head get all cluttered up and busy, there wouldn't be room in it for various specters and heebie-jeebies, and especially no room for the most disquieting fear of all: that Sam Fox, the leading man of her fantasies and the recipient of her deepest and darkest confidences, would turn out to be an imperfect stranger.

THREE

IT WAS BRIAN'S PHILOSOPHY that the drive down to Crystal Cove was best accomplished on automatic pilot. The first half hour or so wasn't bad—was actually pleasant, through rolling oak-studded hills and reasonably clean air. Even as the sand-colored stucco housing tracts began to dominate the scenery, butting their monotonous backsides right up against the freeway, traffic flowed smoothly—at least it did on a Saturday morning. Then, crowning the last hill and descending into a fetid soup in which floated a string of aging suburbs, Brian knew what to expect: For the next couple of hours, the Southern California freeways would thicken and clog at about the same rate as the atmosphere.

How did people live like this? Why did they put up with it? Knowing that those questions would remain unanswered, Brian rolled up his automatic windows and turned on the air conditioning.

He suspected that he often did his best thinking on the freeways. Isolated in a glass and metal box, he became a suspended being—all-knowing, all-seeing, yet shielded from the chaos that surrounded him.

Somebody had once observed that the freeway was the Great Equalizer, Brian recalled. Well, there was a lot of truth to that. During stop-and-slow conditions, the oil sheik or movie mogul in the stretch limo, two lanes over, was just as stuck as he was in his Hyundai.

On this particular Saturday morning, Brian wasn't sure how much thinking he wanted to do. For starters, he'd have to think about why he was blowing a perfectly good weekend—three or four hours of driving each way—to visit his mother. Well, of course, guilt. But why should he feel guilty? He'd always been a good son, a dutiful son. That he had turned out to be the only child of Sid and Sadie Kayne wasn't *his* fault, was it? Nor was the fact that it had taken him several years to put in an appearance. Once he had shown up, he'd done his best to make his parents proud. So he was never class president or a star athlete, but high school salutatorian wasn't exactly chopped liver. He'd even done well at Antioch, managing to eke out a cum laude by virtue of a straight-A final semester. No drugs—well, no drug *trouble*, anyway. And nothing but nice girls—when there were girls.

Brian sighed. He could hardly claim credit for *that* virtue. The only kind of girls he'd ever been able to attract, if you call it that, were "nice" girls.

What more did she want from him?

An outlaw Porsche cut in from the left just as a motorcyclist was threading his way between his lane and the one to the right. Brian came off automatic pilot quick and sweating, braking smartly but not too abruptly. Ahead, a necklace of red brake lights suggested that a major interchange was approaching. Zoo time. Brian almost wished that he smoked. Now would be a good time to light a cigarette. He reached across to the glove compartment and managed to dislodge a calcified pack of Wrigley's spearmint.

An ancient cut-down convertible, coming up fast on the suddenly clotted traffic, screeched to a stop in the next lane, emitting a blast of heavy-metal rock along with flashes of tattoos and earrings. Brian, well schooled in the Helen Keller strategy for subway survival ("I do not *see* this. I do not *hear* this."), stared straight ahead. Yet the intrusion bothered him; it reminded him of his job, of the unending procession of lowlifes and assholes who ran afoul of the criminal-justice system in Paloma County. If by some miracle the DA did manage to get one put away, another was there to take his place before you could say Miranda. Not that they were all male. He remembered, with a shudder, the teenager who had tried to flush her newborn baby down a toilet, the elderly housewife who had blown her husband's head off with a shotgun because he refused to talk to her.

Well, those were just a few of his personal hauntings and hobgoblins. Maybe because he had strived all his life to be a good listener, he often found himself helping to shoulder the burden of Espinoza's black clouds—those cases that nagged his boss, which even once closed refused to stay tidily in the closet, which awakened Lou at 3:00 A.M. with a grinding in the gut and a profound uneasiness in the soul.

Shit, sometimes even *Theresa's* cases gave Brian nightmares. Theresa didn't seem to need anybody, but maybe that was an illusion. He suspected that somehow Theresa had come to need *him*—and maybe vice-a verse-a, as Sadie would say. Of course she'd never let on.

Theresa Scanlon, the only other full-time investigator on the DA's staff, was somewhere in her fifties and didn't try to fight it, although in her own way she projected a powerful sort of earthy attractiveness. A registered nurse, she had married a cop and produced five husky sons. Widowed early, after Joe Scanlon had been fatally shot during a "routine" traffic stop, she had changed careers and eventually obtained a private investigator's license. Since Theresa had joined the DA's staff three years ago—mainly in order to get decent medical coverage and pension benefits—she had become something of a legend. Her methods were psychologically sound and usually effective. Not surprisingly, she had become known—for various reasons—to both the law-enforcement community and the criminal element as Mother Theresa. Nobody but her sons dared call her Mother to her face.

Yeah, Brian reflected, Theresa was one tough lady—as tough in her way as Lou was in his. And yet . . . Sometimes cases got to Theresa, really bugged her. She always hated to admit it. Whenever Theresa asked him to have lunch with her, Brian knew what was coming: A Son Confessor was needed.

Not that it didn't work both ways. Because the DA's staff was chronically shorthanded, he and Theresa rarely worked together on a case. Their periodic lunches served a practical purpose, in that Brian and Theresa had opportunities to exchange casual information about supposedly isolated cases that sometimes turned out to be connected. And sometimes, Brian had to admit, he had done a little dumping on Theresa—all too often in regard to his love life, or lack thereof. And occasionally, the two of them just got silly and generally let off steam and made irreverent and scurrilous comments about their ultimate boss, the esteemed Norman Paloma District.

Theresa was okay, Brian thought. She made his job bearable when things got really rough and he couldn't bring himself to go whining to Lou. And, shit, the lady was probably his best buddy.

Brian's automatic pilot flashed a red light in his brain. Something was stalled in his lane, far ahead. Given that all four freeway lanes were creeping along at about five miles an hour, he suspected that he was among the first of his fellow drivers to recognize the situation. Think ahead!—the first rule of freeway driving. The number-two lane, usually the best choice for a long, steady shot, was about to suffer a major blood clot. He sized up the lanes to the right and left, and pondered his best strategy. Drivers in the number-one lane, by definition aggressive, could not be depended on to let him in. Drivers in the number-three lane, on the other hand, tended to be conservative, or at least not going far on the freeway. And if there *was* a major problem in the number-two lane, the emergency equipment would probably block the number-one lane while trying to clear up the glitch.

Brian considered these options quickly, almost without conscious realization. He looked to his right. Slightly behind him was a middle-aged woman in an elderly Ford station wagon. She seemed perfectly mellow, playing left-hand piano chords on the roof of her car through the wide-open window on the driver's side. Clearly she had a tape going, or the radio. He switched on the right-turn signal and tried to get her attention.

His lane moved forward a few inches. Brian gently nosed the Hyundai slightly to the right, caressing the back bumper of the Toyota pickup that occupied what appeared to be a long-term parking space in front of the Ford wagon. The Toyota lurched ahead in response to a momentary gap in its lane. Brian attempted to make eye contact with the Ford lady—a crucial maneuver, and not easily accomplished. He zapped down the right-side window and did a lot of signaling and smiling. Finally, he caught the lady's eye and she smiled back, waving him into the doldrums of the number-three lane.

Thanks, lady, Brian thought. You won't be sorry that you let me in. I won't let anybody else ahead of us. He fought back a surge of guilt.

His immediate dilemma resolved, Brian free-ranged back to thinking about Theresa. She had seemed down lately. A couple of unsolved cases had been nagging at her. He remembered the last time they had had lunch together, a month or so ago, at the Gorilla Bar. Usually the Gorilla Bar was guaranteed to lift Theresa's spirits, but not that day. A kid had been missing for some time—and the kid's mother was missing, too. Theresa had been furious at the Sheriff's Department—and at the esteemed Norman, who hadn't let her spend any department time on either case. Two runaways—that's how the bureaucracy had read the thing. Or a runaway and a suicide, as another theory had it.

Brian remembered that Theresa had talked calmly, had seemed under control, and then had set down her wineglass so hard that the stem snapped. "Two runaways, yeah. A daughter and her mother, within four days? Well, if you can buy that, I've got a bridge I'd like to sell you. And the worst of it is that I know—I just *know*—that fucking husband was behind all of it. Oh, he's a slick piece of work, that guy. He's a regular Margaret O'Brien; he can cry on cue. But I know. I *know*. For one thing, I caught him out in at least one lie. That sucker killed both of them. I know it. I *know* it. But I can't begin to prove it."

Ah, yes. Knowing was one thing; proving was another. And District Attorney Norman Bascombe didn't like losing in court, except when he felt under political pressure to prosecute—whatever the outcome.

Brian forced his mind back to the present, to the necessity of getting through the weekend. Why did it seem to loom instead of beckon? He loved his mother, didn't he? He had loved his father—perhaps, secretly, more than his mother. Had he asked them to uproot themselves and move out here when Dad decided to sell the store and retire? Certainly not; he had even cautioned against the move. Finally, was it his fault that less than two years later his father had dropped dead on the eighth green of the Sunset Vista golf course?

An impatient honking from the rear made Brian realize that it was his civic duty to move forward ten feet or so. He dutifully obliged, observing to himself that he could be making much better time on foot—even though he was in terrible shape, didn't work out or jog, and thus (not surprisingly) kept failing the physical for Paloma County Sheriff's Department. Which was why he had ended up working as an investigator for the DA's office, having scored top marks on both the written and oral exams and even on the firing range.

Yet he always felt a little self-conscious when he had to deal with the deputies and local cops. His boss, the fabled Jose Luis Espinoza, had been a hotshot homicide detective until an early heart attack had taken him off the street and into a largely desk-bound slot as head of the DA's investigative staff.

Lou had the stuff. Everybody knew it. Even if he could no longer cut it on the street, Lou had been a big man, a tough man.

Brian, dealing with the rank and file on active duty, imagined himself dismissed as a hopeless wimp.

And then there was the matter of women.

The traffic flow burped again. Brian edged ahead, feeling depressed. Another two hours to go, stop and slow, past oil refineries and high rises and high rollers and low riders. Why on earth had he ever promised Sadie that he would drive down to Crystal Cove for the weekend?

FOUR

A RISING CRESCENDO of barking heralded the passage of the postal carrier down Jasmine Way—a daily peak event for many residents thereof. The pair of nasty-natured terriers on the far corner, just the right height to take a chunk out of one's ankle, began the concert in a shrill flutish mode. The basset hound at the next house—harmless, but known to wander down the middle of Main Street if allowed outside untended—chimed in with a stentorious French horn. Two motley, muttlike hunting dogs contributed bright brass sounds—trumpet, or maybe cornet. Finally, the elderly weimaraner who lived adjacent to Blue Cottage filled in the bass.

Joanna, dozing over her account books in the tiny front bedroom that had been retrofitted, with a minimum of fuss, into a tiny office, was jolted awake by the brass sextet. A familiar tingle traveled through her before she quite realized why. Anticipation. Yay, Carly. What might fall through the slot in the door, to land on the floor with a satisfying slap? One could always hope. Even if most of the mail was guaranteed to be junk and the rest of it likely to be bills, there was always a chance. A chance of an actual letter. A letter from Sam.

No, she told herself firmly; there will be no letter to-day—he's been too busy getting ready for the show. Unless there's a letter telling me when he's coming, and what his plans are.

The slap on the floor was promisingly loud, but Jo exercised restraint. She *would not* rush to get the mail. Nor would she fortify herself with a wee nip. What was she expecting, anyway?

A miracle, of course.

In her haste, Jo almost threw away the envelope postmarked Oak Canyon. It was a very small envelope, containing a very small letter. "My dear and lovely collaborator," it began. And it went on to say that his wife was having a nervous breakdown or something, he absolutely could not leave her to drive down to Crystal Cove for the opening of the show, in spite of how much he had looked forward to blah, blah, blah.

Joanna stared at the letter, stared out the window. She crumpled up the letter and attempted to throw it out the window—an attempt that failed, the window being closed at the moment. She considered bursting into tears and in fact made a decent effort to do so. Finally, she wandered into the kitchen, where Gretchen was squeezing whipped cream into fresh-baked pastry horns.

Gretchen looked up. "What's the matter? You look like an unpicked daffodil in late July."

"Sam's not coming."

"Oh?" Gretchen wiped her forehead with her wrist, leaving a streak of white across her eyebrows. "Why? Didn't you tell him that Bill and I would be happy to put him up?"

"Yes, I told him that. He says his wife's having a breakdown or something." Joanna picked up a cream horn and jammed it into her mouth.

"Jo! Do you realize that you've just eaten seventy-five cents of potential profit?" Gretchen relented. "Honey, I guess I'm not really surprised. And maybe it's just as well."

Joanna, her mouth full of whipped cream and crumbs, was unable to respond coherently.

"Jo, you've had a thing about this guy for years. Face it! You've never even met him, but he's ruined you for all other men. *Real* men."

"Sam's real."

"Yes, I'll grant you that, but he may not be the man you imagine him to be." Uncharacteristically exercised, Gretchen came close to losing her grip on the tray of cream horns as she transferred it to the commercial-size cooler that Bill had built into the east wall of the kitchen. "Also, I might remind you that Sam is *married*. You're setting yourself up for a big fall here."

Joanna paced around the center island in the sunny kitchen. "Sam is my friend, that's all. We'll always be friends. Special friends. You can't take that away. And don't knock it."

Gretchen stood her ground. "Okay, that's fine, if that's all you really want. But you *expect* more; you *need* more. You *dream about* more—don't argue with me; I know you too well. And that's—Jo, that's just crazy."

The telephone rang. Joanna and Gretchen looked at one another. Face-off time. Deflating, Jo said, "I'll get it."

"Blue Cottage," she answered, forcing a chirpy tone.

"Joanna? Sadie Kayne here. Did I interrupt something?"

Well, actually, I was in the middle of slitting my wrists. "Oh, no, of course not."

"I know you're busy getting ready for the show, but I'm so excited, I just had to give you a buzz."

"What's happening, Sadiebelle?" Against her will, Jo felt her mood lighten. Sadie was one of her favorites among the senior citizens at Sunset Vista—a feisty little lady who had struggled hard to overcome a severe depression after losing her husband of many years.

"Well, I just found out that my son, Brian—I've told you about Brian, haven't I?—anyway, he's coming down for the weekend. Isn't that wonderful?"

"Yes, it's marvelous. I know how much his visits must mean to you...." Joanna trailed off, feeling puzzled. What did this have to do with her?

"So I'll bring him to the opening today! You two will finally get a chance to meet!"

Ah. The light dawned. But how could she possibly tell Sadie, an undoubted dear but a world-class yenta, that she had absolutely no interest in meeting her son the district attorney, or whatever? Her *available* son, who was certain to be a primo nerd?

"Er, Sadie, I'm not sure that will work out. I mean, we're expecting scads of people (Joanna closed her eyes and crossed her fingers) and I'll be *awfully* busy; I mean, it certainly will be *wonderful* if you can bring him, but..."

"Oh, don't worry; I'll make sure the two of you get together. After all, you have so much in common, at least I'm sure you'll find that you do. And you're about the same age."

Ha, ha, thought Joanna.

"And of course you're both..."

"Available," Joanna finished lamely.

"Exactly!" Sadie's beam was practically visible. "Listen, I won't keep you, I'm late for macramé. We'll see you later, okay? Bye, sweetie!" Jo hung up the phone and willed herself to have an out-of-mind experience. The out-of-body variety was relatively easy to attain, but left one the prisoner of one's personal data bank. Could this day get any worse? No doubt about it.

Gretchen being nowhere in evidence, Jo headed for the cooler and filched another cream horn. Maybe, with any luck, she would drop dead of sheer guilt.

FIVE

AS MOBILE-HOME PARKS GO, Sunset Vista is pleasant, even elegant. A retirement community with myriad amenities, it occupies a choice parcel of real estate on a high bluff overlooking the ocean—high enough, in fact, to escape the worst of the late-night and early-morning summer fogs. The climate is touted as perfect for growing flowers of all descriptions; indeed, of the several dozen "hobby societies" that flourish in the community, more than twenty are devoted to gardening specialties ranging from African violets to zinnias. Demonstrating sagacious foresight, the developers of Sunset Vista had provided not only for a modest amount of private yard around each double-width unit but for ample communal garden space as well. Those particular features had been heavily emphasized in the slick four-color brochures designed to lure retirees from their dank northeastern winters and steaming midwestern summers. And those features had appealed mightily to Sid and Sadie Kayne, as did the prospect of living handily near (or so they had supposed) to their only child.

Florida, they had tried—flying down for a few weeks every year during what they anticipated (they always guessed wrong) would be the worst of the winter. Florida, somebody else could keep. The ritual of emptying creepy critters out of her bedroom slipper every morning soon palled on Sadie; Sid's golf shoes grew mold even as he played.

They had tried Arizona. "This is not America; this is the moon," Sadie had complained.

"They call this landscaping? Cactus and dyed gravel?" Sid had snorted. "Don't they know from lawns? Can't they grow a tree? Who could live in such a place? And I hear that in the summer it can get up to two hundred and fifteen degrees!"

"Sid, that can't be right; water boils at two hundred and twelve. Or maybe you mean metric?"

"No, Sadie, it's the other way around, I think."

"Whatever, Sid. But you're right. We couldn't live here. But what will we do? We have to go *someplace*."

They were in despair. The store was no longer theirs, having been purchased by a discount chain. Their house was sold; escrow would close in less than sixty days. Where would they go?

When the Sunset Vista brochure arrived in the mail, Sid and Sadie had their first mutual orgasm in more than ten years.

As BRIAN PULLED into the VISITOR parking space, he noticed that Sid's roses were looking exceptionally fine—a good sign. Sadie was Keeping Things Up. He'd been worried about her prolonged depression—a natural-enough reaction, for a time. Having read Kübler-Ross, he knew all about Grief. The last time he had seen his mother, about three months ago, she had struggled to drag herself out of bed in the morning; days would go by when she would not bother to dress or put on makeup. He had been concerned, but what could he do? The interim phone calls had not boded well. They would start out determinedly cheerful, then deteriorate into shaky accusations and self-pitying sniffles. Thus he was not prepared for the sprightly—even elfin—figure, clad in shocking-pink sweat suit, that appeared on the veranda.

"Mom?"

"So who did you expect, Professor Kropotkin?"

"Hey, you look great! You've, um, maybe lost a few pounds?"

"Fifteen pounds in less than two months!" Sadie beamed and executed a kick-jump to starboard. "Plus, I'm bulking up in the right places."

Bulking up? Brian felt dizzy. It didn't help that she proceeded to throw herself into his arms, probably cracking a couple of ribs—*his* ribs. Reality swam in a sea of hallucinatory images. "Mom, you'll have to excuse me, but I need to use your bathroom."

"Of course, dear. You have a thoughtless mother. You go ahead and help yourself, and I'll get you a nice glass of lemonade. Or would you rather have ice tea? I only have herbal."

"Anything cold would be great." He let her steer him toward the requisite door. "I'll just be a minute."

Surrounded once again by the suffocating ambience of his mother's various appliances and appurtenances, Brian consciously steeled himself to resist reverting to age fourteen. He briefly considered leaving the seat up, as a token of rebellion, but decided that doing so would defeat his purpose. After conscientiously checking the floor for drips and turning on a faucet for the obligatory ten seconds, he took a deep breath and prepared to face his maker.

Sadie missed nothing, ever. "XYZ," she suggested archly. He could have sworn that she'd been looking out the window. Brian covertly examined his zipper and remedied the oversight. How did she do it? Was it really true that all mothers had eyes in the backs of their heads? Would it ever change? In less than five minutes, she had reduced him to a state of squirming embarrassment. Or was that his basic state, normally disguised by an unconvincing facade of ersatz couth?

He forced himself to take another deep breath, wondering whether—if he stayed much longer in Crystal Cove—he would eventually hyperventilate himself into unconsciousness.

His mother had disappeared into the kitchen. Ice cubes chunked into a glass.

"I'm sort of hungry, too, Mom. Have you had lunch? Can I take you out someplace?"

"Well, I've taken the liberty of making plans, that is if you're not too tired from your drive."

"Oh no, not at all," Brian lied.

"You see, Jo's opening is today, and she's having a buffet lunch. With champagne punch even! I promised her I'd bring you. She's really looking forward to meeting you."

Brian sank back onto the sofa, glaring back at a malevolent-looking spider plant that depended overhead. "Who is Jo? And what is she opening?"

Sadie reappeared, carrying a very tall glass filled with what looked like lemonade, made in the shade, by an old...

Warning bells sounded in Brian's head.

"This Jo person, is she married?"

Sadie plumped her pink self into the bentwood rocker. "Married?" She sounded sincerely mystified.

"Mom, if this is another one of your plots to get me..."

"How can you think such a thing of your mother? I told you about Jo, didn't I? She has turned my life around. She's the reason I lost weight, but that's only part of it." Sadie leaned forward, almost tipping her small self out of the rocker. She looked intense and earnest. She looked, it suddenly occurred to Brian, almost eerily like Dr. Ruth.

"Okay, so tell me about Jo. I'm interested. Really."

"Her name is Joanna Starrett. She's English, I think. From England, I mean. You know, you can tell from the way she talks, sort of like one of those actresses on 'Masterpiece Theatre.'"

Brian blinked. When had Sadie started watching PBS?

"She's a lovely young woman. Very refined. She has a sort of tearoom down in town, with an art gallery. I mean it's a sort of tearoom in an art gallery, or vice-a verse-a, if you get my drift."

Brian nodded, fighting a strong inclination to nod off. "You lost fifteen pounds eating in her tearoom?"

"Of course not. She teaches classes here at Sunset Vista. Dancercize, and yoga, and nutrition. An art class once a week. She's an artist herself."

"So you've been taking her classes..." Brian was sinking fast.

"Yes, and I feel like a new person! I'm a vegetarian now. Not extreme, of course, but I haven't eaten red meat for weeks. Brian, it's amazing; you should try it. I feel— cleansed! And fiber, fiber, fiber! Natural fiber, that's the secret. But at your age, you're probably not concerned about..."

The slightest of snores emerged from the sofa as Brian's head lolled back and then jerked up to full guilt-ridden attention, although his eyelids were clearly fighting a losing battle with gravity.

Sadie observed this phenomenon with an exasperated sigh, which gradually gave way to a tender smile. Well, the boy was tired after the long drive. So let him have a nice little rest. She eased herself out of the rocker and tiptoed into her bedroom to change into something more suitable.

THE TWITTERING BABBLE of well-lubricated female chitchat was audible from well down Jasmine Way. "I hope there's something left to eat," Sadie fretted. Their destination was easy to spot, populated as it was by a clutch of hollow-legged ear-benders mingling on the fuchsia-bedecked front porch. A banner done up in quaint calligraphy advertised the occasion: GRAND OPENING OF "THE PHOENIX GARDEN."

Brian was mystified. "Phoenix Garden?" he muttered to Sadie. "This isn't even Arizona."

"It's the theme of the show," Sadie said impatiently, trotting beside him on her short legs.

"Maybe you should explain this before we go in?"

"Well, not that it should need explaining, but it's about flowers rising from the ashes. Or people becoming flowers. Something like that. It's sort of abstract," Sadie said vaguely. "Mythology, I think. Greek."

Brian was sure that it would all be Greek to him.

"Anyway, Jo knows this writer, she says he's really a genius. He lives up your way, I think, in that artsy town you took us to once, sort of up in the mountains. Sid got sick on the enchiladas."

"He had too many margaritas. Yeah, I remember, Oak Canyon."

"That sounds right. Anyway, he wrote some poems and stories, and she did paintings to illustrate them. Well, I haven't seen it myself. You'll just have to..."

They were abruptly overwhelmed by the elbow-bending chitchatters. Sadie steered him purposefully toward a destination not yet visible. Somehow, as if magically, the minglers made way for them, and Brian found himself confronted by an elongated blonde dressed in a sort of sari.

"Jo, sweetie, I told you I'd bring him!" Sadie crowed triumphantly. The blush that started from Brian's toes and rose rapidly to his incipient bald spot seemed destined to last forever. Speechless, he stared up at the lady.

She gave him a smile on the rocks. "I'm happy to meet you at last. Sadie has been telling me *all* about you. Would you like a cup of punch?"

SIX

IT WAS REALLY AMAZING how stuffed a person could feel after eating a few tiny sandwiches made of whole-grain bread, cucumber, and tofu. The champagne punch was okay, although Brian would have sold his soul for a long-necked Grolsch. Sadie had disappeared into a gaggle of twitterers. Feeling bored but no longer sleepy, Brian decided to see what this show was all about. Few people seemed to be examining the plastic-sheathed writings tacked to the walls or the floral watercolors that accompanied them. What the heck, why not take a look?

Poppy was the nearest work of art at hand. The illustration depicted an almost obscenely burgeoning bright red blossom—a far cry from the delicate native plant Brian remembered. Petals had fallen from the flower like drops of blood. Clearly, the blossom was in its last stages, literally going to seed. Not pleasant, Brian thought. Not pleasant at all. What had inspired such an illustration?

The single page of writing displayed below was inscribed with a dashing signature: "Sam Fox." Intrigued in spite of himself, he stepped closer.

"Where was my child?" he read.

I knew I could not rest until I found her.
And yet I slept, and dreamed that she was calling me,
Calling from the mountain.
I left my bed.
Wrapped in a cape of crimson, with a torch
to light my way,
I climbed the mountain.
The night was filled with light.
Small candles seemed to glow among the flowers.
My torch failed, but the candles marked my path.

The candles drew me on, lured me down
among the blossoms.
They smelled so sweet, so strong.
They promised rest.
I closed my eyes and floated on the fragrance,
The fragrance of forgetfulness.
And thus I left this life.
I dream no more.
I am the bride of Sleep.

Now what was that all about? Brian supposed that this stuff was rich in symbolism, or maybe it was all so much horse pucky. On the other hand, it rang a little bell somewhere in his head. Mythology, Sadie had said. He knew that many myths and symbols were associated with flowers, but his memories of *The Golden Bough* and such had dimmed. An interesting concept, though.

Concept? Whoa, that was wimpthink. To be avoided.

Brian decided to risk a refill on the punch. He grabbed a handful of cheese sticks and proceeded to the next exhibit, *Hyacinth.* Nothing sinister here, surely. He read:

I was born a prince, a beautiful prince—talented at games and clever at my studies. Powerful beings vied for my love, competed for my attention. I took all of this lightly, as my right and due. I did not dream that anyone would want to harm me.

One day, at play, I came to grief. It seemed an accident. We had been practicing at quoits, my mentor and I. A capricious wind turned my plaything against me, smashing my skull.

I know now that my death was not an accident. My mentor, who feared my power to destroy him, had viciously struck me down. And yet in death I enrich the earth, as I nurture the flower called hyacinth—a symbol of beauty and promise wantonly defiled.

"Beauty and promise wantonly defiled"? Really, this was a bit much. Brian scrutinized the watercolor of purplish blue spikes, thrusting upward amid delicate leaves, and could detect no hint of defilement. These flowers looked—pure. Fragile. Innocent. He reread the accompanying text for a clue to what this all meant. "We had been practicing at quoits, my mentor and I," he read again. Quoits? What the hell were quoits? Was quoits? He vaguely remembered rings of stout braided rope that he had been expected to toss over a stake at day camp, decades ago. Sort of like horseshoes. Nothing that could smash the skull. Nothing that could kill.

Freak accidents did happen, of course. He remembered the kid who had been killed by a wayward discus a couple of months ago, during track practice at—where was it? Some high school up in the north county. And, just last month, a toddler who had died from what the doctors called "chemical pneumonia"—who had, in fact, simply inhaled salt, too much salt. Did salt shakers need a warning from the Surgeon General?

Something was nagging at the fringes of Brian's brain. He returned to *Poppy*. "Wrapped in a cape of crimson, with a torch to light my way, I climbed the mountain," he read. That poem was about a woman searching for her child, her daughter. A woman who was committed to finding her child, at the risk of her own life. Mythology, he thought. Ah, yes. Demeter and Persephone. Or was it the other way around?

All these poems were about imaginary people who had disappeared, or died. To be reborn as flowers, as this writer would have it.

This writer. A writer who, according to Sadie, lived "up your way, I think, in that artsy town...sort of up in the mountains."

Oak Canyon. An artsy, sleepy town where real people had somewhat mysteriously disappeared.

Brian walked back to the hyacinth painting and stared at it without seeing it. He thought about the poppy water-color, and was reminded again of the cases—or case—that had so frustrated Theresa—the woman and her daughter who had gone missing. The popular view was that the woman had done away with herself—out of despair, guilt, shame, or some combination thereof. And yet no trace of her had been found; she had simply vanished, as her daughter had done. The daughter had been written off as a runaway, her mother as a suicide. No sign of either one had ever surfaced. No sign, no crime.

Most people, Brian reflected, think that the term *corpus delicti* has to do with a corpse—a human body found, when in fact it refers to "the body of the crime." And there was some truth to that. Absent a corpse, it was not easy to prove that a death had occurred, let alone a crime.

Brian wandered back to the poppy poem and read it again, willing himself to go with the flow of his vibes. Did this fit with what Theresa had told him? He stared at the painting. There is violence here, he told himself. Violence has been done. He dimly remembered that a poncho had been found up on a mountainside, in the ashes of an unseasonable brushfire, shortly after a woman had been reported missing by her apparently frantic husband.

No, this just can't be, Brian told himself, it's just too weird. Still, he knew it was going to keep bugging him until he checked it out.

He looked around the crowded room and zeroed in on the competent-looking little brunette who was replenishing the buffet table.

"Excuse me, do you have a public telephone?"

"No, but you're welcome to use the phone in the office."

"I need to make a long-distance call. I guess I can reverse the charges, though."

"Sure. I'll show you where the phone is. I'm Gretchen Howell, by the way, one of the owners."

"Brian Kayne. I'm, er, here with my mother."

"Oh, you must be Sadie's son. Mercy, we've certainly heard a lot about you. Here you are. I'll close the door and shut out the din."

Brian fumbled in his wallet for Lou's home number. Lou wasn't going to like being interrupted on a weekend, and his wife, Flora, was going to like it even less. If they were home, that is.

They were home, as it turned out, and Lou seemed surprisingly cheerful about being called away from restaining the Espinoza deck furniture. "You're calling from *where*?"

"It's a long story. Listen, Lou, remember that guy up near Oak Canyon? The one whose wife and daughter disappeared a couple of months ago?"

"Sure. The sheriff keeps telling the press that he's treating the case as high priority, but it's been dead in the water for weeks. No leads."

"What was the guy's name, Lou? Was it Sam Fox, by any chance?"

"Nah, Lloyd somebody. Fuller? No, Fulton. Lloyd Fulton. And I'd bet my bunion that he knows what happened to his family. Is this what you called me collect for, Kayne? To satisfy your idle curiosity?"

"No, no—it's just that I came across something weird here. It's probably nothing, but... Didn't those Boy Scouts find a poncho or something up on the trail above Oak Creek, when they were looking for the girl and her mother?"

"Yeah, they found a whole Hefty bag full of stuff. Hikers' litter, probably. I do remember a poncho, because it might have belonged to Fulton's wife or daughter, but he said not. Of course, there was a whole big area that was freshly burned over—too hot to search right away, and there wouldn't have been much to find."

"That poncho—what color was it, do you remember?"

"As I recall, it was red. A sort of bright orangy red, like hunters wear. Hunters with sense, anyway."

"Was that information ever released? I mean, to the public?"

"Not that I know of. No reason to."

"That Fuller guy..."

"Fulton."

"Yeah. Is he a writer?"

"Naw, he's a track coach. At Oak Canyon High School. Don't you remember? We talked to him up there just a couple of days before the daughter was reported missing. After the accident when the kid got beaned by the discus."

Brian felt suddenly dizzy. "That was the *same guy*?"

"Come to think of it, Theresa went out on that one. No reason for you to pay attention, I guess. It was just a freak accident. No charges filed. The poor kid who threw the plate the wrong way is still in counseling, I understand. Say, Brian, can you tell me what is going on? Flora's hollering at me to get back to work.''

"Probably nothing. A couple of funny coincidences is all. I'll try to do some checking while I'm down here.''

"Okay. Well, have fun. I'll see you Monday.''

After Lou had hung up, another question occurred to Brian, but he didn't have enough nerve to call back. What did this Fuller character teach? High-school coaches always had to teach subjects, too, didn't they? Usually something like phys ed or shop or driver training. Wouldn't it be interesting if this particular coach happened to teach English?

SEVEN

THE DUAL REALIZATION that she had, one, absentmindedly exceeded her limit on champagne punch and, two, neglected to nibble made Jo feel suddenly shaky, aware of an impending headache and perhaps worse. She had an overwhelming urge to crawl up to her garret and put a pillow over her head. But clearly such a retreat was not possible. Grazing, guzzling, potential purchasers of her modest works of art were clustered around her, gushing and gabbling. The afternoon was not yet over.

Mercifully, Sadie materialized at her elbow like a miniature good witch, bearing a cup of ice water. Jo sipped a few swallows and regrouped.

"Oh, Sadie, I'd like you to meet Hermione Balsley-Mumble. She's a famous horticulturalist, and I'm sure she'd be interested in seeing your beautiful roses. Joanna winced, hearing herself babble.

There was an icy silence.

"*Doctor* Hermione Balsley-*Mumford*," the good doctor corrected.

"HerMYonee?" Sadie screwed up her face, thinking hard. "Is that spelled like HERmeown?"

The renowned doctor thawed slightly. "Yes. Actually I've found that many people in this country are not clear as to the proper pronunciation of my given name. But do tell me about your roses. Have you any secrets that you might pass along to me?"

"Well, they're really Sid's roses. My husband's, that is. My... late husband." Sadie's face started to crumple. "He loved roses, grew them all his life. He even developed some new varieties. He named one after me. Princess Sadie."

Jo felt a vague impulse to intervene, but Sadie was off and running.

"Since he passed on, I've had this feeling that it's very important for me to take good care of his roses. As though keeping them alive was keeping *him* alive, in a way."

The icy doctor was definitely showing signs of melting. Jo herself was damned close to puddling up.

"I never knew much about growing flowers, and I still don't. But I did do something sort of special to these roses. I'm not sure I should tell you, because I think it might be against the law."

The idea that Sadie might do something illegal seemed entirely bizarre. Even Dr. Hermione Hyphen Mumbles appeared bemused. "And what was that?" she asked.

"Well, Sid always said that when he went he wanted to be cremated, so as not to take up space. And we arranged for that ahead of time. For me, too, of course. Anyway, they gave me his, erm, *remains* in a little sort of jar." Sadie paused to compose herself, reclaiming the cup of ice water. "I'm not sure I should say this to anybody."

Jo took a deep breath. "It's up to you, Sadie."

"Do you promise you won't tell anyone?"

"Cross my heart," Joanna said. She aimed a meaningful look at the hyphenated doctor.

"Absolutely," Hermione promised.

"I mixed them with the fertilizer," Sadie confessed.

Silence.

"Them?"

"Sid's, erm, remains."

"You put them around the *roses*?"

"Could I be arrested for that? I think it's what Sid would have wanted. More than scattering them over the ocean or burying them in a cemetery. But it's not legal, is it?"

"I don't know," Joanna said.

"The roses seem to be doing beautifully," Sadie ventured.

The hyphenated doctor looked at Sadie and then at Jo. "I don't know, either," she said. "But it's a matter that I certainly shall look into."

"Ah, Mom." Brian arrived just in time to administer a sonly hug to the clearly shaken Sadie. "Are you okay?"

Sadie nodded, but Jo grasped his elbow and pulled him aside. "Can I have a word with you?"

"I was about to ask you the same thing."

"Your mother needs help."

"My mother seems to be doing fine, mostly thanks to you, I hear."

"She may be in big trouble."

"What?" Brian chuckled. "Sadie? What did she do, poop in the punch bowl? Speaking of which, I could do with another glass if you've got any left."

"I'm serious, damn it!" Jo maneuvered Brian back into the office and closed the door. "It's about your father."

Brian looked blank. "My father?"

"Look, you're a lawyer, you should know about this sort of thing. I mean whether something is against the law."

"Hey, number one, I'm not a lawyer...."

A wave of dizziness washed over Joanna. She clutched the edge of the desk. Oh boy, she had done it to herself this time. Hoo boy. Please God don't let me lose it, she prayed.

"Maybe you'd better sit down?"

Joanna sat. "Your father was cremated, right?"

"Sure. That's what he always said he wanted. What are you getting at?"

"Do you know what happened to his ashes?"

A long silence. "As a matter of fact, no. Don't they generally scatter them over the ocean or something?"

"Byron..."

"It's *Brian*."

"Maybe *you'd* better sit down."

"Huh?"

"This may come as a shock to you, but Sadie just told us what happened to your father's ashes. She refers to them as 'remains,' but I think we're talking ashes here."

Brian's expression infused a new meaning into the word *dumbfounded*.

"She mixed them with fertilizer and put them around the roses."

"Roses? Sid's roses?"

Joanna could only nod. Several dreadful physical sensations made themselves apparent with awful suddenness. She yanked the wastebasket from underneath the desk, spun around in the swivel chair, and proceeded to heave strenuously into the fortunately plastic receptacle.

Some minutes later, a damp towel and a glass of water appeared at her left shoulder. Jo mopped herself up unprettily, eyes streaming. "Oh, Jesus," she said. "Thank you. I'm so embarrassed."

"Don't worry about it."

"All of this just...got to me, I guess."

"Are you okay now?"

"I think so. For the moment."

"You'd better not push it, though. Just sneak off and have yourself a lie-down."

"You're probably right." Jo sighed, sat back in the chair, and really looked at Byron. No, Brian. Bryan? Nobody you'd look at twice, and yet a nice face. Good eyes. "I was telling you about..."

"My father's ashes."

"If it's true..."

"I'm sure it's true. Sadie wouldn't know how to tell a lie. She's good at omitting and manipulating, but she doesn't make up stories. It sounds like something Sadie would do, actually."

"Could she be in trouble? Because this Dr. Hermione Hyphen Whatever heard all of this, and said something about looking into it."

"I don't know whether it's against the law in this county, or even in the state. There *are* a lot of rules about disposing of remains. Some of them are pretty silly, in my book. The rationale always has to do with health and sanitation, but I suspect that the funeral directors have a very strong lobby. It seems farfetched though, to imagine that Sadie is in danger of being indicted. Who's going to complain? Besides, I love the idea."

Joanna emitted a stray hiccup. "You do?"

"Yes, and I'm sure Dad would have loved it, too. There's nothing he'd have gotten a bigger kick out of than the idea that he would be fertilizing his own roses." Brian glanced at the noxious wastebasket. "Hey, if you've got an outside faucet, I'll go out and take care of this."

"God, that would be wonderful." Jo suddenly realized that she felt absolutely drained—of no use to anyone, not even herself. "How can I thank you? You've been so..."

"You can come to lunch with me tomorrow, if you've recovered by then. Is that possible?"

"Well, tomorrow *is* my Sunday off. Gretch and I take turns. I'm not sure about the prognosis for my recovery."

Brian grinned. "The secret is getting a little food into your stomach, then a lot of water with maybe a couple of aspirin. Eat some cheese. Tofu. Crackers. More water. Hangovers are largely the result of dehydration. Getting totally smashed can be avoided by eating and exercising before and during the consumption of alcohol. The rate at which the body metabolizes alcohol can be controlled, to some extent, by other substances consumed. The trick is to anticipate, and regulate, and..."

"Get stuffed," Joanna suggested.

"Oh. I'm sorry. I did a senior thesis on the subject. I guess I can get a little boring about it."

"Someday I'd like to read it. Not this afternoon. I don't mean to be rude. I do need to crash, and I really would like to have lunch with you tomorrow."

"Well, you have Sadie's number, right? Unless I get a call from you, I'll pick you up—where, here?" Joanna nodded. "At, say eleven-thirty? We'll beat the crowd, and we won't have to eat breakfast."

EIGHT

HAVING PREPARED HIMSELF for the sort of nouvelle cuisine eatery in which the food is difficult to distinguish from the decorative foliage, Brian was pleasantly surprised when Joanna directed him to a homely-looking café on the unchic outskirts of town. He was even more surprised when she proceeded to order a steak sandwich, medium rare, with fries and cole slaw. "I thought you were a vegetarian," he blurted.

"Who, me?"

"All that tofu yesterday..."

Jo shrugged. "That's what people expected."

Well, shit, Brian thought. He ordered a cheese omelet, with fresh fruit and hold the fries.

Served mugs of steaming coffee, they sipped in an uncomfortable silence. Brian kept sneaking looks at Joanna, and got the impression that she was doing the same. He hyperventilated and plunged.

"Erm, I suppose you're wondering why I asked you to lunch."

"Not particularly."

No help. This woman was maddening.

"As a matter of fact, I sort of expected you to."

"Really?"

"I would have been surprised if you hadn't."

Stall, Brian told himself. "And why is that?"

"Oh, give me a break." Jo tore open a packet of raw sugar and dumped it into her coffee. "Sadie's a darling, but she can't resist meddling, can she?"

Brian chuckled nervously, wondering how to reclaim control of the ball. He did, after all, have an agenda for this lunch—a game plan, so to speak.

"It's obvious that she's been dying for a good excuse to throw us together—I'm sorry, does this embarrass you?"

"Oh, no," Brian lied. "But that's not—I mean, I would have asked you to lunch anyway."

Jo raised an eyebrow.

"I'm fascinated by the show, actually. It's such an unusual, er, concept. I mean, showing poems along with paintings. It's sort of like . . ."

"Television?"

Saved by the food, Brian thought as their orders arrived. Jo attacked her enormous steak sandwich with what could only be described as gusto.

"Do you always eat like this?"

"Only when someone else is paying."

"I mean you're so"—he bit off *skinny*—"slender. I guess you don't have to worry about putting on weight."

"Nope," Jo said between mouthfuls. "Not that I can take any credit for it. I inherited a forgiving metabolism. Hey, you're not eating. Shall we send your omelet back to the kitchen?"

"Oh no, it's fine." Brian forced himself to concentrate on the food. It really was fine—delicious, in fact. He speared a chunk of fresh pineapple with his fork. Why was she being so shitty to him? He pondered, fiddling with his pineapple. Well, for one thing, she might be embarrassed. *He* would have been embarrassed, after all, if *she* had borne witness to the limits of his capacity for champagne punch. When somebody has watched you toss your cookies into the wastebasket, and subsequently washed out said wastebasket, a certain humiliation level must make itself felt, mustn't it?

Or maybe she just didn't like him. He twirled strings of melted cheese around his fork. What was there to like?

As he searched for a reflection of himself in Joanna's cool blue eyes, a new thought struck him: Did he like *her*?

He surveyed her objectively as she dissected her steak. Not really his type, even discounting the differences in height and, he suspected, age. (The man was supposed to be taller—and older.) He saw good bones. Bad hair. The lady didn't care. Eye makeup but no lipstick. A Rolling Stones T-shirt worn under what had to be an expensive velvet jacket, or at least a clever imitation of one.

Why was he sizing her up as a potential date? Mate? This was ridiculous.

And how on earth would she size *him* up? Not that he imagined that she was doing so. Far from it. But still. He fantasized: A twerp, a dweeb. A pudgy little man with terrible taste in shirts. He carved out a chunk of cooling omelet. Enough of this, he told himself. I have to Get To It.

"So tell me about this writer of yours, the one who did the poems or whatever—what's his name?"

"Sam Fox."

"How did it come about—this what? Collaboration?"

Jo signaled for more coffee. "I'm not sure. It just sort of evolved, as Jerry Brown used to say—still does, for all I know."

"How did you get to know this guy?"

"I was a free-lance illustrator in New York for a while. A publisher hired me to do some sketches and a cover design for a book of Sam's poems. I thought I ought to get a feel for the man before I went to work, so I wrote to him, and he wrote back. It took. We've been friends ever since."

"Ever since, huh? Since how long ago?"

"I don't know how to tell you this tactfully, but there's a string of what looks like cheese..."

Oh-oh. Examine Your Chin. Why were women compelled to point out these minor social gaffes?

"So, do you get together often?"

Joanna looked blank.

"You and Sam."

"We don't."

"Don't?"

"Get together. In fact, we've never met."

Now it was Brian's turn to look blank. "How long did you say you've known this guy?"

"About ten years."

"And you've never met him?"

"I wouldn't know him if I bumped into him on the street."

"But, how do you...communicate? How did you arrange things for the show?"

"I told you, we write to one another. As a matter of fact, I had expected him to come down for the opening, but at the last minute he had, um, complications."

"Come down from where? Where does he live, anyway?"

Jo swirled a french fry into a puddle of catsup. "You're awfully curious about Sam, it seems to me."

Back off, Brian told himself. "It's just that the whole idea intrigues me. I've always wanted to be a writer but, you know, I never had the time...."

"Yes, that's what stops so many of us," Jo said with a straight face.

"And Sadie did mention that your writer friend lives somewhere in Paloma County, so I thought I might know him. But the name doesn't ring a bell. Where exactly does he live?"

"I don't know the address. His mail goes to a post-office box. But he lives on a ranch near Oak Canyon. He's sort of the caretaker. The ranch is owned by a wealthy couple who aren't there very often. It's not really a working ranch; a lot of the acreage is leased out to other farmers for grazing. The owners keep a few horses there. Sam takes care of them, cleans the swimming pool, generally keeps things in repair. He lives very simply."

"Alone?"

"I beg your pardon?"

"Does he live alone?"

Joanna waved to the waitress. "I think we're finished here. My, er, date would like the check please." She gave Brian a hard look. "If it's any of your business, he lives with his wife and daughter. Stepdaughter, actually. And you are getting to be a royal pain in the ass." She pushed away from the table and strode regally out of the restaurant.

Oh hell, I blew that one, Brian thought. He thought again. Where was she going? They were several miles from the tearoom-cum-art gallery. The chances of hailing a cab seemed slim, to say the least. He chuckled to himself. Could crow be on the menu for this high-handed lady's next meal? Surely he would find her waiting in his car, properly sheepish. Or outside his car, if he had remembered to lock it. Or—

good God, if he had left his keys in the car, as he had been known to do... He groped in his pocket. Keys were present and accounted for. Aha, thought Brian. I am not through with this lady yet.

He took his time about paying the check and tried not to gloat on the way out to the parking lot.

The car was empty. The lady had vanished.

NINE

JO WAS IN THE TUB when the phone rang, trying to soak out the sundry stresses of the weekend in an herbal bubble bath. The hike home from the restaurant had actually felt good at the time, although if she had anticipated the exercise, she would have worn her Reeboks. Now her calf muscles were killing her.

She determined to ignore the phone. Nobody called her unlisted number these days, unless you counted machines. Did a machine really expect her to have a conversation with it? At least junk mail did not demand to be answered. Door-to-door solicitors rang once or twice and then went away. And so far, none had found the way to her private door, disguised as it was by a showy spill of bougainvillea. But the telephone! We are all at its merciless mercy, Jo thought resentfully.

Usually it gave up after five or six rings, but not tonight. Damn it! Jo thought. She felt increasingly edgy. I have neither kith nor kin to worry about, she told herself. Nobody has been in an accident. Nobody is dead. Everybody is dead, already. But what if Gretch needs me for some reason? Or...

By the time she had rinsed and dried herself, the ringing had stopped. She wrapped her body into a long terry-cloth robe, slipped her feet into the fuzzy slippers that had been a birthday gift from Sadie, and scuffed into her tiny galley-like kitchen to top off her glass of wine. She looked at the stack of unread mysteries on the counter—goodies self-denied while she had worked into the wee hours getting ready for the show. The new Teri White beckoned, or was she more in the mood for Elizabeth Peters? Prepared for delicious self-indulgence, she was in the process of pulling out Sue Grafton's latest alphabet novel when the phone rang again.

Oh shit, Joanna said to herself. "Hello?' she said to the telephone.

"Joanna? My fantasy bride, my muse?"

Jo felt the air go out of her in a rush. "Sam?"

"The very same."

"Oh, Sam, how are you?"

"Well, let's say that things could be more sanguine here, but everything's under control. How are *you*? Was the show a smashing success, or should I tuck my tail between my legs and limp off into the sunset?"

"Lots of people came to the opening, but I'm not sure that we sold much. Mostly, I think they came to socialize. But I'm sure that a lot of them will come back...." Jo felt tears rising in her throat.

"Did any critics show up?"

"I don't think so. To tell the truth, I sort of pooped out before the afternoon was over. But then these things take time. Word-of-mouth, you know." Jo managed to keep her voice steady, but tears were dripping into the dregs of the Guenoc chardonnay.

"Jo, I've been thinking about you all weekend. You did get my note?"

"I got your note."

"So you understand why I couldn't come down?"

"I guess so."

"Are we—okay?"

Jo thought long and hard about that one.

"Joanna?"

"Sam, actually I've been doing a lot of thinking." What am I doing? Joanna thought. I'm about to blow a wonderful friendship. "I mean, we've been friends for years, but we don't really *know* one another."

Silence.

"I mean, you know a lot about *me*, but I don't know much about you."

"What do you need to know about me? Beyond the secrets of my soul, of course. What kind of car I drive? Where I park it?"

"Sam, I don't want to make a big thing about this, but it's just that I ..."

"What kind of toothpaste do I use. Do I floss regularly? Where do I buy my underwear? Lady, for the past ten years or so we've been friends. We've trusted one another with all kinds of shit. What's happening all of a sudden?"

"Can you answer just one question? I mean, oh, damn, I'm so tired. I'm about to crash. But this is important."

"Okay, fire away."

"Is Sam Fox your real name?"

There was a pause and then a definitive click, followed by a sustained hum.

Oh Lordy, Jo thought. Stunned, feeling totally bereft, she obeyed a primal instinct and headed for the jar of Jif in her tiny pantry. Now for a spoon . . .

TEN

BY THE TIME HE HAD negotiated the awful Sunday-afternoon traffic and was coasting down into Paloma—flirting with "empty" in more ways than one—Brian's pique had escalated into a full-scale snit. His total failure to elicit any useful information out of the flaky lady painter, and his suspicion that she had outmaneuvered him in all possible ways, combined to lower his always-fragile self-esteem to a windchill reading of twenty below. He was tired. He was starving. He wanted a beer. And before he could satisfy any of his primal needs, he had to pick up his damned cat, who was sure to pretend that she had never seen him before and who was guaranteed to pout for at least a week. At worst, she would pee in his laundry basket. His basket of *clean* laundry. Women! Brian thought savagely.

Mrs. Otani's miniature poodle greeted him at the apartment door, sporting a fresh scratch on its nose. Mrs. O. looked at Brian reprovingly. "I'm not sure I can keep Mabel for you anymore."

Brian professed astonishment. "But you always say that she's no trouble and that you love having her." He knew very well that Mabel took advantage of every opportunity to bait, bedevil, and generally beat up on his neighbor's neurotic excuse for a dog, and that Mrs. Otani would sooner cut off her hand than say so.

Mrs. Otani looked sad. "She will not eat. I tried Kal Kan like you said, and Morris the cat, and the gourmet dinner that costs fifty cents for the tiny can. She misses you. You should not leave her."

Brian affected shock and dismay. "She didn't eat at all?"

"Some of Tamiko's food, she ate."

"Well, maybe that's the ticket." Brian scooped up Mabel with one arm while discreetly depositing a small envelope behind Mrs. O.'s flourishing maidenhair fern. This was a familiar routine, the only variation being the extent and location of the damage to Tamiko.

Back in his own, by-now-stuffy, apartment, Brian opened a few windows and pried off the top of an ice-cold Molson's. Let it go, he told himself. Forget it. It's all just a wild coincidence.

He had been telling himself that for the last three hours, after the obligatory small talk with and distracted farewells to Sadie, who of course had been dying to know "how lunch went." But he knew he had to check all this out, just a little more. He needed to talk to Theresa.

Brian popped a frozen dinner into the microwave and looked at the clock. Certainly not too late to give Theresa a call—not too late at all.

"YOU BET YOUR BIPPY I remember," Theresa said. She sounded relaxed, comfortably into a postprandial nip. "I was damned sure that Fulton was lying through his toupee, and a couple of the sheriff's guys thought so, too, but we couldn't get anything on him. Nothing. Nada. Zip. No case."

"That was the same guy you interviewed after the accident at the high school track, wasn't it?"

"Yeah. That was sort of weird. Less than a week later, his daughter turns up missing—and then his wife."

"Did you ever think that there might be a connection?"

A thoughtful pause. "No. Just a coincidence. What connection could there have been?"

"That's what I'm asking you, Theresa."

"You know, we really didn't look at it that way. But maybe we should go back and take another look."

"What was the chronology of the whole thing?"

"I'd have to check through my notes. But as I recall, the girl was reported missing three or four days after the accident at the track."

"That was when? May?"

"Around the middle of May, I think. I'll have to check."

"You interviewed the parents, right?"

"Yeah. What's this all about, Brian?"

"I think I may have a lead. It's pretty far-out. Look, can you get the file and your notes together and meet me some time tomorrow?"

"You may have to buy me dinner. I'm booked solid all day, and I suspect that you are, too."

"It's a deal. I'll meet you at, when, six-thirty? Where?"

"How about Sandy's? I'm hooked on their mussels."

"At this time of year, they're imported from New Zealand or someplace."

"Who cares? I'll see you then, and meanwhile I'll try to refresh my memory about Mr. Lloyd Sumbitch Fulton."

"We have a date. And, er, Theresa . . ."

"Yeah?"

"Thanks."

ELEVEN

SANDY'S, ONE OF MANY restaurants overlooking Paloma Harbor, eschewed ferns and stained glass. Nor did it opt for sawdust on the floor. The rather haphazard decor had not been designed to attract the tourist clientele. On the other hand, who needed tourists? The reliably superb seafood drew in the natives like moths to a Coleman lantern. Even at six-thirty on a Monday evening there was a bit of a wait for a table.

Brian arrived first and duly registered his name at the front desk. He assuaged his rampant hunger by champing at the bit. Somehow he had neglected to have lunch. Theresa arrived, weighted down by a large briefcase, just as the table was ready.

"So what did you find out?"

"First things first, kiddo." Theresa settled her not-insubstantial self and waved imperiously for a waiter. "A Gibson on the rocks, please. Gin. Very dry."

Waiters always dropped whatever they were doing, sometimes literally, to cater to Theresa's demands. How did she do it?

"I'll have a Beck's if you have it," Brian ventured timidly. "Otherwise, whatever you have on draft that isn't made in the USA."

The waiter gave him a look, the kind of look he wouldn't have dared to give Theresa. "You don't care for Coors, sir?"

"Cat piss," Theresa summarized succinctly.

The waiter seemed to dematerialize.

Theresa reached under the table, opened her briefcase, and retrieved a few sheets of paper. "I haven't had much time to organize all this, but there's enough here to suggest some interesting lines of inquiry."

Brian snapped to attention. When Theresa started sounding pompous, the barbarians had better take cover.

"My notes indicate that my first interview with Fulton was on Thursday, May seventh. This was routine; no foul play suspected. But there had been a critical injury that resulted in death."

"The kid at track practice." Their drinks arrived. "Should we order?"

"I thought you were hungry for my files here."

"I can't eat files, and I'm starving." Brian flagged down a passing waiter—one who looked less supercilious. "Two orders of mussels, plenty of French bread, and a couple of house salads with blue-cheese dressing."

"Well done," Theresa pronounced.

The waiter was confused. "House salads well done?" He was young and nervous, and his green card was showing. Theresa took pity. She beckoned him closer.

"Honey, I was just telling my date that he had ordered well. Comprende?" She patted his wrist. "We'll take the house salads raw, okay?"

"So what have you got?"

"Well, like I said, we first talked to Fulton on Thursday, May seventh, at approximately five-thirty in the afternoon. To summarize the incident, an emergency call was logged by the dispatcher at four-forty-six. An adolescent male had been found unconscious behind the refreshment stand at the end of the bleachers in the Oak Canyon High School stadium. His name was..." Theresa rummaged in her capacious purse and pulled out a pair of half-glasses. "Jason Banks, age sixteen."

"Why was the DA brought in at that point?"

"The kid was comatose and critical. The circumstances were not clear. The paramedics called the sheriff's office because they weren't sure what had happened—there was an outside chance that it might have been assault with intent. The deputies on the scene called for help from us. It turned out that it was my watch. I think you had gone off to the desert with Shirley."

"Shelley."

"Anyway, as I recall, you had asked me to swap a few days with you, so that's why I caught it instead of you."

The French bread appeared, along with a slab of what Brian fervently hoped was butter. He wrenched off a hunk of bread and tried not to feel guilty. "So what did you find?"

"Well, they'd already taken the kid away, of course, but someone had roughly marked the area where he was found. And by then, we had a sort of story from Fulton, who seemed pretty shaken up. The story seemed to fit, after we checked out the scene, so nothing more came of it in terms of our involvement."

"It was written off as an accident?"

The mussels arrived, looking succulent as always in a sinful sauce of red wine and cream. Brian and Theresa both cracked a couple and doused some bread into the sauce before continuing.

"It all checked out," Theresa went on, mopping her chin with her napkin. "We really dug into it, because the kid died the next day. A depressed skull fracture, to put it in layman's terms."

"Thanks," Brian said sarcastically with his mouth full.

"What happened was, this other kid was practicing throwing the discus. I guess in practice, they don't have the same kinds of protective measures that they use in actual track meets. Anyway, he got off a wild toss. Just as he was about to run out to look for the discus, he got an urgent phone call."

"How did he get a phone call in the middle of track practice?"

"The coach had a beeper. He told the kid to go back to the building and take the call, or call back or whatever. The coach—that was Fulton, remember?—said that he would take care of retrieving the discus. And then he said that he got caught up in something else and forgot about it."

"All this seems a little, er, vague, Theresa."

"It didn't seem important at the time."

"Why was that?" Brian retrieved a mussel that had somehow slid down his shirtfront.

"Because we found a discus a few feet away from where the kid was struck down, and his head injuries were consistent with having been struck on the temple by a discus. We put it down as a freak accident. For some reason, Jason was in the wrong place at the wrong time, and he bought it."

Brian cogitated, munching and slurping. "The dead kid—Jason?"

"Jason Banks."

"What was he doing behind the snack shack or whatever when he allegedly got beaned by a discus?"

"Nobody knows. He was on the track team—a hurdler and quarter-miler, as I recall. Only a sophomore, but considered very promising."

"Okay. So when do we next meet Mr. Lloyd Fulton?"

Theresa mopped her mouth and replaced her half-glasses. "Missing-minor call was logged in at seven-thirty Monday morning, May eleventh. Female, age fourteen, five three and approximately one hundred and five pounds."

"Fulton's daughter?"

"Stepdaughter." Theresa balanced another shell on the already-teetering debris pile. "Jessica Stearns. The mother called in, very upset. There being no sheriff's deputies of the female persuasion, of course, yours truly gets elected in such situations. The feminine touch. Sensitive, and all that." She dug around in her bowl for an undiscovered mussel and, finding none, dunked the heel of the baguette into the remnants of the sauce. "You know, in the city they don't do much with these missing-minor complaints unless the kid is under twelve or thirteen. But after I talked to Mama, I just couldn't buy the idea that this girl had run away, in spite of what seemed to be indications that she had."

"What indications?"

"Her backpack was gone, and some personal stuff. Hairbrush, toothbrush, a teddy bear she'd had since she was a baby. A diary, a windbreaker, some changes of clothing."

"So why didn't you buy runaway?"

Theresa sighed, sat back, and lit the last of her daily ration of Salem Ultra-Light 100s. "Maybe because Mr. Hard-Luck Fulton was so damned desperate to sell it to me."

TWELVE

HAVING LET HIMSELF INTO his apartment, his briefcase bulging with Theresa's notes, Brian shifted into his return routine. First on the agenda was feeding Mabel—a task that required some agility, since she insisted on wending a slalom course through and around his legs as he headed for the kitchen. Oh, shit, he thought. Tonight was refrigerator night for the unused half can of 9-Lives. Since Mabel turned up her nose at any food served at less than room temperature, that meant dumping the congealed leftovers into a Corning Ware casserole and popping it into the microwave while Mabel deposited uncounted and unremovable hairs onto his charcoal gray slacks.

Could a child really be more trouble?

Brian dropped his pants and put them out of Mabel's reach. Well, no. Nothing was out of Mabel's reach, if she wanted to reach it.

The next step in his return routine was to check his answering machine for messages. Beep: "Good morning, Mr. Kayne! May I ask if you are already subscribing to the Paloma *Daily*...." Beep: "Good morning, Mr. Kayne. Are you having a good day? This is Tiffany calling from...." Beep: "Hello. I am a disabled veteran of domestic wars and I was just wondering if you...." Beep: "Hi! This is Tiffany calling from Fred's Fantastic Foto Gallery, and I'm pleased to tell you that you have just won...." Beep: "Brian? This is your mother calling. I just wanted to make sure that you got home safe. You didn't call! Well, you know how a mother worries. And I want you to know that Jo called me today to tell me how much she enjoyed having lunch with you."

Unutterably depressed—if you couldn't trust your mother, who could you trust?—Brian flipped the top of a Dos Equis and strolled moodily out onto his "terrace." This consisted of a balcony measuring approximately six feet by three, affording a view of the ocean when the wind was blowing in the right direction, provided that one squinted between a couple of palm trees. The wind was blowing off the ocean. Brian began to be aware of a bit of a breeze, ventilating his Jockey shorts. When the woman across the courtyard began screaming hysterically, Brian beat a discreet retreat into his living room and closed the drapes.

He looked at the pile of files garnered from Theresa's briefcase. He sank down on his sofa. Mabel, fed and feeling fine, immediately jumped onto his stomach and proceeded to growl in three-quarter time. "Mabel," Brian murmured, "kiss me."

THIRTEEN

SOME TWO HOURS and three dead bottles later, Brian found himself pondering and pacing. Theresa's notes had been complete and detailed—if you accepted that there were three separate cases here. But he was becoming increasingly convinced that all the incidents were tied together. The question was, How? And why?

Theresa had interviewed the mother of the missing girl, one Carole Fulton, age thirty-six. She also had talked to Fulton, to a couple of Jessica's friends, to several teachers at Oak Canyon Middle School, where the girl had been an eighth grader. Jessica had apparently been a quiet girl, a good student, something of a loner. No one would have expected her to run away; no one suggested a reason why she might have done so. The usual networks had been notified, with no results. Just another teenage runaway.

Until her mother was reported missing, on May 15. According to Lloyd Fulton, he had last seen his wife on the evening of Wednesday, May 13. Brian read from Theresa's notes, dated May 17.

> L said he went to bed early, exhausted from anxiety about J. C was determined to go to work in A.M. She was gone when he got up Thurs. He called in sick, stayed home, didn't worry until C had not come home by 7 P.M. Called her boss. She never showed up at work. Called around to her friends. No one had seen her. Missing person report noted at 9 A.M. 5/15.

The fact that Theresa's notes about Carole Fulton's disappearance were retrospective was interesting. Nobody had paid much attention to the fact that Mrs. Fulton was missing, it seemed. Nobody from the DA's office had been called in. Theresa had looked into it on her own. The woman was an adult. Her car and her purse had disappeared with her. There were no indications of foul play. Lloyd Fulton's initial theory was that she had set out to look for her daughter. His subsequent theory was that—anguished and distraught over the disappearance of her only child—Carole Fulton had done herself in, somewhere, somehow. "Probably out in the high desert," Theresa had quoted Fulton as suggesting. "She liked to go there by herself when she felt upset."

Theresa had appended a comment to the effect that she personally believed that Carole Fulton, her car, and her purse were probably reposing at the bottom of Lake Chumash. She also had noted that a search of the wilderness area above Oak Canyon had been postponed because of an unseasonable brushfire on Saturday, May 16. Bells clanged in Brian's head. He *knew* that all of this added up, somehow, into an unspeakably vile stew of which Lloyd Fulton was the chef. He was convinced that what had seemed to be an accidental death and two voluntary disappearances were, in fact, three cold-blooded murders.

All of a sudden, he felt totally pooped. He closed the windows, set his alarm and his coffee timer, snatched up a pen and a legal notepad, climbed into bed, and constructed a "to do" list:

1. Talk to friends, etc., of Jessica Sterns.
2. Talk to friends, etc., of Carole Fulton.
3. Talk to Lloyd Fulton.
4. Call Flaky Joanna and try to wring more out of her.
5. Convince Lou that all of this is necessary and important—which would require, of course, getting Lou's attention. Not easy, given the current departmental backlog.

While Brian was trying to come up with strategies for number five, he fell asleep. Seizing the moment, Mabel pressed her paw upon the Off button of his fluorescent bed lamp and nestled herself cozily between his legs.

FOURTEEN

KNEADING, JOANNA REALIZED, was a cathartic occupation. "People...people who knead people," she sang to herself, "are the luckiest people in the world." Streisand's paean to masseurs or masseuses or whatever. She switched songs. "Dough's a knead, a female need. Rye's a tasty loaf of bread..."

Gretchen blitzed in, trailing bags of basic goodies. "Hey, I got some super apples, free! They'll make terrific tarts and popovers." She stopped and looked hard at Jo, then efficiently stowed her provender.

"Jo, do we need to talk?"

Joanna laid a square of cheesecloth over the pile of dough and shoved it into the cupboard. "Maybe yes."

"Meaning yes."

"Yes, I guess."

"Okay, give."

"Gretch, there are certain things we don't, er, talk much about, right? Like my love life, or yours."

"Jo, will you get to it?"

"This is hard."

"So it's hard. Life tends to be that way. Come on, honey, what's on your mind?"

"You and Bill have been married for a long time."

"I guess so. Relatively speaking, anyway."

"Did you ever think that you just didn't know this person? I mean, were there times when he seemed like a total stranger? Gretch, I know that I'm out of line here, but it's important."

Gretchen took a deep breath. She looked out the window. She took another deep breath. She started to speak, and then stopped. She looked at Jo, who was staring at her, waiting for—a stone tablet?

"Marriage," Gretchen said, "is a series of miracles. Listen, don't get me started. Jo, you can't imagine..."

"But that's what I'm trying to do."

"You were married."

"Not really."

"I guess not. So I'm not sure how I can answer what I think you're asking because... well, I don't mean to sound patronizing, but I don't think you'd understand. Even if I could come up with some kind of coherent answer."

"Try me."

Gretchen looked pensive. Then she emitted a sort of chuckle. "Lordy, Jo, this makes me feel a hundred years old." She opened the cooler and took out a bottle of Chablis. "Pardon me." She tipped an ounce or two into the nearest clean receptacle, which happened to be a coffee mug. "You know what jumps into my mind now? This is going to sound silly. But bear with me."

Jo nodded and fetched herself a coffee mug.

"When we decided to make an offer on Blue Cottage, Bill was out of town. So I initially dealt with this real estate guy, who turned out to be a prize asshole. And the first thing he said to me, in his infuriating 'Little Lady' kind of tone, was, 'How much is your husband worth?' Well, it was so crudely put that I was shocked for a minute, and then I blurted out the first thing that came into my head."

"Which was?"

"He's worth every year I ever spent on him."

Jo was sincerely amazed. "But, Gretch..."

"Oh, I know, everybody thinks that Bill is the Perfect Man and that we have the Perfect Marriage."

"Are you going to tell me that it's all a sham? Listen, I know Bill. He's a wonderful man—warm, generous, perceptive. He can't be faking all that."

"No, he's not, and he is all those things. And we have a good marriage, and I know I'm very lucky. It's just that—nobody's perfect; no marriage is perfect. The imperfections tend to get worked out on one's spouse. And that can hurt. It's all a sort of dirty little secret, because if you're a grown-up and you love your man and want to stay with him, you don't run around whining and complaining about your bruises. Oh, not literally. Bill knows I wouldn't put up with that, even if battering was his style. But yes, there have been tears, and not-so-nice surprises.''

"Oh, Gretchen," Jo said. "I'm sorry. I've envied you, I guess. You seemed to have it all.''

"And so I do," Gretchen said firmly. "As much as anyone is likely to have, at any rate. And now I really do need to get to work. Except that—hey, we were going to talk about *you*.''

"Gretch, I'm not sure I'm ready for another crisis. And I suspect that I'm about to have one.''

Gretchen gave her a shrewd look. "Would this have anything to do with Sam, perchance?''

"Don't tell me that you told me so, please.''

"You know me better than that.''

"That's just it. I *think* I do.''

"Don't be so cryptic.''

"I thought I knew Sam, too. Knew him better than anyone. He always told me that he shared things with me that he never shared with anyone else, not even his wife. I trusted him completely with my own feelings. I thought he trusted me. For more than ten years, he's been my rock and my touchstone. But now . . .''

Jo drained the last of the Chablis from her mug. "Now I'm beginning to wonder whether I know him at all.''

FIFTEEN

"MY OWN TIME?" Brian repeated, stunned. "You *want* me to follow this up, but you want me to do it on *my own time*?"

Lou Espinoza looked uncomfortable. He shuffled files on his desktop and peered into the mug of hot water that had replaced (doctor's orders) the endless cups of coffee that had formerly fueled his mornings. "I did check it out with Bascombe, but I knew what he'd say. We're just too bogged down, Kayne."

"Too bogged down for a *murder* investigation? What are our priorities here?"

"What murder?"

"Listen, Lou, you said yourself you thought Fulton was guilty. Of something. Theresa came to the same conclusion. Has there been any sign of his wife or daughter?"

"No, but..."

"Lou, do you think that either of them is alive?"

Lou sighed and fiddled with his pipe. "No."

"Do you think the accident at the track was just a coincidence?"

"Now, there you'd have to show me some information that it wasn't, because I don't see any connection. And I don't see any motive anywhere, for any of it. And I sure don't see any evidence. Poems? Mythology? You don't have a fucking prayer of a case here. Not even a smell of one. Of course Bascombe isn't going to authorize time on this. If it were up to me, I couldn't justify it, either."

Lou sat back and sighed. "Hey, this one is a tough call. It's no accident that I've been putting you off all week. I've been pushing Bascombe too hard lately. I need to watch my ass, kid."

"But you wouldn't mind if I looked into it."

"On your own time."

"On my own time."

"Right." Lou leaned across the desk. "I won't bullshit you, Brian. I think you may be on to something here. That sanctimonious cocksucker Fulton makes my teeth itch. I can't authorize department time, but I'll do whatever I can to help you on *my* own time, and I'm sure Theresa will do the same. She's already done so, I understand."

Brian nodded sheepishly.

"And if you have to take a long lunch break or something in order to, uh, take care of urgent personal business, we can arrange for that. No need for our esteemed district attorney to bother himself with such mundane matters, right?"

"Lou, I appreciate this."

"You appreciate what?"

"Er, nothing, Lou."

Lou grinned and leaned back in his desk chair. "That's my man."

DRIPPING MUSTARD onto Theresa's case notes, Brian nibbled his Dodger Dog and debated how to proceed. Interacting with the sheriff's investigators was always a tricky proposition. They tended to be paranoid, to resent any hint of intervention, of going over their heads. Yet contact had to be made; one needed to liaise at the outset.

Brian consulted the internal directory and dialed 459.

"Sergeant Kopecky."

"Yeah, Sergeant, this is Brian Kayne over in Espinoza's office."

"Uh-huh?"

This did not sound promising. "I wanted to let you know that I'm going to be doing some looking into the Fulton case. You know, the mother and daughter who disappeared, up near Oak Canyon? That's still hi-pri with you, I understand."

"Hi-pri?" Kopecky snorted. "Who told you that?"

Brian tried not to bristle. "I keep reading it in the newspaper."

"Look, I don't know what kind of bug you've got up your ass, Kayne, and I don't *want* to know. But all of that is dead meat, as far as I'm concerned. The kid took off. The wife took off. Nobody seems to want either of them back.''

"So you're not still investigating."

"Like I said, it's dead."

"So you won't be upset if I do."

"You've got something new?"

"Maybe. I'm working it on my own time. Can I count on your help?"

"What kind of help?"

"Well, maybe I could call you as a consultant, sort of."

"On my own time?"

Brian sighed. "That's the way it is."

"That sucks."

"I know."

There was a long silence. "Look, I never liked the smell of this Fulton guy. Just a hunch, maybe. If you've got something to hang on him, I'll help—providing it doesn't interfere with my bowling or my poker night."

"How about access to your notes."

"Notes?"

"You must have taken notes. When you interviewed Carole Fulton. And, after Carole disappeared, her husband."

"Get real, Kayne. You've been watching too many TV shows."

"As a matter of fact, I hardly ever watch—"

"Look, the kid took off. Kids take off every day. The wife took off. After talking to Fulton, I can understand why. No signs of foul play. You really want me to take notes?"

"It would have helped," Brian said stiffly.

"Whaddaya wanna know?"

"Who did you talk to?"

"When?"

"After the kid disappeared. Jessica. She was only fourteen. Didn't you take that seriously?"

"Come on, Kayne, lighten up. As a matter of fact, we turned the thing over to your cohort, Mother Theresa. I didn't interview anyone other than Mrs. Fulton. She gave me a list of the kid's friends, and I talked to one of them.

She didn't have anything to say. Anyway, that list is about all I ever had in the way of notes.''

"Did you give the list to Theresa?''

"Shit, Kayne, I don't remember! We had a major brush-fire the following weekend; we were all working double shifts, trying to evacuate people and close off roads. I think I might have given it to Mother, I dunno. Prolly I gave her a Xerox copy.''

"Well, Kopecky, I'm going to ask a big favor of you.'' Brian felt suddenly strong, even tough. "Find your list and make a copy for me, and I'll pick it up at your office right before five this afternoon. And I'll owe you one, a big one.'' He hung up the phone before Kopecky could protest, and chugged the last of his Diet Pepsi.

A muffled snort erupted from the vicinity of the door that led from the office into the hallway. Brian swiveled around and saw that Espinoza was doubled over, gasping and shaking. Alarmed, he shoved back his chair and loped to the rescue. "Lou, are you okay?'' His boss's face was a peculiar color, and tears seemed to be streaming from his eyes. Oh shit, Brian thought, he's having another heart attack. "Just sit down. Don't try to talk.'' He guided Lou to the nearest chair and eased him into it. "Shall I call nine-one-one?'' That's silly, Brian told himself. We *are* 911. But what did one do in a case like this?

Lou wiped his eyes and seemed to reclaim control of his reflexes.

"Let me get you some water,'' Brian said, scanning the room vainly for a clean receptacle and wondering whether Marge Hedstrom was still out to lunch, so to speak. He came belatedly to the realization that Espinoza's apparent seizure was not cardiac in origin. "Lou, are you *laughing*? What's so funny?''

"You, Kayne,'' Lou gasped, swabbing at his streaming eyes with a wad of tissue. "Trying to sound like a cop.''

Brian felt hurt. He *was* a cop, wasn't he? Sort of, anyway.

SIXTEEN

BRIAN WAS AT FIRST relieved to find that Kopecky's list of Jessica Stearns's friends contained only five names. Then, when the first three turned out to be unavailable for one reason or another—on vacation, away at camp, and so forth—a termite of panic began to gnaw at his always-sensitive innards. Or should he blame the microwaved frozen pizza that he was sharing with Mabel as he hunched over the phone? At least he had intended to share it with Mabel, but Mabel had pronounced it unfit in her unmistakable fashion, and Brian was beginning to think that Mabel had had the right idea.

The late-night fog oozed through the cracked-open sliding door that led to his minideck. Brian got up and closed it as he pried open the top of a Corona. The fourth name on the list was that of one Amy Jurgenson, who turned out to be baby-sitting "down the street." At least this mother was helpful, and not freaked out by talking to an investigator from the DA's office. She gave him the phone number of the family for whom Amy was sitting. Brian dialed the number and got a quick, if distracted, answer. Enraged screaming in the background gave credence to Amy's professed inability to talk to him at the moment, but she did tell him that although she would be out of town for the weekend, on Monday she was planning to go to "the beach—not the real one, you know."

"Lake Chumash?"

"Yeah. My friend's brother's gonna drive us out and back."

Brian did a quick schedule check. "If I show up at about one o'clock, will you talk to me?"

"Sure. We hang out near where the lifeguard sits. Hey, I really have to go."

Progress, Brian thought, taking a long draft of his Corona. And then he wondered how he would find this young
lady amid what was sure to be a large flock of adolescent
lifeguard groupies. Well, he would play it by ear.

ON MONDAY AFTERNOON, feeling ridiculously overdressed
in his sport jacket and tasseled loafers, Brian picked his way
down to the rather pathetic stretch of trucked-in sand that
passed for "the beach" at Lake Chumash. The sand was, in
fact, scarcely visible. A tapestry of beach towels, oily brown
bodies, and ghetto-blasters surrounded the lone lifeguard
tower.

An echo of the chili dog he had chomped down during the
twenty-minute drive from his office rose unpleasantly in
Brian's throat, along with other distressing memories.
"Why I Hated Junior High School," by Brian Kayne. A
rush of ancient, repressed sensations almost sent him reel-
ing: The obligatory naked trip through the showers after
P.E. class, while desperately trying to conceal his infantile
developmental state. The sadistic teachers, all of whom
seemed crazy in their various ways. (The fact that he had
sort of understood why junior high school teachers were by
definition crazy hadn't helped much.) The superior, smirk-
ing, *tall* girls. Girls with boobs. Girls who had "developed." Girls who, of course, were doing a better job of
hiding their general wretchedness than he was. A tsunami of
remembered humiliations left him gasping for breath,
grasping for a foothold. His loafers brought him back to
reality, such as it was. He realized that he was firmly
grounded, breathing fine.

He forced himself to look at this beachful of kids. Some
were, clearly, already in high school, possibly recent grad-
uates. The junior high kids were easy to identify. They
looked—unfinished. Unformed. Unsure. Too loud or too
quiet. Too brazenly self-assured or too nervously gauche.
Brian felt a wave of sadness—for these kids, groping their
way into becoming persons. For himself. For everyone who
had to endure junior high school in one role or another.

And yet, as he headed toward the lifeguard tower in what
probably was a futile effort to pluck the blossom known as

Amy Jurgenson from this manic garden, he steeled himself. Somehow he knew that, fueled by their own tensions and insecurities, these kids were going to brutalize him. Humiliation would once again be the order of the day. Why did his hand keep trying to cover his crotch? He was, after all, fully dressed. Rather too fully, for the occasion. Or was he?

SEVENTEEN

THE VERY APPEARANCE of the lifeguard—scrawny, freckled, wearing an oversized T-shirt over his trunks and a quarter inch of sun block on his nose—took Brian back fifteen or twenty years, to Jones Beach or Coney Island. Lifeguards never change, he thought. Except that some of them, these days, were of the female persuasion. This one looked grimly determined to ignore the cluster of prepubescent females attired in bikinis held up and held together with high hopes and not much else who giggled and gaggled around his underpinnings.

"Er," Brian began. He realized that he needed to shout. "I say, up there!"

The white-gooped nose pointed itself at him. "Yes, sir?"

"I hope you can help me. I'm supposed to meet a girl here, but I don't know what she looks like. And, um, there seems to be a lot of girls here."

"What's her name?"

"Amy Jurgenson. Do you know her?"

"Sure." He scanned the beach with eyes that seemed the color of icicles, and just as sharp. "Yeah, there she is. Here, climb the ladder and I'll point her out. Oops, watch it—are you okay? See over there, on the striped blanket? Three chicks, right? The one in the white suit with green whatevers on it—that's Amy."

"Hey, thanks a lot," Brian said, meaning it.

"No problem, man."

Amy saw him coming up and sat up. "Are you Mr. Kayne?" She was a bit of a surprise. For one thing, she looked vaguely Asian. Jurgenson?

"Yes. You're Amy, right?"

She nodded and stood up. "You probably want a private place to talk."

"That would be best. I really appreciate your letting me interrupt your day at the beach."

"No problem. Summers get boring. And I...let's walk, okay?"

She steered him toward the end of the beach, where grazing land began to take over from the artificial contours of beach and boat dock. "I was glad that you called."

"Why was that?"

"Because it seemed like nobody cared about Jess. She disappeared, and nobody did anything about it. I still think of her, even dream about her. I can't seem to get over feeling upset."

"You were a good friend of hers?"

"Yes, I think so. Maybe I didn't realize it until after she disappeared."

Brian began to realize that he was dealing with a very grown-up fourteen-year-old. "Somebody did come around to talk to you, back when Jessica was reported missing?"

"Yes, a couple of people. A really creepy guy who was a sheriff's deputy, I think, and a woman who seemed nice. But I couldn't tell them anything. I didn't know anything. And both of them seemed to think that Jess had run away. I couldn't buy that. Jess had a hard time at home, but she wouldn't run away. She had no place to run to. I'm...I don't know what more I can tell you." She stood up and walked away from Brian. Her shoulders began to shake. Her lithe young body was so purely beautiful that Brian had to steel himself against reacting. He squatted and toyed with the tassels on his loafers, which by now were thoroughly mucked up with wet sand.

"Amy..."

She paused and then turned toward him, tears running in an ungainly but endearing series of rivulets.

"Listen," Brian told her. "I don't know what I need to know, but I need to know—everything. For example, why was Jess having a hard time at home? Why do you think she wouldn't have run away? And if she didn't confide in you, who might she have told her secrets to? Her diary is gone. Her mother has disappeared, too. And I agree with you."

Brian paused and took a deep breath. "I don't think she ran away."

"You think she's dead, don't you?"

"Yes. And I want you to help me find out who killed her."

"I think I know who killed her." Amy's face took on a look of dumb defiance.

"I think I do, too."

"But you need evidence, right?"

"You're a smart lady."

"I can't give you any evidence. But I had—feelings."

"Feelings?"

"Look, Jess didn't like to talk about her family, even to me. I think I was the only one who ever went to her house. Her dad—stepdad—didn't like her to have friends in. That was pretty obvious."

"How was that obvious?"

Amy paused. "You have to understand that Mr. Fulton is a really weird man. He teaches English at the high school, you know."

"Yeah." Brian tried to ignore his feet, which felt uncomfortably itchy and which seemed to be sticking to his socks, which in turn seemed to be sticking to his shoes. "But how is he 'weird,' Amy?"

"Well, he seems like two or three different persons. The high school kids think he's a wimp, or at least they used to think so. But Jess's mother seemed afraid of him, and I think Jess was, too. He acted like he *owned* Jess. A couple of times, when I was there, he came barging into her bedroom without even knocking. I was feeling some very bad vibes. I was scared, the last time it happened; I just wanted to go home. Mr. Fulton said he would drive me home, but somehow I couldn't let him do that." Amy's composure began to unravel. "I wanted to call my mom, but Mr. Fulton said the phone wasn't working."

"So what did you do?" Brian asked, his gut twisting empathetically.

"Mrs. Fulton came in. She looked as though she'd been crying. She said she would drive me home, and she did."

"How did Mr. Fulton react to that?"

"He looked as though he wanted to kill her. But he didn't say anything, and Jess wouldn't look at me."

Brian glanced at his watch. "Amy, I have to get back. I'm going to be late for court. Can I talk to you again?"

"Sure." Amy set her shoulders and emitted a delicate sniffle. "Just give me a little notice, okay?"

Brian nodded and slogged back down the beach toward his Hyundai, wondering whether he would ever get the sand out of his shoes. He was starting to get a bad feeling about this case. Case? Yes, it definitely was shaping up to be a case—one that would end up, he suspected, providing nightmare fodder for a good while. All because, motivated by his good old friend Guilt, he had gone down to Crystal Cove to visit his mother a couple of weekends ago. If he hadn't succumbed to Good Old Guilt, he wouldn't be here at this moment. He would never have heard of Weird Joanna or her mysterious writer friend, Sam Fox. If he'd stayed in Paloma that weekend, he might have connected with a foxy chick at the Gorilla Bar. His feet would be warm now, and his conscience untroubled.

Why did people have to have mothers?

EIGHTEEN

IN THE KITCHEN OF Blue Cottage, small sad corpses of anchovies lay draining, unmourned, on paper towels. Joanna, blending unsalted butter with whipped cream cheese, fell to meditating on anchovies. What was an anchovy, exactly, and how did it get so salty? Small as it was, of course, eventually it was bound to be eaten by *something*—but who would have expected that human-type people would gobble them up? Small fry, thought Joanna. Anchovies must be the original small fry. Fried anchovies?

The telephone interrupted her fishy reverie. Aware that Gretchen was doubled over with cramps up in the attic apartment, Jo wiped her hands on the nearest dish towel and plucked the receiver from its prongs. "Blue Cottage."

"Jo?" The voice was silky, seductive, unmistakable. Liquid Jell-O flowed down Joanna's legs and congealed in the neighborhood of her knees. She did not need this. She was barely starting to feel normal again.

"Well, hello, Sam."

"I'm, ah, sorry I hung up on you last week. A crisis developed, you see."

Joanna didn't see at all, but she steeled herself and managed a noncommittal "Of course." What was this leading up to?

"But I've been reflecting on our conversation. And I keep wondering why you asked whether Sam Fox is my real name."

"Sam, can you hold a minute?" Without waiting for an answer, Jo gently laid down the receiver and headed for the wine cupboard, where a bottle of sherry was waiting to be decanted into a handy teacup. How was she going to answer this one? Oh, damn you, anyway, Sam, she thought. Why did you have to call? Armed with her gobbet of Spanish courage, she tentatively returned to the telephone.

"Sam, it's just that . . . I think we're talking trust here."

"Funny, I think so, too."

"I mean, we've been friends for so long, but I've started to wonder exactly who it is that I'm a friend of. I mean, you know me, inside and out; I've never kept anything from you . . . ."

"Is that entirely true, Joanna?" The voice was suddenly icy cold. Jo felt a shiver travel from her heels to her eyebrows. What was going on here? She took a deep breath and tried to feel her center, tried to stay balanced and controlled.

"Sam, I've been totally candid with you for more than ten years—sometimes against my better judgment. But recently, I've begun to suspect that you've been less than candid with me about yourself. I don't feel comfortable about our friendship anymore. I feel awful about this; I feel a real sense of grief. I feel as though I've lost something that had been really important to me."

"This is your imagination working, Jo, your paranoid side. I'm still here. The same as always. But you still haven't answered my question."

"I've forgotten your question," Jo said truthfully.

"My question was, why did you ask whether Sam Fox is my real name?"

"I don't know. I really don't know." Jo felt herself coming unglued.

"Has somebody been down there asking questions about me?"

Jo felt dizzy. "What?"

Sam chuckled. "I guess I can't tell you to read my lips, since we're talking on the telephone. Let me repeat myself: Has somebody been asking you questions about me?"

"Why would anybody do that?"

"I have no idea. But can you give me a yes or no answer?"

"Sam, what's going on?"

"I wish I knew."

He sounded so pathetic all of a sudden, so lonesome and abandoned. Jo felt her defenses crumbling. This man had, after all, been her dear friend for many years. Her solace.

Her support. And what, in fact, *was* going on here? Suddenly, the whole business—Brian's questions, her own suspicions—did, indeed, begin to seem paranoid.

"Well, there was a guy from Paloma County—a sheriff's deputy or something—down for the show. Visiting his mother, who's a friend of mine. And he was curious about the person who wrote the poems and pieces. He asked a few questions."

"What did you tell him?"

"Not much. I mean, how much could I tell him? Actually, I thought he was getting a bit too curious, so I walked out on him."

"You walked out on him?"

"He took me to lunch."

There was a long silence.

"Well, I felt I sort of owed it to him. I mean, the afternoon of the opening, I practically threw up in his lap, and he was nice to me and very sensitive, and then I let him take me to lunch and I was in a shitty mood and he started sort of *grilling* me, and I ended up walking out and walking home. Almost ten miles. It felt pretty good until the next day."

"What was he *grilling* you about?"

Joanna was unable to conjure up a response.

"Never mind. I can imagine. What did you tell him?"

"I told him—what could I tell him? What do I know about you? Your name. Your post-office-box number. Which I didn't tell him, by the way." Jo sighed. "Sam, why does all this seem so heavy, all of a sudden?" She looked at the congealing anchovies on the kitchen counter and began to fantasize about botulism. "Look, I'm in the middle of something, I really have to go."

"Not to worry, lady. We're in good shape, okay? I don't want to lose you, either. Tell me you still love me, huh?"

"I still love you, Sam," Joanna said dutifully into the phone.

Did she mean it?

NINETEEN

BRIAN SQUISHED UP the stairs to his apartment, precariously juggling two bags of groceries and a six-pack of Beck's. His loafers were still soggy and sand-bogged after an uncomfortable afternoon in court, where he hadn't dared to take them off to dry. At the supermarket, out of force of habit, he had as usual requested paper bags instead of plastic—a decision he regretted even before a leaky milk carton had made its existence belatedly known. Please, God, Brian prayed. Sort of. He wasn't really big on praying, a fact that apparently was not lost on God. The bottom of the sopping paper bag gave way even as Brian pondered on how to insert his key in the door without dropping the six-pack.

He watched numbly as the milk carton ruptured with a splat on the aggregate concrete landing and a fusillade of Campbell's cans bounced and careened down the stairs. Mrs. Otani emerged from her apartment below just in time to catch a rebounding roll of Nice'n Soft on the chin. "You okay, Blian?" she inquired—forgetting in her anxiety, her usual careful attention to r's.

"Oh, sure. Fine. A little accident." I will sue, Brian resolved. I will sue Safeway for 10 million dollars.

Mrs. O. scuttled up the stairs, bearing soup cans. "You should ask for the prastic bags. They don't blake."

"Hey, uh, Mrs. Otani, look out for all this milk. It's a mess up here."

"Wait!" Mrs. O. disappeared while Brian gathered up a dented head of lettuce and a thoroughly squashed tomato. She reappeared with a large watering can. "We just frush it out, you see?" She poured liberal doses of water onto the spilt milk, which obligingly ran off down into the open stairwell. Brian realized how lucky he was to be living in a California apartment instead of a flat in the Bronx. Even the most luxurious of California apartments did not have carpeted stairwells. Everything was open in California. The spilt milk could easily be frushed away.

Most of the time.

"Hey, thanks." Brian gave a hug to Mrs. O. Mabel could be heard inside, complaining. At least the Tender Vittles had survived unscathed. "It's been a tough day."

"I can cook you something."

"Oh, no. Thanks. I have a microwave dinner."

Mrs. Otani's nostrils flared and her eyebrows arched, but she withheld negative comment. "I cook real food for you. I am good cook. You can smell, right?"

"Oh, yes," Brian said with feeling. The aromas of Mrs. Otani's cooking had frequently produced pools of saliva on Brian's floor. It was clear that Mabel, along with Brian, had been doing her share of drooling.

"But I have no one to cook for, now that Shigeru is gone."

Oh, Lord, Brian sort of prayed, let us not get into this. I'm just not up to it.

"Mrs. Otani, I'm really—I'm working overtime right now, and I'm—maybe next week. I'd love to have you cook for me."

BRIAN PRIED OFF THE TOP of a cold Corona and looked at Kopecky's notes. The last of the five names on the list of Jessica Stearns's friends seemed a strange amalgamation: Kerry Perez. Well, anything was possible in Southern California. Amy Jurgenson had certainly been Eurasian in some way. There was no helpful phone number appended to the name of Kerry Perez, only a scribbled note that seemed to read "See Quintanero."

Mabel complained, loudly, depositing a drift of cat fur onto his still-damp trousers. He sighed and opened a cat can. The contents smelled rather enticing. Good grief! Brian realized that if the smell of cat food appealed to him, he needed to devote some attention to feeding himself, as well. He selected a box from the freezer at random, shoved it into the microwave, and pulled out the telephone directory.

Praise be, only two Quintaneros were listed. The first try produced a recording telling him that the number had been disconnected, with no new number available. On the second try, a young man answered.

Brian's microwave oven beeped at him repeatedly. He ignored it. "May I speak to Kerry Perez?"

"You've got him."

"Him?" Brian did a mental doubletake.

"Yeah, I know. It's a bummer. I thought of having my name changed to Kelly, but it wouldn't help much. Does it matter?"

"Does what matter?"

"That I'm not a girl. You were expecting a lady, right?"

Brian felt befuddled. "I guess I was. But it's not really important." He paused to regroup. "My name is Brian Kayne. I'm an investigator for the Paloma County District Attorney. The reason I'm calling you is that I understand that you were"—he caught himself up short—"that you're a friend of Jessica Stearns."

There was a long silence, then a sigh. "Jessie."

"You do know Jessica?"

"Yeah, what a punkin. Wherever she is, I hope she's flyin'."

"Flyin'?"

"With the angels. 'Cause that's what she was. An angel."

"You say 'That's what she was.' Does that mean that you think she's dead?"

"Where else, man?"

"Why do you think that?"

There was a very long silence.

"Look, I shouldn't be talking to you. I don't want to be talking to you. Whatever happened to Jessie, *it happened*, okay? Nothin' I say can undo it."

Brian felt helpless. "Look, I don't understand this. I talk to you; I've talked to Amy Jurgenson. You both seem to care about Jessica, and yet you won't tell me anything. What's going on here? I'm trying to find Jess. If she's dead, I want to find her killer. Why won't any of you help me?"

Brian wished with all his heart that he was in the same room with this young man. It had been a mistake to do this over the phone. But then he had assumed that Kerry Perez was a girl, and somewhat younger than this guy seemed to be. He had blown it, once again.

"I'll help you," said Kerry Perez. "If you don't say anything about me. I won't be a witness. I've got a juvie prior, and I'm still on probation, and my P.O. is real tight with...well, certain people that I don't want to piss off. But I'll help you, because Jessie was special. Can you meet me on the beach tomorrow at six in the morning?"

"Which beach?" Brian asked.

Kerry laughed. "The *real* beach, man. The one down by the *real* water. McGraw State Beach. By the lifeguard towers."

"Are you serious. Six?"

"Are *you* serious?"

"Kerry, I've never been more serious. I'll see you then."

Brian hung up the phone and contemplated his frozen microwave Gourmet Surprise Delite. Was it still edible? Did he need to give it another shot in the microwave? Had it been edible to begin with? He didn't even remember what it was supposed to be, and he was too pooped to grope in the undercounter trash bin for the discarded box.

What kind of life *was* this, anyway? Didn't he deserve an identifiable dinner at night? Even Mabel knew her 9-Lives from her Tender Vittles.

Maybe he should let Mrs. Otani feed him, after all. Maybe he should *marry* Mrs. Otani. She couldn't be more than forty years his senior, and at the rate he was going, she was likely to outlive him.

Brian sighed and fished his Gourmet Surprise Delite out of the microwave. With any luck, he would at least lose a few pounds of flab out of all this business.

TWENTY

ALTERNATELY SWEATING AND shivering, Brian coaxed his Hyundai down the narrow road that led to the state beach. Tentacles of dense fog embraced the car and rendered his windshield inscrutable, in spite of the fact that he had the defroster set on high. In his head, he could hear his father's voice: "So what kind of car is this? Made in *Korea*? So at least you should buy Japanese, if you can't buy American."

Brian's paranoid side fed him messages: What was he doing here? What did he know about Kerry Perez? Why had he agreed to meet this kid—an admitted juvie offender—at 6:00 A.M. on a deserted beach, a beach that didn't even open officially until 9:00, if his memory served him right? And why had the kid chosen this time and place? Kerry Perez lived twenty-five or thirty miles away, up in Oak Canyon.

Uh-oh, Brian thought. I am being set up. I'm doing exactly the kind of stupid thing that a private eye tends to do in the next-to-last chapter. Except that fictional private eyes always managed to rescue themselves, not to mention distressed damsels—usually in spite of grievous wounds. And your prototypical hard-boiled hero generally wasted a half-dozen lowlifes in the process.

That's why he never believed those books—well, hardly ever. It was tempting to believe them. They fed his post-adolescent, or maybe preadolescent, fantasies. But how could anybody be dumb enough to agree to meet a possible suspect at 6:00 A.M. on a deserted beach? Without, of course, notifying the law, or at least arranging for backup. If he only had a Hawk...

Shit, Brian thought. I don't even have a gun.

Realizing that he had arrived at the last-ditch, last-chance parking area, Brian coasted to a halt and killed his lights. The fog was as thick as Sadie's Cream of Wheat. The lifeguard tower, if he remembered correctly, was about fifty yards to his right. He unclipped his flashlight from its place under the dashboard, aware that it would be of little use. He sat for a few minutes, debating whether the best course of action would be to retreat. Wimp! he scolded himself. An urgent need to urinate made itself apparent. He sighed, zipped up his jacket, and abandoned his Korean cocoon.

Nagged by a vague notion of ecological propriety, he aimed himself in the direction of what he imagined was the Pacific Ocean. His ears tuned in to a subtle susurration. The surf seemed to be low. And so did the tide, gauging by the succession of scalloped ridges in the hard-packed sand which revealed themselves in the beam of his torch. Just as he came to the place where sea met land, at least for the moment, there was a sudden break in the fog. The sunrise, reflected and refracted by the fragmented low clouds, created a magical panoply of light and color. Brian stopped, transfixed. He looked, really looked, at the ocean.

Oh, God, he prayed, semidevoutly but sincerely, I wish I were an artist.

He scanned the scene made unexpectedly visible by this sucker hole in the sky. Ripples of waves rolled in, gently, sporting frothy tiaras of spume. Litters of baby sandpipers skittered alternately surfward and landward, staying a whisper ahead of the miniature breakers, learning the rules of the waves.

Oh, hell, Brian thought. He unzipped his Land's End cords and let loose.

The muffled hum of an engine in the distance reminded him of why he had come here in the first place—not to enjoy the delights of sunrise on the West Coast. He rezipped and prepared to face the worst.

Threads of fog drifted in again. The sound of the engine amplified. Brian splayed his flashlight around and homed in on a sort of tractor, pulling something. When it ground to a halt, Brian headed toward it. Whoever this was, he needed a human contact. He felt lost. He needed help.

The figure that descended from the tractor was large, and muffled in a hooded parka. Brian briefly considered making a break for the Hyundai, but decided to stand his ground.

The voice that emerged from the hood was clearly young, marginally past changing.

"Hi! I'm Kerry. You must be the guy from the DA's office. Nobody else would be out here at this hour, huh?"

"Yeah." Brian stepped forward, feeling relieved. "I'm Brian Kayne. And I'm freezing." Which was true. A windbreaker over an Irish fisherman's sweater wasn't enough if cap and gloves had been forgotten. "Can we talk in my car?"

"For a while. Then I have to get to work."

Brian beckoned to Kerry and groped for his keys. "Work?"

"I clean the beach, see?" Kerry loped after Brian like a half-grown—no, make that full-grown—quarter horse. He seemed as friendly as a retriever pup. "That's why I asked you to meet me here. I have to start at six-thirty. I do beach cleanup until nine o'clock, when—Allakazam!—I am magically transformed into a lifeguard."

Brian opened up the car and got them settled in. "Aren't you a little young to be a lifeguard?" He finally got a good look at Kerry Perez as the overhead lights kicked in: green eyes in a tanned face, curly reddish hair. A good-looking kid in more ways than one. He seemed like a good kid, a bright kid. Maybe there was hope here.

"I'm sixteen. I've had my senior-lifesaving certificate for two years, and I'm working toward my paramedic license. I'm a pretty good surfer—a board's the only way to rescue people on this beach. And I hold the county record for the fifteen-hundred-meter freestyle." The kid seemed to collapse a little. "Good enough?"

"I'm impressed," Brian said, meaning it. "Are you going after an athletic scholarship? Sounds like you might have a good chance at a school that puts some money behind its swim team."

"I hope so. My first choice would be Indiana, but I'd be really happy with UCLA. Without a scholarship, I can't afford to go away to school; it'll have to be Paloma Community College. Which would be okay for a couple of years."

The kid sighed. "But I'd really like to get away from ... Of course getting an athletic scholarship is a lot harder than it used to be. My SATs have to be pretty good. I'm working on that now. It's tough, because by the time I can get to dealing with the study tapes, I'm so wiped that it's hard to stay awake."

"Lots of partying after you get off work, huh?"

Kerry snorted. "It seems like I never get off work. I don't know what partying is."

"But surely there's a limit to how long a shift you can take here?"

"Oh, yeah. I'm a lifeguard from nine until noon, no breaks. Then I grab something to eat and head over to Green Valley to baby-sit my sister's kids while she works the afternoon shift at Paloma County General. When her husband gets back from his job at about five-thirty, I make a beeline for home, so my mom can take off for *her* job."

Brian digested and pondered. "Why is that necessary?"

"Huh?"

"To be home before your mother leaves. Do you have to baby-sit at home, too?"

Kerry sighed. "In a manner of speaking. My dad had a stroke last year. He, er, can't be left alone."

Good Lord. Why did people keep saying that kids had it too easy these days? They sure weren't talking about *this* kid.

"That sounds like an awfully strenuous schedule."

"It's not so bad. During the school year, it's worse. I have to get up every morning at four-thirty to drive down to Paloma for swim-team practice. Oak Canyon High is too small to have its own pool."

The mention of Oak Canyon High reminded Brian that he needed to change the subject. And Kerry seemed to be getting fidgety. The kid had responsibilities here, after all.

"Kerry," he began gently, "about Jessica ..."

Kerry stiffened, and visibly reverted to his flip, streetwise persona. "Man, I don't know ..."

"Just tell me how you got to know her," Brian said in what he hoped was a relaxed, nonthreatening manner. "I mean, you're in high school and she was only in junior high. Were you neighbors?''

"Naw, she lived—lives—out in the boonies somewhere. I met her at a church group for kids. Youth for Christ. It's about the only action going in Oak Canyon if you're under eighteen. There are almost two hundred members. It's weird, because the church that sponsors it is pretty small. Most of the kids aren't members of the church; they don't even go to services there. But it's open to everyone, and the people who run it are a lot of fun. They have neat ideas about projects and things to do, and they don't get too involved with all this fundamentalist sh . . . stuff. Otherwise I wouldn't feel comfortable about going, because I'm Catholic.''

"Was Jessica a member of the church?''

"Yeah, I think so. Her father, I mean stepfather, was superreligious, a real nut. He wouldn't let Jessie do *anything*. But he did let her go to Youth for Christ meetings. And that's where she . . .'' Kerry shot the cuff of his parka and looked at his watch. "I really have to get out there and do my job now, I'm sorry. I'm late getting started already.''

Oh, no. He was just getting this kid to open up. Brian frantically groped for innovative strategies. "Can I come with you?''

Kerry stared at him. "Come *with* me?''

"Yeah. I mean, can I ride pillion, go along with you? Then we could keep on talking. Is there a place on your, um, beach-cleaning machine for me to sort of latch on to?''

Kerry thought for a moment. "I guess it might work. It won't be very comfortable. You'll have to hang on tight. If you fall off the tractor, you won't be a pretty sight.''

Brian heroically repressed images of being raked over with the rest of the beach debris. "If I feel myself losing my grip, can you stop fairly quickly?''

"Shit, yes. I go about five miles an hour max, and it's a struggle to do that. But I could lose my job if we screw this up, and my brother-in-law could lose his.''

"Your brother-in-law?''

"Yeah. Mark's in charge of maintenance for McGraw State Beach." Kerry stifled a giggle. "I may be qualified for this job, but you don't think that's why I *got* it, do you?"

"Erm," Brian replied.

"Anyway, I gotta boogie. Are we on for this? Make up your mind before I change mine."

Brian sighed and reflected that his will and his life-insurance policies were in order, and that Mrs. Otani would surely break down and take in Mabel.

"We're on," he said resignedly.

TWENTY-ONE

OH-H-H-H MY-Y-Y-Y God-d-d-d, Brian thought. Weren't beaches supposed to be smooth? This was like battling the mid-February ice ruts in Queens—on a pogo stick. He tried not to concentrate on his tenuous foothold as he attempted to hug Kerry Perez, whose water-repellent parka was much too slippery for comfort, in a life-or-death grip. His teeth juddered. He needed to keep his tongue out of the way of his teeth, Brian told himself. Otherwise, he might bleed to death out here. The ensuing publicity would not be appreciated by the Paloma County District Attorney's office.

How could he possibly talk to the kid under these— OOF!—circumstances?

He realized belatedly that the kid was talking to *him*—in fact, had embarked on a sort of monologue—and that if he stopped worrying about his precarious physical situation he might be able to hear. Snatches, at least. He hugged Kerry tighter, at the risk of having his intentions misunderstood.

"...Easter Parade," Kerry seemed to be saying. Huh? "We ended up on the same float committee, and so we got to be pretty tight."

"P-p-arade?"

The tractor seemed to leave the ground entirely, having encountered a sort of Grand Canyon of ruts. "Hi-yee!" Kerry yelled. Brian was incapable of speech. He was barely able to breathe. The kid is enjoying this, he thought. Okay. He attempted to readjust his feet on the slender bar at the rear of the tractor, thanking Something Up There that he had had the foresight to wear his New Balances instead of the usual loafers. He clawed for a better grip on Kerry's parka, which was getting slipperier by the second.

In an instant, the fog was somehow, magically, gone. "All right," Kerry said. "Whoa, I need to take off this thing or I'll be steamed pig in ten minutes." He cut the engine on the

tractor. Brian slid off the rear, feeling miraculously re-
deemed. He could not have lasted much longer, he was sure.

Kerry unsnapped his parka and stowed it somewhere under what passed for a dashboard. "Where was I?"

"Something about a float?"

"Oh, yeah. Are you still game for this, by the way? It's
been pretty rough, I know."

"I think it's going to get better."

Kerry laughed. "And it's going to get warmer. Tell me
when you want to take off your jacket, and I'll stop." He
climbed back onto the seat and kicked in the tractor engine. Brian resumed his precarious perch with mixed emo-
tions. But it *was* a lot better, now that he could see where
they were going and anticipate the ruts.

"Well, Russ and Kathy—the couple who run Youth for
Christ—got this idea about having an Easter Parade, with
floats. They divided us up into teams of four or five. It was
going to be a competition. They got the Oak Canyon
Chamber of Commerce involved, and the high school, and
all sorts of people. We had a real Easter Parade right down
the middle of Main Street. Man, it was a blast!"

Brian, by now used to the jouncing and feeling more
confident about his physical security, began to realize that
he was losing the thread of Kerry's narrative. OOMP! He
was also forgetting to watch out for ruts. Clutching Kerry's
sweatshirt, he centered himself.

"Sounds great. Tell me about your team. And what all
this has to do with Jessica."

"Well, I mean, that was the team. *Our* team. Me and
Jessie and Amy and Jason. None of us really knew each
other that well before, but we got—close. Working hard together, for a few weeks, you get close. It's tough to explain."

"I think I understand."

"Jessie was so quiet." Kerry expertly detoured around a
clump of rocks. "At first, she seemed scared of us. I mean
physically scared. She'd stiffen up and sort of shiver if one
of us accidentally touched her. Amy really worked at making her feel easy, and I think that helped. She and Amy got
pretty tight after a few days."

"Amy seems like a very mature young lady," Brian observed. He was starting to get into the rhythm of the thing now, sort of like riding a horse.

"Yeah." Kerry went suddenly, self-consciously, silent.

Aha, Brian thought. He quickly shifted back into the Jessica mode. "And then what happened?"

"Well, I didn't realize it right away, but Jessie and Jason—they were getting a *thing* for one another. Jason was pretty shy, too; I don't think he'd ever had a girlfriend, and..."

"Wait a minute." Brian connected, belatedly. "Jason?"

"Jason Banks. He was killed right before Jessie disappeared. It was one of those fluke accidents. He got hit in the head by a discus, during track practice. That was hard enough to take, but then when Jessie went, I..."

Brian said nothing for a while. He could feel the kid's shoulders shaking. Finally, the tractor pulled up in front of an equipment shed. Kerry went inside and reemerged wearing stout gloves and carrying a box of heavy-duty lawn-and-leaf bags. He disengaged the rake/disker contraption from the tractor and replaced it with a small open trailer.

"I take a little break now," Kerry said. "Maybe ten minutes. Then I have to go around and pick up everything that isn't biodegradable."

"Will you talk to me for ten more minutes?"

Kerry looked down at the sand and sighed. "I guess."

"Why did you tell me that you were sure that Jessica is dead? What do you know—or suspect—that you haven't told me?"

The kid took a deep breath and let it out slowly. "I don't *know* this, understand? I guess it's what you guys call hearsay evidence."

"Hearsay evidence is not admissible in court," Brian said very carefully. "But it's often important to an investigation."

"Well." An even deeper breath. "Like I said, Jessie and Jase got close. She wasn't allowed to go out on dates, but sometimes Amy and I would sort of cover for her, you know? So they did manage to have some time by themselves. They'd go hiking up in the hills, and sometimes they'd come over to my place in the evening and go down in the basement and listen to records. Jason didn't have wheels, so there wasn't much they could do. But they spent as much time together as they could.'' Kerry stripped off his gloves and threw them down on the sand. His face was a study in wretchedness.

Brian forced back his impatience. "What is this leading up to, Kerry?"

"I promised Jason I'd never tell anybody!"

Brian held his tongue and his breath.

"One night, after we'd driven Jessie home—she lived out of town on a ranch up toward the hills—Jason got really upset. I mean, he wanted to go out and get a couple of six-packs and get wasted, which was unreal because the guy was seriously into training for track season and, I mean, *clean*. Totally into this 'my body is a temple' business. I knew something had to be really wrong, so I encouraged him to talk about whatever it was. And afterward, I was sorry. Because he told me something I didn't want to know."

Brian waited. "But now you do know."

"I don't *know*. I only know what he told me. What he told me Jessie told him. So that's sort of double hearsay, huh?"

"I'm not a judge. But it might be important. So why don't you tell me?"

Kerry walked a few paces toward the breaking waves and stared out at the horizon. When he turned back toward Brian, his jaw was set in an expression of intense determination, but his eyes . . .

"You have to understand something, Mr. DA. A year or so ago, I did a really dumb thing, and it got me into a whole shitload of trouble. I don't want to get into the details, but I'm still on probation. Okay, I was willing to pay the price and I'll never do anything like it again. But I need to clear my record in order to get any kind of scholarship, to a good college or even a bad one. It's my only ticket out of here, out of this life."

Brian, puzzled, remained mute. "So?" he finally said.

"Jessie's stepfather is Mr. Fulton. He teaches at my high school. And he's the chairman of the committee—that's a laugh; he *is* the committee—that writes scholarship recommendation letters."

"I don't understand how this connects," Brian said slowly.

Kerry picked up his gloves. He stared at them as though they were Slime from Another Planet.

"I told you that Jase was upset that night. He finally told me why. Jessie wouldn't let him kiss her, even touch her. He didn't understand. She would freak out if he put his arm around her. And yet she seemed to trust him, he said. And then, that night, she told him why she couldn't let him touch her, even though she wanted to."

An awful certainty clamped itself around Brian's temples, metastasizing into his gut. Somehow he didn't need to hear the rest of this story. He *knew* the rest of it, or so he was very much afraid. "Why *was* that, Kerry?"

Kerry's face scrooonched up and he suddenly looked about four and a half, fighting back unmanly tears. "Because Fulton had been *doing it* to her for years. Since she was nine." The tears spilled over the dam, and Kerry turned his back quickly.

Brian took a deep breath. "That's very bad. Very bad. I can't think of many things that are worse." He felt totally inadequate.

Kerry picked up the box of lawn-and-leaf bags and dropkicked it forty yards down the beach. "Well I can."

"You can?"

"Yeah. Jessie thought she was pregnant."

TWENTY-TWO

IGNORING AT HIS PERIL Mabel's loud complaints that her litter box was no longer in a condition that could be tolerated by a fastidious feline, Brian hit the shower and changed into nonbeach gear. He slung a Great Starts breakfast (French toast with sausages) into the microwave and poured himself a large glass of orange juice. He needed to talk to Theresa. Mabel continued to complain. He checked her dishes and replenished the dry cat food and water.

Oh, shit, he thought. He knew he'd be sorry if he didn't strain out her box. She was a worse nag than his mother.

Half an hour later, he was loping into the office suite inhabited by the famous Norman Paloma District, wincing only slightly from the effects of his morning workout. He knew all too well that he'd feel worse tomorrow.

"Where's Theresa?" he gasped at Marge Hedstrom, who seemed to be sporting a mauve rinse on her colorless hair. No, *colorless* wasn't the right word—Marge's hair was always *some* color, but seldom the same color two weeks in a row. Was that why he secretly thought of her as Marge Headstorm?

Marge looked irritated. "How the hell should I know?"

"You're supposed to keep track of us!"

Marge rolled her eyes and refrained from comment.

Brian blitzed down the hall and slid into home base, so to speak. Lou Espinoza looked up at him from the perspective of his pipe.

"Where the hell have you been, Kayne?"

"On the beach, actually." Brian checked himself for lingering sandburs. "Did I miss something?"

"Theresa's been trying to get hold of you."

"Theresa?" Brian barely kept himself from yelping. "I need to talk to *her* too. Where is she?"

"She had to go out on a juvie call. A thirteen-year-old girl beat up her mother, bad."

"Oh, my God," Brian said. "Beat up her *mother*? How can that be?"

"Easy," Lou said. "The kid is maybe five eight, one hundred and fifty, from what we got. The mother is pretty frail and has multiple sclerosis."

"Oh, shit. East Paloma, right?"

"Wrong. El Rancho Rio. That fancy-schmancy development of avocado miniranches up Santa Rita way. Those people act rich, but they're all going broke; they can't pay their mortgages; they can't even take the tax deductions anymore. And their kids go crazy because they're out in the middle of nowhere. They can't get to anywhere. They get cabin fever and go bonkers. The mothers get cabin fever and go bonkers." Lou sighed. "I don't know, Brian. I think I need to take my retirement and go...where? Bonkers?"

Brian chuckled nervously. "Bonkers, New York?"

Lou banged his meaty fist down on the desk. "I'm serious! There's a real issue here. Flora sells real estate, right? At least she tries to. But she has a problem with that. These people come out here on weekends, in their RVs. They come out from the Valley or from the West Side, for the most part. They're all looking for the same thing: a custom home on a half-acre, a place where they can keep a horse or at least a pony—for their kids. They want to be out in the country. They want some land around them. No crime. And, of course, they want all this for less than two hundred grand. With full-service amenities. Flora tries to tell them that they're chasing an impossible dream, but they don't listen. They don't want to listen. And the ones who finally give up the dream are the lucky ones, because the people who *do* find a place and buy it end up in shit up to their armpits. Every time."

Brian did his breathing exercises and absorbed Lou's data dump. He cogitated.

"This family—the situation Theresa went out on—Lou, I don't want to poke my nose in where it doesn't belong, but did Flora by any chance sell that house to those people?"

There was a long silence. Lou stood up suddenly and hurled his pipe across the room. It shattered against a bank of filing cabinets. Lou said nothing. Brian said nothing. There was nothing to say.

BRIAN WAS ON THE VERGE of going out for lunch when Theresa finally checked back in at the office, looking dangerously surly. He intercepted her, managing to fend off the briefcase that she had hurled in the general direction of his desk. "A bad one, huh?"

Theresa looked every one of her fifty-umph years and then some. "God, Brian. I don't believe people. I used to think that if kids did bad things, it was because grown-ups had done bad things to *them*. I tried to believe that for a long time."

"Some kids are just—evil, I think," Brian ventured. "From the beginning. Who knows why?"

"The 'bad seed' syndrome, huh?"

"It happens, I think. Not often." Brian approached Theresa and gave her a tentative hug. "We need food. What are you in the mood for?"

Theresa let out a long breath. "How about a tuna salad on whole wheat with plenty of mayo. An ice-cold beer. Maybe two."

"Sounds great. Where can we get that?"

"My house," Theresa said. "You can make the sandwiches while I take a long, hot shower."

"That bad, was it?"

"That bad. You drive."

BRIAN LET THERESA cool out while he negotiated the narrow roads and hairpin bends that led to her comfortably funky house up in the high Paloma foothills. It was far too large for a woman living alone, but it was paid for, and sometimes Theresa needed a lot of space. Besides, the "boys" came home from time to time and brought their wives and children; during the Christmas holidays, the house was always packed to the rafters.

Theresa coped with all of this in a kind of absent-minded way. She cooked, after a fashion. She let the daughters-in-law clean up after and take care of their own kids. She was glad to see them all arrive and relieved when they left. She had her own life to live. She didn't try to live their lives for them. She left them alone, and they left her alone. If alone was sometimes too much alone, Theresa never let on.

"I need to talk to you," Brian ventured. "About this Fulton thing. I guess you tried to reach me, too."

He pulled into the driveway of Theresa's 1950s-vintage cutesy split-level ranch-style house. Cunningly tucked into the hillside, it seemed in imminent danger of being devoured by the surrounding vegetation.

Theresa groped in her purse for the house key. "Yeah. I'd almost forgotten. Oh, boy, many more of these cases and I'm outta here." She dragged herself up the curving steps that led to the front door.

Brian felt suddenly scared. Lou. Theresa. He realized, suddenly, that they were—well, not old, but getting there. Wearing out? Oh, no. He depended on them. He looked up to them. What would happen when they were gone? Not dead, necessarily, but gone. Maybe even dead. You never know. Look at his father.

He shuddered. He knew what would happen. He would move up to the head of the line.

Brian sleepwalked through Theresa's house to the kitchen, moving on automatic pilot. Anyone entering Theresa's house went directly to the kitchen. That was a given. The kitchen had a wonderful view of the Pacific Ocean, unless there was a fog. And the kitchen was where the food was.

There was also a cheery eating area in a sort of benched bay window. Theresa plopped herself down and put her head on her hands. "Bring me a beer, honey."

Brian had spent enough time in Theresa's kitchen to know his way around. He checked the refrigerator and found some cold Buds. Also some celery and scallions. The bread was reposing therein, as well. The pantry yielded many cans of Chicken of the Sea tuna, water-packed. He went to work.

"Theresa, I can't find the mayonnaise."

"I just bought a new jar. It's in the closet."

Could Theresa be crying? No, probably just coming down with a cold, or an allergy. It was getting to be allergy season. Brian steeled himself not to look at her. If Theresa was coming apart, what hope was there for him? He hauled out the breadboard and chopped some celery and scallions and lathered four slices of Oroweat with whipped margarine. He found the paprika and a plastic lemon and mooshed a tuna salad together, mourning the absence of a handful of chopped hard-boiled egg.

"Dill pickles?"

"Top shelf of the fridge, on the left."

He speared a couple of Vlasic wedges and laid out lunch on the two mismatched plates that happened to be on the top of the pile. He cracked the last two Buds, ripped off a couple of paper towels in lieu of napkins, and presented his peasant repast.

"God, Brian, this looks great." Theresa tore into it. She was obviously hungry. Brian felt good. Was this how women felt, he wondered, when they gave you good food and you ate it with gusto? He had a sudden flash of understanding as to what had motivated his mother over the years. Here, eat! So enjoy, already! He realized that he was starving himself, and attacked his own sandwich.

Their initial hunger sated, Theresa and Brian tried to talk at the same time.

"Why did you call me?" Brian got his question in first. "Does it have anything to do with the Fulton case?"

"It might," Theresa mused. "I was taking a break with the deputy who originally caught this...situation I went out on this morning, and he just sort of mentioned casually that his kid had found a bone. Well, his kid's *dog* had found a bone. They had been hiking up in the hills, and the dog—a golden retriever—came loping back, all wagging and drooling, with a bone. The kid is some sort of science whiz, I guess. He pegged the bone as a human femur, even though it was charred and partially destroyed."

"Femur?" Brian did a frantic data search of his brain.

"A thighbone. The kid was all excited. He told his dad that the femur is an important bone, forensically. He was convincing enough so that his father—Rich Wing, a good guy; I think you know him—bagged the bone and had it sent down to the lab."

"That's interesting." Brian washed down a bite of sand-wich with a swallow of beer. "But how do you figure that it ties in to the Fulton case?"

"Well, as I said, this kid is a science nut. His ambition, for Christ's sake, is to be a forensic pathologist—a sort of Quincy. And before he gave the bone fragment to his fa-ther, he did some measurements and calculations."

"Whoa." Brian crunched a chunk of pickle. "No, I won't ask why. Go ahead. What did he calculate?"

"That the bone had belonged to a young adult female, whose height was somewhere between five feet two and five feet four. That the bone fragment had been buried for more than a month but less than six months."

"That's a pretty sharp baby pathologist, if he knows what he's talking about."

"His father seems to think so. And we don't have a whole shitload of missing young adult females around here."

Brian chugged the rest of the bottle. "You're thinking Jessica Stearns, right?"

"Right." Theresa sighed and her face seemed to sag. "And so was he."

TWENTY-THREE

PROBING WITH HIS TONGUE for stray shreds of tuna that had lodged themselves between his molars, Brian mentally reviewed the sparse scraps of information he had elicited from Theresa during what had turned out to be a largely liquid lunch. Kerry Perez's revelations about possible sexual abuse and pregnancy had shocked and upset Theresa; no one she had talked to had hinted at anything of the kind. Certainly Jessica Stearns's doctor—she had still been seeing a pediatrician—had not suspected that Jess was sexually active. Theresa's notes from that interview were sketchy and brief; her questions had been geared primarily toward determining the girl's probable mental state. But the biggest shocker, to both Theresa and Brian, had been the connection between Jessica Stearns and Jason Banks. A *direct* connection—independent of the relationship of each to Lloyd Fulton.

Brian believed in coincidence up to a point. He knew, somehow, that he had passed that point. But he didn't have a clue as to what to do next. Well, yes he did. But he didn't much want to do it, and he was *very* much afraid that whatever he did would blow the whole investigation.

The Hyundai had been heading down the hill from Theresa's house like a well-trained and docile milk horse, homing in on the Paloma County Government Center. Brian had persuaded a drained Theresa to take the rest of the day off, promising to pick her up first thing in the morning. Now he forced himself to concentrate. He had to talk to Fulton eventually, he told himself. Why not now? He worked his way into the right-hand lane and turned onto the artery that connected with the road that snaked its way up into the foothills, toward Oak Canyon. Toward, he hoped, a man who had a lot of explaining to do. Toward a man named Lloyd Fulton—and also, perhaps, Sam Fox.

A COUPLE OF MILES after he had passed through the center of Oak Canyon, Brian began to lose whatever trust he'd had in Theresa's quickly scrawled map and haphazard directional notes. As he headed east out of town on the main drag, past spotty suburban tracts and roadside fruit/nut stands and a variety of rural detritus, he could detect no evidence that any roads penetrated the dry-looking, brush-covered hillsides to his left. He pulled over onto the gravel shoulder and looked again at Theresa's map. A landmark was indicated: "RD WTRTWR"; just beyond, a series of dashes had been hazily traced, with an appended: "UNPVD RD—NO SIGN." Well, Theresa wasn't too good at estimating mileage, but she *had* said, "a mile or so outside of town." "RD WTRTWR?" What on earth did that mean? Road Where the Rolling Tumbleweed Whirls Round?

He pulled back out onto the highway and cruised at a slower pace, trying to get a better look at what was passing on his left. Not much. A couple of old nut ranches, looking marginally viable and barely habitable. A peeling billboard advertising waterfront acreage on Lake Chumash. A funny-looking reddish structure—serving what purpose? Certainly not habitation, although it did have a couple of small, oddly placed windows. It was built in the shape of a sort of elongated pyramid, with a bulge at the top.

Brian had passed this strange edifice before his right brain clicked in: "RD WTRTWR." Red water tower?

He spun a U-turn on the empty highway and headed back, looking to his right for an unmarked gravel road. As it turned out, it *was* marked, after a fashion, by a couple of battered tin mailboxes. This had to be the road.

Soon after he had hung a right onto the dusty lane, Brian began to feel that he had made a bad mistake. But there was nowhere to turn around. The silence was spooky, eerie. And yet it was not silent. There were, actually, myriad and various sounds, albeit not the sort of sounds to which he was accustomed. The windows of his Hyundai were open—driving around in Paloma County, he rarely turned on the air-conditioning system. As he eased the Hyundai up the graveled incline, aware of the damage that ricocheting pebbles might cause to the paint, he could hear the buzzing of what must be thousands of bees in the commercial sunflower field to his right. On his left was a jumble of weeds and thistles that seemed inhabited by hyperactive flocks of small birds, which periodically rose in an agitated cloud, regrouped, and resettled. The air smelled sweet, spicy and dry.

Brian sneezed. He sneezed again. Oh, dear, he thought. He knew he was in for a siege. He stopped the car and groped in the glove compartment for a box of tissues. As he waited for the predictable series of spasms to play itself out, he looked up at the sky. Large-winged birds swooped and soared against a backdrop of the palest blue, which blended into a grayish beige around the edges. Hawks? Eagles? Condors? Surely not condors.

I am engaging in avoidance behavior, Brian told himself. He put the Hyundai into gear and forged onward. The open fields metamorphosed into a dense eucalyptus forest. This had to be wrong, he thought. How could there be a ranch up in here? And why hadn't the whole place burned out years ago? He followed the yellow gravel road, feeling more and more that he had made a bad mistake and halfway imagining the smell of smoke. What would he find at the end of this road?

A pair of disused ruts off to the right did not look promising. He kept on, through the dense overgrowth, feeling a bit claustrophobic. The road began to climb more steeply. Negotiating a series of hairpin bends, Brian once again questioned his sanity. He realized that he had not called in to the office, that no one knew where he was. He wondered belatedly whether he had been scheduled, at the last minute, for a court appearance. He checked his gas gauge and nervously scrutinized the dashboard for warning lights. That ominous rapping noise—did he have a flat tire, or had he merely picked up a stone in one of the treads?

The eucalyptus grove ended abruptly as the Hyundai crowned a final ridge, and Brian found himself looking down into a narrow, sloping valley that had obviously been carved, over time, by the year-round creek that bisected it. The broader, higher end seemed to expand into a series of mountain meadows; a group of buildings occupied the lower glen. The whole spread, as far as Brian could determine, was enclosed within a businesslike barbed-wire fence. He let the Hyundai coast downhill to the gate, where a small parking area and turnaround had been graded out of the hardpan. The gate appeared to be secured by a padlock and chain. Brian got out of his car and surveyed the scene.

His first impression was one of absolute stillness. Then his eyes caught traces of motion: a raptor hang gliding on a thermal over the far ridge, a few animals—horses, surely—grazing on the tawny hillsides. A monster hornet began to buzz angrily, somewhere. Brian struggled to identify the sound; then he had it; a chain saw, gasoline-operated, probably. He had seen no indication that this ranch was connected to electric power lines, although signs along the road had warned of a buried telephone cable.

The buildings below looked an ill-assorted lot. There was a sprawling house that appeared to have been constructed from river rock and giant Lincoln Logs, and an even larger barn; both buildings were equipped with elaborate roof-mounted sprinkler systems. He could see, behind the house, a piece of artificial-looking blue water—a swimming pool, no doubt. A variety of smaller buildings obtruded here and there. A well house would be needed, Brian thought, and a generator, an equipment shed of some kind, and a place for the caretaker to live.

The caretaker; one Lloyd Fulton, providing that he had the right place. The angry hornet was still buzzing sporadically, creating echoes that reverberated across the valley. Brian could not pinpoint the source of the buzzing, nor could he see the sawer. He looked at the gate and wondered what to do next.

Well, check it out, said Sweet Reason. Never assume. Brian walked up to the gate and discovered that the chain was merely looped between the gate and the gatepost, with the padlock depending nonfunctionally from an odd link. He unwound the chain and opened the gate, wondering why his gut was enjoining him to be stealthy, to walk on tiptoe. He got back into his car and started the engine. The Hyundai had never seemed so noisy. He chastised himself. Why was he being such a simp, such a wimp? What would Lou do in this situation? Shit, how would *Theresa* handle it? What on earth was he expecting, anyway?

Brian swallowed hard and mentally answered himself as he eased the car down the hill toward the ranch. Son of Texas Chainsaw Massacre, he told himself: That's what.

TWENTY-FOUR

FEELING WEIRDLY AS THOUGH he were having an out-of-body experience, Brian aimed his car at the sporadic grating buzz of the chain saw—a course that led him past the main ranch house and around the expansive stock barn. The absence of signs of human habitation was spooky. He cut the engine when the farm track seemed to end, and reconnoitered. No sound. No body—at least of the human variety. And yet, Brian reasoned, if a horse could be trained to operate a chain saw, it surely would have appeared by now on the David Letterman show. Therefore, a human being must be on the premises.

Brian opened the door and stepped out of the car and looked around. A frenzied explosion of deep-throated barking sent him diving back into the Hyundai, rolling up the windows fast. He sat there, feeling every bit as stupid as he was sure he looked, and watched a man and a dog approach. The dog was approaching at a much faster rate than the man was. Worse, the dog was audibly snarling and visibly drooling. Brian could not, at first, identify its breed. It reminded him, somehow, of a Nazi. As it hurled itself against the window of what suddenly seemed a totally flimsy and defenseless vehicle, Brian thought to himself, rottweiler. So this is a rottweiler. Aha.

Preoccupied as he had been by the dog, Brian paid little attention to the man until he summoned the dog sharply to him. A chain appeared out of a pocket; the dog was abruptly clipped and leashed. The man disappeared, with the dog, around the corner of the nearest outbuilding.

Brian waited, mentally squirming. Obeying a subconscious message from his Fairy Godmother of Belated Foresight, he backed and filled and got the Hyundai turned around, heading out. And then he waited for the man to return.

In his rearview mirror, the man seemed less than threatening. Not very big. Slight, even; yet the bare arms and shoulders revealed by the cutoff T-shirt were wiry and sinewy. Skintight sun-bleached jeans topped a pair of scuffed cowboy boots. The guy was not carrying, clearly. There was no place to conceal a weapon. Well, maybe a knife, or a small gun inside one of his boots. But certainly not a chain saw. There was no way that this man could be arrested for carrying a concealed chain saw.

Tired of feeling silly, Brian got out of the car. Up close, he could see the man's face. Colorless eyes behind rimless eyeglasses. No, upon closer scrutiny, make that wire-rimmed. Old-fashioned. The guy's hair seemed old-fashioned, too; he affected untrimmed sideburns of a muddy gray blond hue, as well as a scruffy mustache with reddish tendencies.

"Hi!" Brian ventured, extending a jovial hand. "Brian Kayne."

The man looked at him. He said nothing. He did not move. Brian began to wonder whether he was dreaming, having one of those dreams where you know you're dreaming and you try to wake up but even that effort becomes part of the dream and it endlessly recycles until you...

Brian resolutely centered himself. If this is Lloyd Fulton, he told himself, he probably killed his wife and stepdaughter, and maybe a kid on his track team. I need to *deal* with this asshole!

"I'm looking for Lloyd Fulton." Brian consciously forged a harder edge to his voice. "Would you be Mr. Fulton?"

The man nodded. "Yes, I would be. And am. Who did you say you were?"

"Brian Kayne. I'm an investigator for the Paloma County District Attorney's Office." Hoo boy; the fat was now in the fire. "You've had some personal problems lately, I understand. We're just trying to follow up on them."

"What good would that do?"

"I don't know," Brian said honestly. "But can we talk?"

Fulton led the way to a rustic sort of thrown-together house, hardly more than a shack, and pointed him toward a scarred oak rocking chair. He disappeared into another room and reappeared, bearing a couple of sweating cans of Pepsi. "So talk."

Brian cut his thumb trying to open the Pepsi—an inauspicious beginning. He frantically groped for a tissue to staunch the flow. Fulton disappeared again and reemerged with a gauze pad and a roll of adhesive tape. Efficiently, he bound up Brian's wound. Brian began to realize that this was no ordinary lowlife here. This was a complicated guy, maybe more than a match for him. The usual strategies would not be operable.

Nevertheless ...

"I told you that I'm from the district attorney's office." Fulton nodded.

"We're looking into Jessica's disappearance. What do you think happened?"

Fulton shrugged. "She ran off. That's what I told you people a couple of months ago."

"Why would she have done that?"

Fulton shot a wry look at Brian. "You don't have kids, do you? With a fourteen-year-old, anything can happen. They think they're grown up. They take a big dive, and find out too late that there's no water in the pool."

"Is that what happened to Jessie? There was no water in the pool?"

Fulton shifted uncomfortably in his chair. "I don't know. We tried to find her."

Brian took a couple of deep breaths. Don't blow this, he told himself. "What was happening with Jessie? Didn't you have any clue? And what did you do to try to find her?"

Something strange happened to Fulton's face. His mouth began to work, but no words came out. Brian stared, fascinated.

Fulton stood up abruptly and walked toward the window. No, *walked* wasn't really the right word. He sort of shuffled, zombielike. He began to mutter. Brian could not make out what he was saying. The muttering increased in volume, became a shout and then a shrieking. Every hair on Brian's body stood on end. This man is totally mad, he thought.

Then Fulton seemed to collect himself. He sighed and returned to his chair. "Would you like another Pepsi?" he asked. He seemed to be a reasonable man, a good neighbor, a good guy—and a consummate actor, clearly.

Brian felt dizzy. What was happening here? What sort of person was he dealing with?

He made an effort of will to glue Fulton's eyes to his own, to intimidate him. "So you don't have any idea why Jessie might have run away?"

Fulton fidgeted.

I've got him, Brian thought. I've almost got him.

"Well, I don't know this for a fact, because Jessie and Carole didn't tell me much, but I think that the girl might have been in trouble."

"Trouble?"

Fulton sighed and put his head in his hands. "Yeah."

"What kind of trouble?"

"Boy trouble."

Ease off, now, Brian told himself.

"Can you be more specific?"

Fulton seemed to collapse. "We didn't let her go out on dates. We thought she was too young. But she got involved in Youth for Christ, and we thought that was fine. Except that she started doing stuff with this boy."

Brian took a slow breath. "What boy?"

"I don't know."

"What do you mean by 'doing stuff'?"

"Do you want me to spell it out? She got herself in the family way, that's what! And I think she couldn't face the shame of it. That's what I think. And I don't think Carole could face it, either."

"And so Carole 'ran off' too, is that what happened?"

Fulton drained his can of Pepsi and crunched it in his fist. "I think that Carole is dead. That's what I think. I think she killed herself."

"How about Jessica? Do you think she's dead, too? Or do you *know* she's dead?"

Fulton seemed to glaze over. His lips moved but nothing audible emerged.

"What happened to Jessica, Lloyd?" Brian persisted.

Fulton was silent. When he finally spoke, he seemed to be addressing himself. "She ran off. She probably ran off with whoever got her with child."

Brian took a deep breath. "But I understand that was *you*, Lloyd."

TWENTY-FIVE

CAREENING TOO FAST BACK down the gravel road that led to the Fulton ranch, still sweating, Brian wondered how he'd gotten himself out of that situation alive and intact. He should have bitten his tongue. He had given away his game. Why on earth had he put into words his strong suspicion that Lloyd Fulton had knocked up his stepdaughter?

The moment hung suspended in his mind; he heard the echo of his own words: "But I understand that was *you*, Lloyd." The silence that had followed had seemed so full of tension that Brian had found himself quivering and shuddering, had felt a tic nibbling at his left eyelid.

Fulton had stared at the floor for what seemed like a week. When he had at last looked up at Brian, his eyes had been full of tears.

"Oh, no," he had said in a voice at first barely audible. "What you speak of is—bestiality. To despoil an innocent, a child who has entrusted himself to you—that is bestial, brutish." The tears had run unchecked down Fulton's face as he continued. "I am a scholar, a teacher, a writer. Yes, I do physical labor, to support myself and my family, but the meaning of my existence is to celebrate the sacredness of being, of myth and magic. I sing of gods and mortals, of truths eternal, of beauty transcendent."

Or something like that. And then the guy had seemed to go into a trance. Brian had sort of slithered out of the room, hoping that the rottweiler or whatever was securely chained. Nutso, nutso. The Hyundai had started on the first try. And now he was outta there. But what next?

Brian reflected on what Fulton had said, leaning heavily on his famous aural memory—which was close to perfect even over the long term. Something had struck a false note—what? He mentally replayed Fulton's monologue. Yes, that was it. Fulton had referred to a perhaps (or perhaps not) hypothetical child who had entrusted *himself*—not *herself*—to someone. Why not *herself*, if the conversation was supposed to be about Jessica?

Everything about Lloyd Fulton touched off weird vibes in Brian, sent him back to his Abnormal Psychology class at Antioch—the initial impetus for his interest in a law-enforcement career. At that time, of course, he'd had no way of knowing that most law enforcement deals with the normal and subnormal, that the abnormal criminal is an anomaly.

Wow, Brian thought as he finally reached the highway that led west back to Oak Canyon, this guy Fulton is a strange piece of work. He's almost surely a killer.

But was he Sam Fox?

And did it matter?

TWENTY-SIX

JOANNA SQUINTED AGAINST the blinding glare of the sinking sun as she tooled her little Honda hatchback into the parking area that adjoined the Sunset Vista Recreation Center. Tuesday meant Art Night, a weekly event that she usually enjoyed. But tonight, she felt a bit nervous. Tonight was an experiment. How would her various protégés respond to an exercise in drawing from life? Limning, in particular, the luscious limbs of Luke, Sunset Vista's seasonal summer maintenance man?

She had checked out Luke. Boy, had she checked out Luke. Shirtless, barefoot, his integral parts concealed within raggedy cutoff jeans, Luke was a hunk. Jo wondered whether his mind would turn her on, as well. Luke was, it was said, an English major at the university. An English major? What a waste. Well, maybe he majored in body English. Knowing that she was out of line—after all, she was clearly old enough to be Luke's mother, was perhaps even *older* than his actual mother—Joanna had permitted herself some lascivious daydreams about the luscious Luke. Mentally slapping herself down, aware that if she possessed legs like Ann Bancroft's she would not be a believable Mrs. Robinson to even an *under*graduate, she had compromised by employing Luke from time to time as a model. Tonight was one of those times. Some senior citizens were about to be mightily surprised.

She checked the sign-up roster posted outside the meeting room she used for her weekly classes. Only six names—a smaller group than usual. Which was just as well; she didn't want any heart attacks on her conscience. Six regulars—all in good health as far as she knew. The long folding tables were already in place, as were the ad hoc platform and screen she had asked Luke to set up earlier in the day. As she positioned six chairs and distributed the large pads of newsprint she had cadged from the local paper—carved out of roll ends that otherwise would have been discarded—she mentally reviewed her students of the evening.

Admiral Tidworth, of course. Horace R. Tidworth, USN, ret. He rarely missed a session and was usually the first to sign up. Also, he frequently was the only man in the group. The admiral dealt with his retirement as though it were just another tour of duty, except that he no longer controlled the helm. His wife, Henrietta ("Call me Hank!"), who was built along the lines of an aircraft carrier, clearly ran the ship, and it was just as clearly a tight one. Jo liked Hank, an open, earthy lady who could talk your ear off and then give you the shirt off her back. (Hank did, alas, tend to talk in clichés, and thus one tended to think in clichés when one thought of Hank.) The worthy Mrs. Tidworth was not shy about boasting that she had raised four children and run several sequential households essentially alone, "While Tiddy was steaming off to Raratonga or wherever." Joanna did not doubt that the lady spoke the truth. The admiral, on the other hand, sorely tried her patience. Her art classes were intended, after all, to stimulate people's repressed creative instincts—but "Tightass Tiddy," as she had privately come to think of him, persisted in doing every exercise according to some unwritten book. On more than one occasion, Jo had restrained herself from jamming his hand into the paint and smearing it over the paper. "Go crazy, Tiddy! Make a mess!" No, alas, it wouldn't have worked. What Tiddy did in the privacy of his own bathroom, she would let Hank cope with.

And then there were the Misses Bunker and Stufflebeam. Jo had often wondered whether many of the Sunset Vista residents had pegged them for what they obviously (to her) were—a devoted and durable lesbian pair—but there was no doubt that they were well liked and valuable residents of the complex. Hazel Bunker, known to one and all as "Bunky" and a dead ringer for Gertrude Stein, had a knack for fixing any nonelectronic appliance and was a fabled cook, a veritable one-woman potluck supper; she was more than generous about sharing both talents. Eleanor Stufflebeam, who submitted good-naturedly to being called "Stuffy," was tall and improbably skinny; a retired registered nurse, she was always on call for emergencies and had on more than one occasion kept a neighbor alive until the paramedics arrived. Together, Bunky and Stuffy more or less ran the board of directors of the homeowners' association and were undisputed queens of the Contract Bridge Club. Joanna smiled as she distributed sticks of charcoal, reflecting that every neighborhood could use a Bunky and Stuffy. Precluded from making a biological family of their own, they made all of Sunset Vista their family. And a more stable "marriage," she thought, probably did not exist.

She looked at her watch: fifteen minutes until class time. Luke should be arriving soon; he needed to change into his minimal costume and review some last-minute strategy. She wandered back into the hall. No sigh of Luke. Who else had signed up for tonight? She looked at the roster.

Well, a surprise, Miss Margaret Pultney, the last of the old-maid schoolteachers. Miss Pultney had occasionally turned up in her Dancercize classes, but seldom at Art Night. Miss Pultney, Jo had often thought, should be preserved in aspic. Actually, she seemed to *be* preserved in aspic. A tiny, birdlike woman, she affected what Jo assumed was a 1940s hairstyle (congealed ringlets, set once a week and imprisoned in a net) and what looked for all the world like Lanz dresses. Did Lanz still make dresses? Well, Jo had cheated once, during a Dancercize break; she had peeked at the label in Miss Pultney's dress as it hung on a hook in the changing room. Yup. Lanz, size seven. Well, either Lanz was still in business or Miss Pultney kept her clothes for decades, which was entirely possible. Not that she had anything against Miss Pultney, whose wellness statistics could have served as a model for residents of the complex. Miss Pultney was terminally earnest, almost pathetically eager, and obviously *determined to do the right thing at all times*. But someone ought to gently suggest to her, Jo thought, that a woman of seventy or so might—let go a wee tad? Stop trying so hard to be a good little girl?

And then there was Mrs. Spofford—now there was a good old gal, and pretty cute to boot. Jean Spofford described herself as a "happy widow." For years she had been openly having an affair with a married fellow resident, with the apparent blessing of the latter's wife. In fact, the three were close friends. How things do work out, Jo thought. Jean's lover boy still had plenty of juice; his wife had lost interest in sex long ago; Jean's marriage had been unhappy, but she had stuck with it. And now, Jean was having the time of her life. She loved to talk to Jo about the flowering of her sexuality in her eighth decade. Jo listened avidly; in fact, she was learning a few tricks. I should be so lucky, Jo told herself; maybe, I will be. But can I wait that long?

And, of course, there was Sadie. She was the first to arrive, followed closely by the admiral and Miss Pultney.

"Hi, Sweetie!" Sadie cried, giving Jo a hug. "What's on for tonight?"

"Life drawing," Jo said. "Drawing from life," she added in response to three blank looks.

"You mean with a live model?" Sadie asked.

"Erm, yes."

Miss Pultney seemed to shudder. "The models—I mean, in such circumstances, are they not usually, um..."

The admiral seemed to come to life. "Nekkid," he croaked. "Bare-ass nekkid. Perverted, that's what I say. I blame the French. They never had any morals to speak of."

"Oh, no," Jo reassured them. "This model will not be nude." Not entirely, she hoped. "Listen, I have to check to see that the model is ready. You all go on in and sit down, okay?"

Jo slipped down the hall to the men's room and knocked discreetly on the door. "Luke?"

"All ready." The door opened and Luke appeared, clad in a spandex bikini that left to the imagination only what Luke's dimensions might be in an excited state.

Joanna managed to refrain from swooning. "You've got my little cue cards, huh?"

"Yup." He grinned. "I think this is going to be fun. I've been practicing my pose. Maybe I can make some serious money doing this."

"I hope so. Well, put your robe on and go get behind the screen. I think we're ready to start."

Jo took a deep breath and reentered the ad hoc classroom. Her students were visibly exhibiting varying degrees of nervousness. She hoped that all this would work out. I could get fired, she thought. No, they can't fire me; they don't pay me anything.

"Okay, gang, I want you to listen carefully. Put down your charcoal; you won't need it quite yet. We're going to start out by training your eyes to form an image, and letting your hands practice tracing that image. Luke—I think you all know Luke—has agreed to model for us tonight. When I give him a signal, he will step out from behind the screen and hold a pose for two minutes. As you watch him, let your hand move over the paper in an imitation of what you are seeing and noticing. Don't be concerned with details. Experience the flow of his body..." Jo had to stop for a moment, being on the verge of giving herself an orgasm. "What I mean is, you want to look at line, at curves and angles. And don't be concerned about getting the proportions right. Let your hands draw what you see."

"But how can we draw without these coal sticks?" Sadie protested.

"Imagine that you're finger painting, or that your hand is dipped in ink. Don't look at what your hand is doing, look at the model."

Bunky snorted. "Okay. Then what?"

"After two minutes, Luke will go back behind the screen. Then, pick up your charcoal sticks and quickly sketch what you remember. Try to let your hands do what they did before. Don't look at what you are doing. You'll have one minute to do your first sketch. Don't expect it to look like anything other than a scribble."

The admiral raised his hand. Jo repressed an urge to tell him that it was okay to go to the little boys' room. "Yes, Admiral?"

"I, er, don't pretend to know anything about *creative* art, but one minute doesn't seem enough time to do any sort of drawing."

"Let's not think of it as drawing, just yet," Jo tried to explain. "We'll give it a shot, and then we'll try again a few more times. You all have plenty of sheets on your pads, so don't worry about spoiling them. This is an experiment. I think you'll enjoy it, and I suspect that most of you will surprise yourselves."

Jo looked at her class and observed that *dubious* was the operative word for the expressions that looked back at her. Well, carry on. She had noticed, out of the corner of an eye, that Luke had unobtrusively taken his place behind the screen. In front of the screen was a camp stool. The plan called for Luke to slouch on the camp stool facing the class, legs spread, head and arms dangling down between his legs in an attitude that suggested extreme exhaustion or dejection. It was a classic life-drawing pose, one that effectively concealed perhaps embarrassing parts of the anatomy.

"Okay, Luke," Joanna sang out with a confidence she didn't feel. The tension in the room increased palpably.

Luke stepped out from behind the screen, golden and splendid in his purple bikini. He had oiled his skin, to Jo's surprise. Nobody breathed until Miss Pultney emitted a gasp and knocked her stick of charcoal off the table. It hit the floor with a shattering crack and pulverized itself into dozens of skittering pieces. Almost as one, the Art Night students ducked under their tables and scrambled to retrieve the pieces—almost as one. Jean Spofford gazed at Luke with a dreamy smile as he arranged himself in the predetermined pose. As Jo watched, not sure whether to crack up or throw up, Jean's hand moved rhythmically, lovingly, over her pad of newsprint. She seemed to be casting a sort of spell. Jo was entranced. This little pudding of a lady, a couple of years into her seventies, was turning magically into an eager young blossom of a girl; she was projecting this image into the room, filling the room with it. One by one, the other class members resumed their seats and stared at her. They looked at Luke. They looked back at Jean, who seemed to be caressing her pad of paper.

Sadie was the first to respond, albeit tentatively. She looked back and forth between Luke and Jean, and finally began to imitate Jean's hand tracings. Bunky and Stuffy made attempts to get into it—stiffly, at first, but then with

increasing enthusiasm. Miss Pultney, supplied with a fresh
stick of charcoal, made an earnest effort. The admiral, his
eyes fixed firmly on the floor, left the room.

Oh well, Jo thought. Five out of six ain't bad.

TWENTY-SEVEN

JOANNA WAS DEEP INTO *Trace Elements*—a so-far wonderful book by a writer she'd never heard of—when the telephone summoned her back to the real world. She let it ring a couple of times and then resentfully slipped an emery board into the book to mark her page. "Yeah?"

"Yeah?"

"I mean, hello. Whoever you are, I'll warn you that this isn't a good time."

"So when *is* a good time?"

"That depends."

"On what?"

"On who you are, for starters. And what you want?"

"Okay, I can dig that. I've often felt the same way myself."

Joanna sighed. Well, now wasn't this wonderful? The Communication Generation, featuring the famous "I" statement. The generation that majored in "I" but so often failed to communicate anything of consequence. "Shit or get off the pot, buster," she communicated, graphically if inelegantly.

"Jo, this is Brian Kayne. I'm sorry if I've disturbed you, but I need to talk to you. It's important."

Joanna silently whistled for her wits and attempted to gather them about her. Somehow, she had been expecting this phone call. But she had no idea how to handle what seemed to be a living nightmare that was taking a shape entirely beyond her control.

"Okay," she said. "Hold on a minute, huh?" She gently laid down the receiver and recklessly filled her wineglass with brandy, tossing in a couple of ice cubes for good luck. "I'm sorry that I walked out on you, by the way. I was upset. It really had nothing to do with you. Directly."

"I understand that, at least I guess so. And *this* has nothing to do with *that*. Directly."

Joanna felt spasms in her gut, spasms of anticipated pain, loss, grief. "This has to do with Sam, doesn't it?" I have lost Sam, she told herself.

Brian's voice was gentle and hesitant. "I don't *know* whether this has anything to do with your Sam. I don't know who your Sam is, but I think I very much need to find out. And I would like your help."

"I think we'd better be straight with each other," Jo said. "First, he's not 'my Sam,' and I'm beginning to think that I don't really know him all that well myself. And maybe I'm starting to feel a little bit scared." There. She had said it. She felt a little better. Fear and rage and grief continued to do battle in her gut, but somehow she instinctively trusted this man. Any son of Sadie's had to be trustworthy, by definition. Both of her feet had left the dock; she had damned well better land in the boat—any boat. If the boat happened to be named Brian, so be it.

"I went to see a man today, and I had a very interesting conversation with him."

Joanna felt befuddled. "A man? What man?"

"A man who goes by the name of Lloyd Fulton."

"I don't understand."

"Your Sam—I'm sorry. The Sam you know, the writer. I'm blanking out on his last name."

"Fox. Sam Fox."

"Did it ever occur to you that Sam Fox might be an alias? A pen name, I guess you'd call it. A pseudonym. You know, like George Sand."

"I know what a pseudonym is," Joanna said curtly. A lump of ice seemed to invade her upper intestine. "You'd better explain all of this."

There was a pause, and what sounded like a gurgle. Jo took a deep swallow of brandy and almost choked on an ice cube.

"It all started with your show. No, I don't mean that. It all started long before your show, but it wasn't until I went to your show and read Sam's stuff that I started to notice, um, some remarkable coincidences."

Joanna realized that she was sweating; she felt frozen inside and feverish from the neck up. Was this what a hot flash felt like?

"Go on," she said weakly.

"A couple of Sam's poems, or whatever, sort of rang a bell. They sounded familiar, somehow. I didn't realize why, right away. And then I started to look into it."

"Into it?"

Another gurgle. "This is hard to explain." Gurgle. "Hold on a minute, huh?"

He's going to the refrigerator for another beer, Jo thought. She reached for the brandy bottle and topped off her glass. I will regret this in the morning, she thought, but it may be the least of my regrets.

"Still there? Okay, let's go back to Lloyd Fulton. He's a weird man. He's had lots of problems during the last few months. His stepdaughter disappeared, and then his wife. We had our suspicions, at the time, but we didn't connect those cases with another incident that this Fulton guy was involved in just a bit earlier. Hey, are you still with me?"

"I'm here." Actually, she was several sentences ahead of him, but she'd be damned if she'd let him know it.

"This Fulton guy teaches English at Oak Canyon High School, and he's also the track coach. There was a tragic accident during track practice one afternoon; a kid was killed, hit on the head by a discus when another athlete got off a wild toss. At least that's how we pegged it at the time. But now I'm wondering. Because the kid who was killed turns out to have been Jessica Stearns's boyfriend."

"Jessica Stearns?"

"Lloyd Fulton's stepdaughter. The one who later disappeared. Fulton says she 'ran off' because some boy had gotten her pregnant, and that his wife probably killed herself because she couldn't deal with her daughter's disappearance, or maybe couldn't face the shame. But I've been talking to a couple of Jessie's friends, and the picture that emerges is that . . . anyway, before I go on, does any of this ring a bell?"

The bells are ringing, all right, Jo thought. Death knells. The party's over. "Ring a bell? What do you mean?"

"Sam's writings. The stuff in your show. About the kid who was killed while playing at quoits, whatever that is. And the mother who died when she went up onto the mountain to search for her missing daughter. There are too many parallels. Sam Fox is just too mysterious. You told me that he lives on a ranch outside Oak Canyon, acts as a sort of caretaker. So does Lloyd Fulton. Joanna, I think that Sam Fox is really Lloyd Fulton, or vice versa. And I think he's a killer."

"Oh, no." Jo desperately tried to center herself. "Not Sam. Maybe I don't entirely know him, but I can't believe this."

"Joanna, the man is weird. Schitzy. But there's no evidence to build a case around. Just a bunch of hunches. Fulton has the reputation of being a religious fanatic—is this the Sam you know?"

"Lord, no," Jo almost whimpered.

"Lloyd Fulton is a high school teacher, but when I talked to him today, he came across more like an uneducated hillbilly, a redneck. Part of the time, at least. He seemed to flip-flop back and forth between being two different people, maybe more than two. Could he be Sam Fox? I need to know what you think. Please stop worrying about protecting Sam, and tell me whatever you know about him that might help. Maybe we can at least eliminate him, if he and Fulton are not the same person. And if they *are* the same guy, we need to nail him. We need to find out how a nice young kid died, and what happened to another nice young kid—and to her mother. You could help me a lot."

Jo drained her glass, feeling a bit dizzy. "What if I don't choose to help you? Or what if I can't tell you anything helpful? I'm...I'm not sure why I should get involved in all this."

There was a pause and another gurgle.

"Because you might be in danger yourself. I've been to see Lloyd Fulton. If he's Sam Fox, he might get the idea that you sent me."

TWENTY-EIGHT

THERESA'S DAY WAS NOT proceeding according to schedule.
It was, in fact, clear that her day was falling apart, even
though the hour was barely past 9:00 A.M. She had planned
to get to the office early, to make up for taking yesterday
afternoon off. Then she had remembered that she lacked
transportation—that her reliable little Toyota was parked in
the lot at the County Government Center, and that Brian
had promised to pick her up this morning. She had phoned
his home number to remind him of his promise, with exas-
perating results: After five or six rings, the headset had been
picked up, but what followed was an unintelligible mum-
ble—and an abruptly broken connection. She had summoned a cab, resigning herself to a long wait: Taxi "service"
in Paloma was a local joke.

Amazingly, a cab had arrived within fifteen minutes, and
at 7:45, Theresa was groping in her purse for her key to the
DA's suite of offices. But the doors had been open; Marge
Hedstrom was storming around the reception lobby, looking exceptionally surly. The copier was down, it seemed, and
likewise the computer. The junior college student who acted
as office gofer had neglected to replenish the coffee supply.
And there was a message for Theresa to call her son Patrick
up in Portland.

Now, Theresa's stomach did somersaults as she repeatedly tried to get through to what obviously was not her son's
home number. Beth wasn't due for at least a month; something had to be wrong. Patrick was her eldest; he and Beth
had been married for eight years; they had been trying to
make a baby. Pat had endured massive kidding from his
colleagues because of being called out of meetings when
"the time" was just right. Beth had taken a leave of absence from her good job as a personnel administrator in order to concentrate on conception. She had finally conceived,

and up until now everything had gone well. Please, God, Theresa prayed. Don't let them lose this baby. She dialed again. Another busy signal. Were the bleeping *telephones* down, too?

It wasn't as though she was hurting for grandkids. Mike and Cathy had produced a set of twins before they'd been married a year. Joe Jr. and Becky had a boy and a girl and, she suspected, something in the oven. Matt and Claire had a beautiful three-month-old daughter. And Jonathan, her youngest, her free spirit, was far from being ready to settle down; a fledgling archaeologist, he was at the moment on a dig in—Turkey? Theresa tried not to keep track. It really was better not to wonder too much about what Jon was doing. But Patrick! Her firstborn—her most-special son, if the truth be known. And his sweet Beth. Wanting so much to be parents, wanting this baby desperately. Oh, please!

Brian blundered—no other verb quite fit—into the communal office shared by the DA's investigative staff, his briefcase under his arm, bearing two Styrofoam cups that contained a turbid liquid which the Government Center cafeteria fraudulently misrepresented as coffee.

Theresa glared at him. "What happened to you this morning?"

"Huh?"

"You were supposed to drive me to work. I called, and you hung up on me."

"Naw." Brian set down a cup on Theresa's desk. "Is that black? You'll have to check." He shambled, yawning, over to his own desk. "Where's Lou?"

"Don't change the subject," Theresa snapped. "You stood me up. You hung up on me. I'm supposed to forgive all of that because you brought me a cup of this crap?"

"Hey, Theresa, I'm really sorry. But I didn't hang up on you. I was waking up; I was getting my act together. Really."

He looks awful, Theresa thought; he must have had a hard night. Oho. "Somebody else hung up on me, huh? None of my business, but who might that have been?"

Brian looked embarrassed. "Actually, it was Mabel."

"Mabel?"

"You know. My cat."

"Your *cat* hung up on me?"

"She's developed this fascination with buttons." Brian hung his jacket over the back of his chair and slurped coffee. "She likes to push them. She turned off my clock radio this morning, too. I think she got the idea from watching that TV ad."

Theresa rubbed her eyes. "Okay, I guess I should ask; What TV ad?"

"The one where the dog hangs up the phone by pressing his paw down on the button. It's for some phone company, I think. You know, the guy in the ad looks sort of like Axelrod on 'St. Elsewhere.'"

Theresa realized that she was close to exploding. She took three long, deep, measured breaths. She forced herself to speak calmly. "Look, Brian, we have some problems here. The copier is down. The computer is down. My daughter-in-law may be losing her baby." She felt herself start to lose control. "Brian, Marge is coming unglued. *I* am coming unglued. Lou will not be here today. Lou is at a seminar down in San Miguel, remember? Nothing is working. I am due in court in less than an hour and I don't have the printouts that I need. This goddamn coffee is lousy. You are a disaster. We need to get together on this fucking Fulton thing."

Brian gaped at her, not really tracking—not really awake, Theresa thought.

Suddenly she was furious at him; she wanted to put him over her knee and whale him with a hairbrush. All he could think about was his goddamn cat. Whoa . . .

She felt tears rising in her throat. And then Brian was there, giving her a good substantial hug. She took another deep breath and tried the Portland number again. This time, she got through. And after a couple of transfers and holds, she found herself talking to Patrick. "What's going on, honey?"

"We have a son, Mom!" Patrick sounded exhausted but ecstatic. "He's a little small—just under four pounds—but the doctors say he's going to be fine. No lung problems, and with any luck we'll have him home in three or four weeks. And Beth is doing great.''

"Oh, Pat..." Tears ran freely down Theresa's face now; she had given her troopers a break. "I'm so happy for you both, and so relieved.''

"Yeah, we were pretty scared when we realized that Beth was going into premature labor. There's a lot of technical stuff involved, I guess, which had to do with why it took us so long to get pregnant."

Theresa smiled bemusedly, wondering at the mind-set of a generation that thought in terms of a conjoint pregnancy.

"Mom?"

"Yes, I'm here."

"Anyway, the good news is that Beth's doctor says he thinks that whatever, er, bugs she had in her system have been worked out, and that we shouldn't have any trouble having more children."

"Oh, God, that's wonderful," Theresa said. She thought, More children? You barely have this one. "Have you named him? I know you were going to wait until just before the baby came, but since he came so early..."

"Yeah, Mom; in fact, we decided on a name just a few minutes before you called. We're going to name him Terrence Joseph Scanlon, after Dad—and you. We'll call him Terry."

Theresa hung up the phone and bawled.

TWENTY-NINE

AS PLEASED AS HE WAS that Theresa's new grandbaby seemed to be okay, Brian felt impatient: He needed Theresa now, needed her full concentration. At the very least, he needed her notes on the accident involving the Banks kid. He hoped that she had saved them. There would be no file on that one, since nobody had ever contemplated bringing charges. An accident, pure and simple. Yeah. How had Fulton pulled it off? Would anyone involved remember anything, after three months? Was anyone involved even available?

Theresa's sobs had diminished to sniffles. "Oh, dear," she said to herself. "Should I go up there? I ought to go to Portland immediately." She fumbled with phone books. "On the other hand, what could I do? I'd only be in the way. The baby will be in the hospital for several weeks; they might not even let me *see* him. And if I *see* him, I'll want to *hold* him, and they certainly won't let me do that. And maybe I won't want to hold him. Maybe—oh God, Brian!" She looked at him imploringly. "I've never seen a premature baby, not up close. Maybe he'll look like one of those little ratty Mexican dogs. Maybe I won't *love* him!"

"Theresa..." Brian ventured a tentative pat. "Of course you would love him. But you're right; there wouldn't be much you could do now. Maybe when the baby is ready to come home, you could go up and give Beth a hand for a week or so, if she seems to need help."

Theresa shook her head. "She won't need help. She and Patrick will want to be alone with the baby. I'll just be in the way. They won't need a houseguest. I know how *that* feels."

Brian nodded, attempting to encourage her accelerating train of thought. "Besides, brand-new babies aren't all that interesting, are they? Not that I'm an expert, of course, but it's been my observation that they don't start acting like

people until they're—oh . . ." Shit, Brian thought. He had
no idea how old any given baby was. Three months, six
months, nine months—it was all the same to him. "You
know, when they start to grin and drool and jabber."

"Three months is the magic age." Theresa gave him a
rueful smile. "You know, Brian, for someone who by all
rights should have no sense at all, on occasion you can come
up with very sensible advice."

"Well, thank you. I guess that's settled, then."

"What's settled?"

"You're not going to Portland. At least immediately,"
Brian hastily amended.

"I take it that you have an alternative plan in mind."

"I do. We have to be sneaky here, though. Official time
has not been authorized, remember?"

"You're still after Fulton. But what have you got? Anything new?"

"Yes and no. I went out to see the dude yesterday." He
quickly summarized his experience for Theresa, realizing in
the process of doing so that what he had was a bunch of
ephemeral nothings. A pronoun, inadvertently of the wrong
gender? An elusive, mysterious man who seemed to change
personae by the minute? He lamely wound down his narrative, feeling more than a bit foolish and naïve, and waited
for Theresa's reaction.

"Brian, this guy is bad news. Serious bad news. I've always felt that, and the things you keep coming up with
confirm my suspicions.

"But suspicions are all we have. And until we have more
than that, Lou's not going to let us work the cases. Whatever. We're not going to get backup, lab help—we're on our
own. Theresa, I think this guy's got us licked, and he knows
it."

"Fudgsicle!" Theresa stood up and hurled a phone book
across the room. "I'm not ready to quit. Are you?"

"No way."

"Then let's get us a game plan." She looked at her watch.
"Now's out; I'm booked. I'll meet you at Sandy's at six."

THE GAME PLAN, which turned out to be largely Theresa's, seemed simple enough on paper. Theresa would talk to Amy and Kerry and any other of Jessica's friends who might be resurfacing from summer vacations. Brian would attempt to replow the neglected field in which the investigation of the Banks "accident" had been buried. And then there was the matter of the human bone, found up on the mountain.

Brian felt furiously frustrated. Three people were dead—well, one was known to be dead. Two others were missing and presumed dead. And who was working the case? A couple of DA's investigators—*on their own time*. After the so-called Black Dahlia's murder was discovered, he seemed to recall from a book he'd read, the LAPD had assigned a hundred officers to work the case full-time. And the lady had been a tramp, by all accounts. These were three innocent people—people who were disturbingly fleshing themselves out as personalities, in his head. Now, it would not do to become personally involved. But how could he avoid becoming personally involved? Maybe he had chosen the wrong line of work.

He forced himself back to the task at hand. Theresa's notes on the Banks kid's death were fragmentary, but—bless her pack-rat tendencies—she had saved them. He scanned the basics and mentally constructed a checklist. Top priority was interviewing the boy who supposedly had hurled the fatal discus: one Brett Miller, if Theresa's handwriting could be deciphered. He looked in vain for the name of a school secretary or whoever had answered the phone call for Brett and activated Fulton's electronic pager. Whoa! A big gap, there. The names of a few track-team members were included; none had observed anything relevant.

Brian felt himself dozing off. He mechanically disrobed, brushed his teeth, and nudged the already-snoring Mabel over onto her side of the bed. "No buttons!" he whispered firmly.

THIRTY

BRIAN WAS NOT SURE whether anyone would be answering the phone at Oak Canyon High School during summer break, but he tried the number, anyway. An exceedingly bored-sounding female voice finally responded, after the seventh ring. He steeled himself for the standard petty-bureaucratic runaround, and he was not disappointed. After several false starts and devious end runs around stone walls, he finally elicited the information that Brett Miller had graduated the previous June. Combined threats and cajolements eventually provided an address and phone number for the kid.

Another dead end, probably. And yet, a place to start. A new place to start. Every so-called dead end yielded a new place to start.

Brian knew he thrived on this sort of stuff, that he was stubborn, that he would not accept *impossible* as a given. If humans could be compared to dogs, he was a terrier. He would worry a thing, chew it and pursue it, until he had it cornered in its burrow.

Maybe he wasn't in the wrong line of work, after all.

"BRETT? YOU WANNA TALK to Brett?" The voice sounded female and preadolescent. "I dunno. Lemme ask my mom."

Brian flipped off the top of an icy bottle of Beck's while he cooled his heels. Mabel watched impassively from the top of the refrigerator. Brian looked at her nervously, wondering whether at a critical moment she would leap down and break the connection with a precisely censoring paw—and hoping that this conversation might yield a critical moment or two, given that he had been trying all morning to get through to the Miller residence. At least he hadn't had to contend with an answering machine; the Millers seemed, simply and honestly, not to be home.

Brian was halfway through his first long swallow of brew when a fully mature female voice came on the line.

"This is Mrs. Greenberg. Who's calling, please?"

"Mrs. *Greenberg*? I'm sorry; I guess I have the wrong number. I was trying to reach Brett Miller."

"I am Brett Miller's mother, but my name is not Mrs. Miller. And I get really tired of having to explain this to schools and doctors and insurance companies and whoever. I mean, in this day and age, when the nuclear family is supposed to be largely extinct, wouldn't you suppose that people might not be so quick to assume that a mother's last name is the same as that of her child?" She seemed to run out of gas, with a sigh.

Brian took a deep breath. "You have a good point there, Mrs. Greenbaum."

"Green*berg*. And you haven't answered my question. Who are you, and why do you want to talk to Brett?"

Brian covered the speaking end of the receiver and took another swig of beer. "Look. Please give me a little room here. My name is Brian Kayne. I'm an investigator for the Paloma County District Attorney. And I need to talk to your son about the accident at the track last May."

There was a long pause. Suspicious vibes seemed to transmit themselves through the telephone lines. "I think that I'd better refer you to our attorney."

"No, you don't understand..."

"We were told that no charges would be filed against Brett." Mrs. Greenberg's voice rose and began to tremble. "The coroner ruled that it was an accident, that no negligence was involved."

"Look, I don't think for a minute that Brett was to blame in any way for what happened. That's the point. That's why I need to talk to him, to find out more about the situation. I think it might actually be helpful to your son."

"How? How is this going to help? We're already spending hundreds of dollars a month on therapy. The psychologist says it may take him years to work through his feelings of guilt."

"Look, Mrs. Greenberg, I can't get into the details now, and I'll have to talk to your son before I can confirm my suspicions, but I'm pretty much convinced that your son has no reason to feel guilty. You see, I don't think that Jason Banks died because Brett got off a wild discus toss."

There was a long silence.

"What are you saying?"

"I'm not sure, exactly. But I need to talk to your son, to ask him about what happened that afternoon. And then I'll do some more investigating. All I can tell you is that I don't think your son killed Jason Banks, accidentally or otherwise. I'd like to have a chance to prove it. Will you cooperate with me?"

A short silence. "Are you bullshitting me, Mr. King?"

"Kayne. And no. I'm absolutely serious. Serious enough to be working this case on my own time."

"Hold on a minute." The minute stretched out into two, and then three. Mabel stretched, leaped lithely down from the top of the refrigerator and languidly made for her litter box, which she proceeded to fussily tidy before getting down to business. Brian averted his eyes and drained the Beck's bottle.

"Hullo?" The voice was male and tentatively deep, still exploring the depths.

"Brett?"

"Yeah."

"Did your mother tell you who I am and why I called?"

"Yeah, I guess."

"Would you be willing to talk to me?"

An exhausted sigh. "Why not? What have I got to lose?"

"When can we do that?"

"Well, maybe on my lunch hour tomorrow, if you can brown-bag it. I've got a summer job, thanks to my mother. She's a librarian, right? She got me a job shelving books at the Green Valley branch of the Paloma County Library. That's a gas, huh? Here I am, shelving books. Oh, shit."

"Hey, nothing wrong with working for a library. I'm a big user, myself. I'll even bring lunch—do you like calzones?"

"Fuckin-A. And don't hold the onions. What time can I meet you? My lunch hour's from eleven-thirty to twelve-thirty."

Brian consulted his Day-Timer and realized that he had a problem. Well, he would fudge a bit here, do a little side-step there. If he remembered correctly the location of the Green Valley library, it was a good fifteen minutes' drive—maybe twenty—from the Government Center, given the best of traffic conditions. Which were not likely to prevail during the lunch hour.

"I'll meet you at eleven-forty-five outside the library, with all ingredients for lunch, okay? Then you can tell me where we should go to eat lunch—and have a little talk. Are we square, Brett?"

The voice took on, at last, a trace of enthusiasm: "Rare as a bear, confrere! Dig ya tamale, and don't forget the Pepsi."

"Hokay José. Light, caffeine-free, or what?"

"Straight up, my man." The kid was showing some signs of normalcy, or abnormalcy, or whatever boys of eighteen or so ought to be showing signs of. Brian felt encouraged. Out of the corner of an eye, he observed that Mabel was approaching him with a purposeful expression in her normally limpid yellow eyes.

"See you then," Brian managed before Mabel yanked out the phone jack with her teeth. Jesus. Where had she learned *that* trick?

THIRTY-ONE

BRIAN WAS RUNNING FIVE minutes late when he pulled into the parking lot of the Green Valley branch of the Paloma County Library. Not bad, he thought, given that he had backtracked twice trying to find it and that one of the Pepsi containers had fallen over and was leaking into his loafer. The brown paper bag containing the calzones had slid over to nestle into the right side of his sport jacket, oozing garlic-scented grease. He hoped that all of this was going to be worth it. He hoped that Brett Miller would have something useful to tell him. He hoped that he would be able to find Brett Miller, or vice versa. Why hadn't he asked the kid what he looked like?

The Green Valley library was new, and bare. Embryo bits of planting struggled to survive in a landscaping scheme that obviously had not run to a sprinkler system. Poor budget management, Brian thought. He levered himself out of the car and looked around. A large young man was stretched out on the ground in the scanty shade of an adolescent fruitless mulberry tree. Brian took a closer look and realized that the kid was deeply asleep. His features seemed cherubic, his complexion the color of espresso *au lait*.

Brian looked around. No other human presence was in evidence. He cleared his throat. "Brett?"

"Ummph." The kid sat up abruptly, looking dazed. Brian was struck by the beauty of his face: the melting brown eyes, the long eyelashes, the full and slightly pouty lips. Below the neck, though, he was built like a nose tackle. And here again was a rainbow kid for sure. Some black blood, certainly, and maybe Irish? Scandinavian? Mixtures, Brian thought, usually turned out well. He cleared his throat again. "Are you Brett Miller? I'm Brian Kayne. We talked last night, remember? The calzones are in the car, getting cold."

The kid look sheepish. "Yeah, I'm Brett. Sorry I fell asleep. I didn't get too many Zs last night." He held out a hand that looked like the meaty end of a leg of lamb.

Brian shook it nervously. The kid was gentle with him, praise be. "Are you hungry?"

"Starving."

"Can we eat right here?"

"Sure, providing we pick up our litter."

"Okay, José." Brian retreated to the car for the provisions, reflecting that Brett could easily put away a couple of calzones and then some, and preparing himself to sacrifice his own lunch if he could get something out of the kid.

The kid was nothing if not forthcoming, as it turned out—and he politely confined himself to a single calzone.

"So you think you remember this pretty well, Brett?"

"Aw, sh—ucks, I've gone over and over it all so much, it's just like a nightmare that won't quit." Brett drained his Pepsi container. "I keep telling it and telling it. And it still doesn't make sense. My therapist says I have to 'work through the guilt.' But that's my problem. I'm not sure that what I feel is *guilt*. I think I was a medium, somehow, that some weird higher power took over my arm and aimed that discus. I think I was *used* to kill Jason."

Brian looked at him gravely. "I think you're right, in a way."

"And you know, that doesn't make me feel guilty. But it does make me feel scared."

"Scared of some supernatural power?"

Brett hung his head and shrugged. "Yeah, I guess so. Pretty flaky, huh?"

"Brett, what if I told you that you didn't kill Jason at all, that some entirely *human* being had been manipulating you. How would you feel about that?"

There was a long silence. "Are you serious?"

"Absolutely."

"You mean, maybe I *didn't* do it?"

"That's what I'm saying."

"Well then, who did?"

"That's what I'm trying to find out. And I think you can help me. Can you remember the day of the accident?"

"I can't forget it. The seventh of May. It was a Thursday. We were getting ready for our last track meet of the season. It was tough to get psyched up for practice, because we didn't have a prayer of doing anything in the tri-county finals. I mean, we were the dregs of the league. The best chance we had was Jason in the quarter-mile, he might have placed third, with luck. And he wasn't bad in the hurdles. But otherwise, the team was a disaster, and we all knew it. It was really hard to go out and practice every day."

"So what happened on that day that made it different from other days? Besides the accident, I mean."

"Well, it was weird. I didn't feel right, hadn't felt right all week. I mean, I knew I wasn't all that good, but I was even worse than usual. I doubled in the discus and shot put, and the discus was usually my stronger event, but I was having a lot of trouble switching back and forth between the two. More trouble than usual. I don't know why."

"Had you discussed this problem with your track coach?"

"Mr. Fulton? Yeah. He didn't have much to offer. I don't think he knows a lot about the field events. He's pretty good on track stuff—I think he's done some himself, still does. Runs 10Ks and so forth. But with a small high school like Oak Canyon, you're lucky if you don't have somebody's *mother* for a track coach. And maybe that wouldn't be so bad. She might know what she was doing."

"Okay. So that particular afternoon—Thursday, May seventh—you were having problems in practice, right?"

The kid shrugged. "I was terrible. I was getting off so many wild throws that I wanted to quit. I was afraid that I might hurt somebody." He shuddered and seemed to repress a sob. "Mr. Fulton told me to hang in there and keep trying, so I did."

"And then what?"

"I got off a really crazy toss. I couldn't even see where it went. Way off to the right. I was about to go look for the plate when Mr. Fulton stopped me."

"He stopped you?"

"He said I had a phone call. That seemed pretty crazy at first, and then I got really worried. I mean, nobody would call me out of track practice unless something was wrong. Bad wrong. Like at home.''

"Did you expect that something might be wrong at home?''

"Well, my mom was on chemo at the time. And you just never know, do you?''

"No,'' Brian said. "You sure don't. Were you surprised that your coach knew you had a phone call?''

"Naw, he made a big deal about this electronic pager he had, a Radio Shack special, I think. There was some arrangement that he let the school office buzz him and leave a number. I never really understood what it was all about, but he had all our home numbers in a little book, so he'd know who to notify in case of an emergency, and I guess he recognized my number when it showed up on his beeper.''

"So what did you do?''

"Well, like I said, I was on my way to go looking for where the discus had landed and Coach told me to forget it, to go back to the school office and call home. He said he'd take care of finding the discus. And I was worried about that, because if we lose or damage a piece of track equipment, we're supposed to pay for it.''

"And then what happened?''

"I hustled my butt back to the school. There was nobody in the office. I looked all over the building and couldn't find anyone. I went down to the locker room and got some change out of my pocket and called home on the pay phone, but I didn't get an answer. That's when I got seriously worried—maybe my mom had been taken to the hospital or something. So I hit the shower and got dressed, and by the time I was outta there, I was hearing sirens all over the place and the shit had hit the fan.''

"They had found Jason?''

The kid's face seemed to melt. "Oh, man, I never felt so bad in my life. They told me at first that he was still alive, that he might make it. Jason was a good guy. We weren't close, but I liked him. When they told me he had died, I felt like I had died, too. Sometimes I still feel that way. Why couldn't it have been me? I'm the clumsy one; I'm the one who put that discus where it shouldn't have been. *I'm* the one who deserved to die, damn it!''

Brian felt totally inept. Ye gods, why wasn't he better at this sort of thing? Theresa would know how to handle it. Even *Mabel* would know how to handle it. His instinctive reaction was to back off, run away. Another part of him wanted to cradle and comfort this oversized kid who had suffered so much pain—needlessly, Brian suspected. But, if he tried to cradle and comfort, what would the kid think?

Brian put a tentative hand on the kid's shoulder. "Brett," he said gently. "You didn't do this. Believe me, you did *not* kill Jason Banks. I need you to help me prove this. I hope that you will help. But meanwhile, you need to take care of yourself, keep yourself sort of centered. And talk to me, huh?''

Brian's options were abruptly limited when Brett threw himself against him and began to sob mightily. Barely able to remain in an upright position, Brian shut his eyes and turned off his brain and let primordial instincts take over. He found himself patting and then rubbing an enormous back. He heard himself crooning an ancient lullaby. He realized that it felt good. It all felt pretty good.

Maybe he wouldn't be such a terrible father, after all.

THIRTY-TWO

THERESA WAS SLIPPING OFF the brink into deep sleep when her telephone rang. Cruelly jarred, she took a few deep breaths before she groped for the headset. This is how people die of heart attacks, she thought. The phone rings at the wrong time. Please God, let nothing be wrong up in Portland. But it probably was a wrong number. She picked up the phone midway through the fifth ring.

"Mrs. Scanlon?" The voice was whispery, definitely female.

Theresa's adrenaline surged. "Yes?"

"He killed them. He killed them all."

"Who is this?"

"I can't tell you. But I saw something. And I know some other things."

Theresa sat up and turned on her bedside lamp. "What are you talking about?" She reached for the pad and pen that did duty next to the phone.

"I know you talked to Amy. She told me. But she doesn't *know*."

Theresa fumed. What kind of games were these kids playing? "Look, I'm going to hang up unless you tell me who you are and what it is you want to talk to me about. I'll give you thirty seconds."

"I can't tell you who I am. But I'll tell you what I saw."

Patience, Theresa told herself. "So what did you see?"

"I saw enough to be pretty sure that Mr. Fulton killed Jason."

"*What?*" Theresa's pen dropped from her suddenly numb fingers and rolled under the bed.

"I used to sneak in to watch track practice—this is embarrassing. I was really hung up on a guy on the track team, but he didn't know I existed. And I didn't want anybody to know how I felt. So I used to stand under the bleachers, over toward the refreshment stand. I could see the field from between the rows of seats, but nobody could see me.''

''Yes?'' Theresa encouraged, hardly daring to breathe. ''What happened?''

''Well, I wasn't paying attention at first; I was watching Darren. He's a pole-vaulter. And then I heard Mr. Fulton call out for Brett Miller. Brett had been getting off some really wild throws—I thought one was going to hit me once, but it sort of did a curve and landed down behind the snack shack. Mr. Fulton talked to Brett and then Brett took off toward the school building. And then Mr. Fulton motioned for Jason to come over to him.''

''Jason Banks?'' Theresa frantically groped under the bed for her pen.

''Yeah. I couldn't hear what they were saying, but it looked like Mr. Fulton was telling Jason to go get the discus and bring it back—just from the way he was making arm motions, if you get me.''

''Sure,'' Theresa said, rapidly making notes in her eccentric shorthand. She drew in a quick breath. ''You're telling me that when Brett got off the wild toss that landed behind the snack shack, Jason was still out on the field?''

''Yes.'' The voice wavered a bit. ''I may have to hang up now.''

''NO!'' Theresa tried not to shout. ''You've got to finish this.'' *Damn it*, she thought. ''Then what did you see?''

''Jason ran back toward the snack shack. Mr. Fulton followed him. Jason looked around, and bent over to pick up the discus. Mr. Fulton got him from behind in a sort of armlock. He reached into his pocket and pulled out something; I couldn't see what. And then both of them disappeared behind the snack shack. I couldn't see anything else.''

''What did you do then?''

''I ran home. I was scared.''

''Have you ever told anyone else about what you saw?''

''No.'' The voice began to whimper.

''Why? My God, don't you realize what you're covering up?''

"Brett never got in trouble. They said it was an accident."

"Look, you've got to give me your name, your telephone number. If you give me a deposition, maybe you won't have to testify, but you're the only witness...." Theresa took a deep breath. "You called me tonight. You said, 'He killed them all'— do you mean Mr. Fulton? And who else did he kill? And why did you call me if you aren't willing to testify to what you saw?"

There was a teary pause. "I don't know. I just want *somebody* to do *something*."

"Why can't that somebody be you?"

"I have to hang up now," said the whimpery, whispery voice. And it did.

THERESA HATED TO CALL Brian at such an ungodly hour. She knew he would be surly and probably incoherent. He was both—in spades.

"I just got a phone call, and I need to tell you about it," she told him, and proceeded to do so. "It's nothing we can take to court, or even to Bascombe. But I think it's a breakthrough, of sorts. Tomorrow's Saturday. Are you free?"

"Mmmrrummph," said Brian.

"I'd like to go up in the hills and poke around, check out where the Wing boy's dog found that bone. Are you game?"

"I guess so. Let's not make it too early, though. Hey, this kid on the phone—do you think we can track her down?"

"I doubt it, Brian. And even if we could, I don't think she'd testify. And she didn't really *see* Fulton kill the Banks kid."

"Ayahh," Brian observed profoundly.

"Pick me up at nine. I'll call the Wings first thing in the morning; with luck, we can get Rich's son to go with us. Maybe the dog, too. Deal?"

"Deal," Brian grunted, rolling back into sleep.

THIRTY-THREE

BRIAN REMEMBERED Paloma County Deputy Sheriff Richard Louis Wing as a tall, rangy blond with a ginger-colored mustache. Cable-muscled, lean as a bean, Wing was nobody you'd want to mess with. Yet he had a solid reputation as a nice guy. As Brian and Theresa headed up into the foothills in his Hyundai, she filled him in on personal details: The Wings had a sort of ranchette on which they supported a large and varied menagerie of animals that had been abandoned or found injured. There were three or four young Wings. Mrs. Wing worked with 4-H kids to train guide dogs for the blind, and gave private obedience classes. (No, Theresa didn't think she accepted cats—only dogs and the occasional recalcitrant horse.) From time to time, Theresa told Brian, the Wings had been known to take in a foster child on a temporary basis.

Rich Wing was waiting to open the gate for them as they pulled into the gravel driveway. He wore an amateurishly stenciled T-shirt that proclaimed PIGS NEED LOVE TOO, faded denim cutoffs, and hiking boots. As Brian braked in a puff of dust, he could see that a scaled-down version of Wing, sans ginger mustache, was sitting on the porch steps with his arm around a golden Lab who seemed to be quivering with excitement.

"We're all set to go unless you'd like some coffee first," Wing said, shaking Brian's hand through the open car window and aiming a lascivious wink at Theresa.

"No coffee, honey, but how about a kiss?" Theresa made movie-vamp eyes at him.

Wing loped around the car and obliged, making a hammy exhibition of it. Wing's kid laughed so hard that he let go of the dog, who galloped to the Hyundai and did a good job of Frenching off Theresa's makeup before she figured out how to roll up the window.

"What's this dog's name?" Theresa sputtered, groping into her purse for tissues.

"I dunno," Wing managed between whoops of laughter. "Which one is this, Ben?"

"Tawny." Up close, the kid didn't look so much like his dad, Brian thought. He looked as though he *wanted* to look like his dad. He was a true towhead, even at age—twelve? Thirteen? It was hard to guess the age of a boy who was on the verge of spurting into his growth and turning into a bewildered Martian. Ben was finer of bone, fairer of complexion than his father, and his nose was peeling. "You know, Dad, I think we'd better take the four-by-four."

"Okay, if you say so. Let me go get the keys." Rich Wing jogged back toward the house, which looked comfy in a sagging sort of way, the kind of place where dogs and cats might bed down on the furniture without making much of a dent in the ambience.

Theresa had exited the Hyundai and was fondling the dog. "She's a female, I'd guess," she said to Ben. "I mean, she seems very open about expressing affection."

"Labs are like that. They're loving dogs. Tawny's the one we kept out of that litter. We fed them all with baby bottles."

"How did that come to be?"

Ben took a deep breath and seemed to struggle with a combination of pride and sadness. "The bitch died about two weeks after the pups were born. The vet called and asked whether we could take the litter—six pups. Good, registered stock. But of course they weren't weaned yet, nowhere ready to leave their mother. So we raised them until they were two months old. One of them didn't make it. Four of them went to 4-H kids to be trained as guide dogs. I got to keep Tawny because she was too hyper to be a good guide dog, shucks, even *I* could tell that. But she's a good dog. We've got other goldens, but she's my favorite."

"Ah, she's a sweetie," Theresa crooned, totally in love. "Is this the dog that found the bone?"

Ben allowed a grin to escape from lips that had concealed a formidable armory of hardware. "Sure. That's

Tawny. She's a digger. She dug up the remains of a horse we lost two years ago.''

Theresa looked at Brian. "Should we hire this dog?"

HALF AN HOUR OF teeth-grinding travel later, Ben indicated that his father should stop the truck, that they were as close to the archaeological dog dig as they were going to get via modern technology. They had been traveling through depressingly burned-over hillsides and ravines; the lingering acrid stench of charred wood and perhaps animal matter still pervaded the area. Brian wished that he had worn his climbing boots; he noticed that Theresa was nervously eyeing her Nikes, preparing to kiss them off. At least, in late summer, it was dry, so there would be no mud to struggle with.

Brian tried to ignore the damp patch in his crotch where Tawny had been depositing her ecstatic drool; during the trek up into the hills, Theresa had been fondling her constantly. "How are we going to proceed here?"

Ben was fumbling into the glove compartment as Rich detached a compass from the dashboard. "Huh?"

"I mean, what are we going to do? You don't know exactly where the dog dug up the bone, do you?"

Ben turned around from the front seat. "No, but Tawny will lead us to the place." He held up a plastic bag that contained a bright blur of fabric. "See, when she brought me the piece of bone, I wrapped it in my headband so it would retain whatever scent might have been there. If there's anything, Tawny will recognize it. Here, girl!" He reached over and clipped a long lead onto the Lab's collar.

Rich turned around and looked hard at Brian and Theresa. "Ben was way ahead of us," he said quietly as the boy maneuvered the dog out of the backseat of the truck. "He expected that it would all come down to this. You see, he knew Jessie from the church group and from school. He had a sort of crush on her. Please don't let on that I told you this. He'd be embarrassed."

"Gotcha." Brian unfolded himself from the backseat and tested his knees: stiff, but functional. Theresa's expression seemed a bit pained. Incipient degenerative arthritis, Brian thought. Theresa really ought to exercise regularly.

After letting Tawny do her obligatory dribbles and bits around several surrounding bushes, Ben removed the headband from its plastic shroud and shoved the dog's nose into it. At first, Tawny seemed less than interested. Then her ears began to quiver and she aggressively nuzzled and scruffed. Brian cast a glance at Rich. The elder Wing's face was a study in contrasts: one part "Okay, so we'll humor the kid," the other part "Hey, the kids not bad, huh?"

Ben bent down and whispered something into Tawny's ear. The dog bounded up as though released on a spring, then she and Ben disappeared into the underbrush.

"Jesus," Brian said. He looked up at the lanky deputy. "How do we keep track of what's happening?"

Rich Wing yawned and stretched. "We wait until we hear a beep from this." He reached under his T-shirt and pulled out a pager. "The kid's got a homer on his belt. When he thinks he's got something, he'll activate a signal. We'll zero right in on the place—if he finds it. Until then, we might as well relax." He settled himself into the front seat of the truck and leaned back against the headrest.

Brian looked at Theresa, who was looking as astonished as he felt. He looked at Rich. "Hey, I had no idea that you guys had such sophisticated equipment. I mean, I've been given to understand that the Sheriff's Department was really hurting for high-tech help."

"Who said anything about the department?" Rich turned around, opening one eye and then the other. He winked at Brian. "We've got a high-tech family, that's all. I've got a high-tech kid. We write it all off against the ranch expenses. And let's say that today we're doing a little volunteer public-service work. Now, you wouldn't tell on me, would you?"

"No way," Brian said fervently. Theresa had already curled herself up into the backseat of the truck. "I'll just wait for the beep, maybe count some sheep." He opened the back door and nudged Theresa to move over a smidgen. "Let the next generation take over."

THIRTY-FOUR

SCRUNCHED UNCOMFORTABLY into a corner of the back-seat of Rich Wing's four-wheeler, Brian felt himself dozing off. His major talent, he had often thought, was dozing off. He had been known to doze off while practicing his guitar, while waiting to testify in court, even (O Shame! O Major Embarrassment!) during leisurely foreplay, not to mention afterplay. Some guardian angel had so far kept him from dozing off while driving a car. But the truth of the matter was that if Brian remained in a reasonably relaxed position for more than five minutes, he was apt to doze off unless someone engaged him in conversation.

Well, Brian thought, why not? Everybody else seemed to have dozed off. Periodic apneic snorts erupted through Rich Wing's mustache; Theresa seemed to be snoring delicately. The hypnotic hums and buzzes of various insects formed a shroud of white noise around the truck; the air smelled spicy sweet when the breeze was from the right direction.

Brian felt himself letting go, drifting away. His eyes were closed, he realized. But he was still awake. Of course he was. He was looking at the insides of his eyelids. Well, this was fascinating. All sorts of images were being projected onto the insides of his eyelids. A progression of faces, faces he didn't remember ever seeing before. Where had they come from? He decided to enjoy the movie, not try to direct it. The human faces were replaced by flower faces: pansies, daisies, and then poppies. Poppies dropping petals, dripping blood. The drops of blood formed and reformed into a melange of innards: his first and last autopsy.

Brian jerked awake, shaken. Rich and Theresa were still catnapping. What had happened to the kid? And the dog? He fidgeted. What could he do? Nothing, now.

He thought about how all this had come about. He had gone down to Crystal Cove to visit Sadie. She had taken him to a weird sort of art show. And now here he was.

He thought about Joanna, and realized that he had been trying not to think about the lady. How was she involved in all this? Or was she? I need to call her, Brian told himself.

This time, his eyes closed of their own volition. The dream began before he was quite asleep. He was running down a gravel road, holding a fuzzy little dog on a leash. The road wound through fragrant fields of sunflowers, hollyhocks, poppies. The dog's leash kept getting longer; he was losing track of the little dog. Incipient panic swelled in his chest; it was important that he not lose this dog. He wanted desperately to cry.

A water fountain appeared at the side of the road. Holding grimly on to his end of the leash, he made a detour to get a drink. The water tasted like ice-cold strawberry Kool-Aid. Large birds circled above him, laughing. He looked up and saw Mabel, perched in the crotch of a live oak. "Ma—" he tried to say, but could say nothing.

He realized to his horror that he had somehow lost hold of the little dog's leash. He looked up again, but the tree and the cat had disappeared. He looked down, and found himself surrounded by tiny people who looked like his mother. "I told you so," they all cackled. "I told you so."

I need to find the dog, Brian told himself in his dream. *I need to find the dog.*

Suddenly he found himself on a beach, groping his way through wafting ghosts of fog. Fog, dog, fog. The dog is in the fog. He could hear the wavelets breaking against the shore. He aimed himself toward the sound. A sudden break in the overcast revealed a sodden furry body washed up on the beach.

Oh, no! Brian cried out, in his dream. Sobbing, he waded out into the breaking waves and gathered into his arms the corpse of the drowned dog. Oh, poor doggy! Why didn't I take care of you?

Brian's armful of drowned canine seemed to be increasing in both substance and viability, becoming harder to hold, dragging him down. He sank toward the sand, finally, as the armful entwined her arms around his neck. Somehow he was not surprised to see that he was looking into Joanna's face. But it was all so wet everywhere, so very wet.

As it was, for Brian, when Rich Wing's beeper went off.

THIRTY-FIVE

BRIAN EMERGED SUDDENLY, jarringly, from his damp dream. The guilty flush that washed over him went unnoticed by his companions, who were engrossed in waking themselves up and regrouping. He reflected that his crotch had been wet anyway, thanks to Tawny's drool. In an hour, he would feel sticky and uncomfortable, but there was nothing he could do now to rectify the situation—not without totally losing face.

Theresa mumbled and rubbed her cheeks. Rich Wing yawned and unclipped some sort of device from his sun visor, then reached under the dashboard for a backpack that Brian had not noticed before. "Let's go fetch," he said.

The going was not easy; they were not following a path, but, rather, homing in on Ben and the dog. The conversation en route was largely limited to comments not suitable for publication in a family newspaper. Machetes all around would have helped, Brian thought as he tried to wrestle his way through the tough and thorny chaparral. Bushwhacking, that's what the hiking guidebooks called this sort of excursion. Except that in this case the bushes were doing all the whacking, and Brian had nothing with which to whack back. And he could sense all too vividly that they were climbing, climbing all the time.

The dog's excited high-pitched whimpering was the first indication that they were nearing their goal. "Ben?" Rich called.

"Over here, Dad!" Ben blundered through the brush toward them, his face tear-streaked. "Oh, Daddy." He ran into his father's open arms.

Rich knelt and hugged the boy tightly; they talked for a few moments in tones too low to be intelligible. Then he straightened up and looked at Brian and Theresa. "The dog's found some more bones. Some of them are charred, and they're mostly fragments, but Ben thinks that they're human, and that they match the profile. We'll have to ship them off to the state forensic lab to be sure. And there's a big problem, Ben says."

"What's the problem?" Brian felt a cold shuddering in his gut. Could he stop the action, rewind the film, and take it back to the video-rental store?

"Ben didn't see anything that looked like part of a skull. And you know what that means."

Brian did indeed: almost no chance of making a positive identification, no chance of determining whether these bones belonged to Jessica Stearns, no chance of nailing her weirdo stepfather. The bone fragments could belong to at least a few of the dozen or so people who had disappeared up in here during the past several years. Some of them had been females, young females. He groaned aloud.

Theresa was already following Rich and the kid through the chaparral. Brian took a deep breath and tagged along.

The dog, barely recognizable in her new coat of soot and ash, obviously had been digging furiously; scattered mounds of earth dotted an area that had been burned over down to bare soil. Burned over so intensely, Brian thought, that the brushfire must have started in that immediate area. He looked for evidence that a tree had been struck by lightning, but he saw none.

Then he looked at the dog. She was resting now, panting, worrying something in her mouth. Ben went over to her and replaced what she had been mouthing with a shot of water from his canteen. He brought the object to his father.

"Part of a human pelvis, I think." The kid's eyes squinched shut, briefly, but he managed to hang on. "I tried to mark all the places where Tawny found the bones. It was hard, because I had to get them away from her before she chewed them up, so sometimes I lost track of the exact places. I just stuffed everything into my backpack—bones and fragments and dirt and whatever. I know it wasn't the best forensic procedure, but I couldn't think what else to do."

"You did well, son," Rich said, whomping the kid gently on the seat of his pants.

Brian stared, transfixed at the bit of bone that Ben had retrieved from Tawny's mouth. Well, it was more than a bit. He looked at Theresa, who seemed a bit queasy but determined to rise to the occasion.

"How much have you got in there?" Theresa asked, pointing to Ben's backpack.

The boy removed the pack from his shoulders and handed it to her, mutely.

"It's heavy," Theresa observed, surprised. The kid nodded. She looked inside.

"Oh, my God." Theresa looked at Brian and then at Rich. "These are human remains, no doubt about it." She looked at Ben. "Did the dog find all of these fragments right around here?"

Ben nodded.

"What does that tell you?"

"Somebody buried a body." Brian, Ben, and Rich seemed to speak at once.

"But didn't bury it deep enough," Rich offered.

"The coyotes got at it," Ben suggested, looking sick.

"Makes you wonder about the fire, doesn't it?" Brian wondered out loud.

"If we got a scene-of-crime unit up here, could they possibly come up with anything?" Theresa asked Rich.

"Doubtful."

Brian closed his eyes and flashed back on camping trips with his Boy Scout troop, twenty years ago. Well, more than twenty years ago. Working on his woodsmanship merit badge. A kid from Queens transported via chartered bus to the fearsome wilds of New Jersey.

Spoor, he remembered. Tracks.

"Let's look around for a bit," Brian said. "Split up, spread out. Let's look for things other than bones, okay? Things that maybe didn't get burned—or eaten." He swallowed back bile.

Rich shrugged. "Can't hurt."

"I'm exhausted," Theresa said. "But I don't know how to get back to the truck."

"I'll take you," Ben told her. He looked at the dog, who was fast asleep and snoring. "I think Tawny's pooped, too." He refastened her leash and tied it to a branch of blackened brush, then hoisted the bone-filled pack. "Dad, bring her when you come back, okay?"

"Okay. We won't be long. Will we?" Rich tossed the truck keys to the boy and looked meaningfully at Brian.

"Not long," Brian promised.

He began to wander aimlessly, not sure what he was looking for. There had been a grave of sorts, and in this immediate area. Why? Why here? The site was remote—a plus, if one did not want a body to be discovered, but a disadvantage if one wanted to dispose of a body without shlepping it over a mile or so of hostile terrain. Why this place?

Brian looked around, trying to envision the site before it had been burned over. It seemed to have been a natural clearing, a sort of glade. He noticed, for the first time, an outcropping of rocks. He took a closer look. The rocks were rather interesting; their natural grouping was pleasing to the eye. The site, he realized, was actually the crown of a smallish hill; some of the rocks had crumbled and broken away in a sort of minuscule avalanche. He followed the trail down the slope, becoming aware of a gentle rushing sound, and realized that he was descending into the ravine of a year-round creek, that the microenvironment was changing with every step he took, that in fact he was entering a forest of ferns—a magical place. He kept slipping and sliding on the gravel and stones underfoot, more so as the slope grew steeper, and finally stopped himself by the simple expedient of sitting down on his butt and digging in his heels.

Brian came to rest just above a quiet pool in the tiny stream, a miniature reservoir created by a tree stump that had worked its way downhill to form an accidental dam. He looked around and breathed deeply, absorbing and enjoying the scents and sounds and scene.

But something was bugging him. Something was not quite right, not natural. A Coors can in the creek? No. A discarded bit of plastic wrapping?

He closed his eyes, willed himself back into the persona of a twelve-year-old Boy Scout, and then opened his eyes and did a quick scan.

Aha.

Aha, he thought.

That rock is wrong.

There is something wrong about that rock.

It was a largish rock, too big to have been carried down the hillside by runoff. And it looked wrong. Why?

Brian crawled over and touched the top of it. It looked black, darkened with dried mud.

It hasn't rained here for months, Brian thought. Something unnatural has turned over this rock. Some*body* has turned over this rock.

He turned it over.

The underside of the rock obviously had been touched by a human hand, had been crudely inscribed with some sort of message, in fact. Brian could not make out the inscription. He groped in his pocket for his reading glasses and realized that he had left them in his briefcase, which was in his car, which was back at Rich Wing's place.

He heard the other rock coming before he realized what he was hearing. It bounded down the slope, caroming wildly. Brian looked around frantically for some kind of cover and realized that he had none, that he had no way of knowing what kind of bounces the rock might take. When it finally came to rest harmlessly in the creek, Brian began to ask himself an uncomfortable question: Where had it come from?

When the shotgun blast echoed down into the ravine, Brian thought he knew.

THIRTY-SIX

FOR A PERSON WHO HAD failed the Sheriff's Department physical four times, Brian told himself, he was not doing badly. Sure, he was gasping, but the important thing was that he was still breathing. He had crawled on his belly like a snake, stopped, listened, and sniffed. After a while, he had come to the conclusion that whoever had been shooting at him—if, in fact, *he* had been the target—had given up. No other rocks had come tumbling down the steep slope. He seemed to be safe for the moment.

He took a deep breath and pushed himself up into a tenuous crouch. Uh-oh. Well, plenty of bushes, and no witnesses. He unzipped and watered a particularly parched-looking adolescent oak tree. Now what?

Rich Wing, Brian reasoned, must have heard the shotgun. But what would the deputy have done? Waited for Brian to return? Hightailed it back to the truck to go for help? Or taken off to look for him on his own?

Brian realized that he had no idea where he was or how to get back to the clearing, let alone the truck. He had belly-crawled a long way in a state of sheer panic, paying no attention to landmarks. Gradually, he seemed to have worked himself uphill; the creek was no longer visible or audible.

"If you realize that you are lost," he remembered vaguely from the *Boy Scout Handbook*, "stay where you are." The first rule of woodsmanship. "Construct a crude shelter if you can; drink sparingly from your canteen. Eventually, someone will find you."

Canteen, ha! Crude shelter, double ha! Yeah, in New Jersey someone would have found him fast, even if he had been deep in the Pine Barrens. Someone would have ripped off his wallet and stomped him to death. But this was California wilderness, and if anything found him, it would probably be an endangered and hungry condor who had not yet been rescued by environmentalists.

You are being a shmuck, Brian told himself. Think!

He had gone downhill to the creek, but he had lateraled for a ways. Downhill was supposed to be the safest route, following a watercourse, but he suspected that he would encounter an impenetrable jungle if he followed the creek downstream, that the ravine would peter out in a tangle of chaparral. If he went uphill, he might be able, eventually, to see where he was.

Brian listened again, hard. He heard the buzzing of sundry insects, the cries and caws and cackles of swooping and diving birds.

He voted for uphill.

Brian kept telling himself that he was not that far from civilization as he knew it. He envisioned his mother, as he scrabbled and clawed his way up the slope. Sadie would never forgive him if he didn't survive. So what was he worried about? Was there guilt after death? All he was sure of was that he was scared—and terminally thirsty. He yearned for a cold brew, or a wet Canada Dry, or even a reasonably clean puddle. He had stopped looking where he was going—a bad sign. He realized with a start that he might actually die here, sprawled without dignity on an anonymous hillside. Shit, where were all the search-and-rescue people?

Refueled by an unexpected dose of adrenaline, Brian scrambled up another fifty feet of hillside and encountered a sort of plateau. Upon further inspection, it appeared to be a well-traveled trail. He sprawled facedown and panted.

Surely he was dreaming, maybe hallucinating. He heard women singing. He could not recognize the melody, but the sound was sweet and pure.

I am dead, Brian thought. There really are angels, and they are singing. Am I in heaven? Gosh, how on earth did I manage that?

The next thing he knew, water was being gently dribbled into his mouth. Someone was holding up his head.

Brian awoke quickly and attempted to sit up.

"Not too fast," a voice admonished. He looked around, and found himself surrounded by an oddly assorted group of females. Some were rather elderly and wearing what he recognized as being traditional nuns' habits; others were youngish and wearing jeans and sweatshirts. All sported functional-looking backpacks and hiking boots.

"Erm," Brian croaked. "Sister, I presume?"

A tall brunette crouched down to his level. "Sisters of the Immaculate Conception, at your service. And I am Sister Bernadette O'Rourke, registered nurse and certified paramedic. Are you having trouble breathing?"

"Just a bit," Brian breathed, gazing into a wonderfully Irish face. "But I think it will pass."

"Can you walk?"

"Yes, I'm sure I can. With a little help, maybe. My problem is that I don't know in which direction to walk. What I mean is, I'm lost."

"Not to worry." Sister Bernadette hoisted him to his feet with practiced ease. "We're only about a half a mile from our van. We can carry you, if necessary."

Brian was tempted for a moment. "No, Sister. I'd better walk. But you may have to go slowly." He looked into her Irish eyes, which looked back at him with a definite twinkle.

"Slowly is my middle name," said the beguiling Sister Bernadette. She bent down and whispered into his ear, "And don't worry; we won't eat you. We're vegetarians."

THIRTY-SEVEN

AFTER ABOUT FIFTEEN minutes of slow going up the path, supported altogether agreeably by Sister Bernadette, Brian began to feel somewhat recovered. The other nuns had gone on ahead. He looked up at Sister Bernadette and wondered why he always seemed to find himself looking *up* at women he found attractive. "I think I can make it by myself now," he told her.

"Are you sure? Not feeling light-headed anymore?"

"No, I think I'm back to normal." He disengaged himself and took a few tentative steps. "I seem to be fine. But I don't know what I would have done if you hadn't come along."

The nun laughed. "Oh, someone would have. This is a popular hiking trail, especially on weekends. And you're really not that far from civilization, you know."

"That's what I kept telling myself," Brian said ruefully. He looked out of the corner of his eye at the statuesque sister. Her dark curly hair had been pulled back into a hasty ponytail; her habit consisted of a gray T-shirt that proclaimed LOYOLA MARYMOUNT and faded blue jeans worn through at one knee.

"It's funny," he mused out loud, "but come to think of it, I've never known a nun before." He considered the biblical implications and blushed profoundly.

"Oh, you probably have, without realizing it," Sister Bernadette said cheerfully. "We nuns have changed a lot during the last couple of decades. Well, some of us have, anyway." She turned to look at him. "Are you doing okay?"

"Yeah, but I hope we're almost there."

Bernadette scanned the scenery. "Five or ten minutes more, I'd say."

A scrabbling sound preceded the appearance of a small figure who scurried down the path in their direction. "Sister, Sister!" it called in a hoarse whisper. Brian realized that he was looking at a dumpling of a middle-aged nun whose full-length habit had been haphazardly shortened by virtue of (he supposed) safety pins, revealing a pair of sturdy hiking boots.

"Sister Rosella?" Sister Bernadette seemed astonished. "What on earth is the matter?"

Sister Rosella dithered. "Oh, dear, we didn't know what to do. I mean, everyone is just hiding in the bushes. Sister Loretta said we all ought to arm ourselves with branches and stones and attack, but of course she watches too much television. Anyway, we thought you'd know how to handle this."

Bernadette took the older nun by the shoulders and gave her a good shake. "What's 'this'? What's going on?"

Sister Rosella shuddered. "A man. There's a man. There's a man in our van." She let out a muffled shriek. "And he's got a gun!"

HAVING CALMED DOWN Sister Rosella sufficiently to elicit a description of the ominous gunman and his weapon, Brian felt reasonably confident that the man who awaited them at the trailhead parking area was Rich Wing—armed not with a shotgun but with a smallish sidearm, small enough to have been concealed under Wing's admittedly baggy T-shirt. Still, he approached cautiously; he didn't know the deputy well enough to guess how quick he might be on the trigger, if caught by surprise.

"What's our game plan?" Sister Bernadette whispered.

"Stay here," he whispered back. "I think everything's okay, but stay under cover until I give you the high sign."

"And what sort of sign will that be?"

"I don't know. You'll be able to tell, I'm sure. I'll…" Wet my pants, Brian thought.

He crept up the path until he could see Wing—slamming the van door in disgust, walking dejectedly around the vehicle, finally slouching against the front bumper. "Rich?" he called tentatively.

Wing wheeled around and reached under his T-shirt.

"Don't shoot! It's me, Brian. And some friends." Brian stood up and made himself visible. "That's their van you were checking out, and you scared the, erm, blazes out of them." Brian staggered up to Wing and clapped him on the back. "Rich, I found something down there," he gasped. "I think it's Jessie's gravestone."

Rich stared at him, not computing. "Shit, man, I thought you were dead!"

"Shhh! Watch your language!" Brian turned toward the trail and waved energetically. "All clear, ladies! Allee allee in free!"

Rich Wing took in and let out a long breath. He looked hard at Brian. "What the hell happened?"

"I once was lost but now am found," Brian explained. "By the Sisters of the Immaculate Conception." The nuns were tentatively gathering, emitting nervous giggles.

"This is their van, I take it."

"So they say. I have no reason to disbelieve them, do you?"

Sister Bernadette stepped up and offered Rich her canteen of water. "You look to be a bit dry under the tongue, Deputy."

Rich stared at her.

"We've met before, I think," Bernadette said quietly. "At a bad road accident. We were both in uniform. I'm a paramedic."

Rich drank gratefully from the canteen. "I'm sorry," he said. "I think I need to regroup here." He looked at Brian. "When I heard the shotgun, I had no idea what was going down. I didn't know where you were. I had a pretty good idea where *I* was, so I started looking around near what I remembered as being access routes to the creek. I knew that this trailhead was close by, and the van was the only vehicle parked here. So I checked it out." He looked at Sister Bernadette. "I'm sorry, Sister, if I caused you any alarm."

"No problem," she said. "But what do we do now?"

Brian looked at Wing. "Do you have any idea where we *are* in relation to where we *were*? And, in particular, how far we are from your truck?"

Rich shrugged. "A good bushwhacking mile, I'd say, cross-country. Now let me ask you one: How long would Theresa wait for us before she'd head out for reinforcements—especially if she heard the shotgun?"

Brian's head swam. "How long has it been since Theresa and Ben went back to the truck?"

Rich looked at his watch. "An hour and change. Close to an hour and a half."

"You can't be serious!" It had seemed, Brian thought, more like four or five hours. "You don't have a radio in the truck, do you?"

Rich shook his head.

Something pinged in Brian's brain. "What happened to the dog?" *I need to find the dog*, he thought. Oh, no, poor doggy. He clenched his grip on the edges of consciousness. Was all of this a recycled dream?

"I let the dog loose when I went to look for you," Wing told him. "She was awake by then, but she wouldn't have been any help, and I figured that she'd go back to the truck."

"Are you sure? Aren't you worried about the dog?" Brian realized that the nuns were looking at him impatiently. He resolutely centered himself. "We have to figure out what to do. I'm not sure how long Theresa would have waited for us. And I don't know whether she can drive a four-by-four."

Rich shrugged. "Ben can drive the truck, if it comes to that."

"Ben can drive that truck? How old is he, twelve?"

"With a pillow under his butt, he can drive it just fine."

"But what about the keys?"

"I gave him my keys when he and Theresa decided to head back."

"So the question is," Ben observed—to himself as much as to anyone else—"are they still there or did they go to call for help?"

Sister Bernadette spoke up. "Can we get from here to there in our van?"

Wing looked dubious. "You mean, from here to where the truck was parked?"

"That's what I mean. This van doesn't have four-wheel drive, but I've taken it up and down a lot of roads that mountain goats would think twice about attempting."

Wing debated for about five seconds. "Sister," he said, flashing his badge, "I hereby commandeer this van in the name of the Paloma County Sheriff's Department."

"Okay, Sisters," Bernadette hollered. "Pile in!"

A VANFUL OF NUNS, Brian reflected, might make a charming pen and ink sketch for *The New Yorker*. A vanful of nuns plus a large deputy sheriff and an overweight DA's investigator made for discomfort, to say the least, both physical and emotional—especially when the van became periodically airborne, headed for a crash landing guaranteed to loosen a few teeth and bowels.

Sister Bernadette drove. Rich Wing, as navigator, shared the front seat, which was bisected by the gearbox. Brian found himself squeezed into the second seat, with Sister Rosella on his lap. The little nun obviously was as tense as a concrete slab; Brian wondered whether she'd had a fatal heart attack and rigor mortis had set in. Well, the lady probably hadn't sat on a man's lap for a half century or so. Sensitive creature that he was, he tried not to touch her, but of course that was impossible. From time to time, he needed to grab her firmly to keep her from catapulting through the roof.

The overloaded van strained and shuddered as it hauled its cargo up the deeply rutted fire road. Both Rich and Sister Bernadette muttered and sometimes shouted imprecations. Bernadette's comments were unintelligible; Brian suspected that she was cursing in Latin. Was that possible? The other nuns seemed to be muttering, too; what Brian vaguely recognized as rosaries had materialized from the pockets of Levis. This van, Brian thought, is going to need a new set of shocks.

Finally, just when Brian had decided that he was going to need a new set of kidneys, the van pulled up behind Wing's truck. There was no one in sight.

"Honk the horn," Rich told Bernadette. "Two longs, two shorts." He jumped out of the van and headed for the truck.

"Erm, Sister." Brian attempted to address the apparently paralyzed nun on his lap. "I, um, need to get out. Can we open the door?" He managed to slide himself out from under the nun and work himself down to terra firma—always an iffy proposition in Southern California. Sister Bernadette was already out of the van and conferring with a worried-looking Wing, who was shaking his head.

"This doesn't look good," Wing was saying as Brian approached. "Why would they have taken off on foot? The keys are in the truck, and Ben's backpack is still there. But there's no sign of Ben, or the dog, or..."

Brian's stomach lurched and he closed his eyes, feeling suddenly dizzy. An eruption of noise and movement shocked him into sensibility: the dog had burst into the clearing, followed by the boy. Both made a beeline for Rich Wing, almost knocking him over.

"Oh, Dad!" The kid stopped and looked around. "Who are all these people?"

"Never mind." Wing's gruffness failed to conceal his damp-eyed relief. "Where were you? What happened?"

Ben paused to catch his breath. "I was asleep, and Tawny jumped through the window and woke me up. And then she took off. I didn't know what was going on, so I went after her. It took me a while to catch up. She didn't have her leash—I don't know how she got loose—so it was hard to get her back here."

Wing, obviously embarrassed, reached into a back pocket and pulled out the dog's leash.

Ben looked puzzled. "But Dad, you said you were going to bring Tawny back to the truck when you came." The tears he had been choking back all day began to spill out.

"I'm sorry, son. Things got complicated in a hurry. I just let the dog loose. I thought she'd head back to the truck. And she did, didn't she?"

The nuns murmured sympathetically. Well, Brian thought, it had all worked out. The doggy was okay. Everybody was okay. Except for...

"Ben," Brian began as a chill rose through his body.

"Yes?" The kid let out a hiccup.

"Where's Theresa?"

"Theresa?"

"The lady who came with us. The lady you took back to the truck. Do you know where she is?"

The kid looked back at him blankly. "I brought her back to the truck. We both sort of zonked off, I think."

"And then what?"

Ben shook his head. "When Tawny woke me up, she was gone."

THIRTY-EIGHT

THERESA REALIZED THAT SHE had no idea where she was.

The echoing gunshot had abruptly penetrated an unfocused half dream. She had recognized the sound even before she was fully awake. The kid, more deeply asleep, had just begun to stir. Theresa had cautiously opened the door of Wing's truck and listened. There had been no answering gunfire, nothing to hear but the somnolent humming and buzzing of cicadas and tree frogs. Fueled by uncharacteristic panic, she had set out blindly in what she thought was the direction of the sound—which had seemed to correspond roughly with the place where Tawny had dug up the bones.

After a few minutes, she realized that she had made a dumb move. She had abandoned the kid—mistake number one. She had no way to orient herself, no idea what was going on.

You hopeless cretin, Theresa told herself. You should have stayed with the truck.

But by that time, she knew she was lost. She looked at her watch. The time was fast approaching noon; the sun ought to be almost overhead and no help in determining direction, even if she had known in what direction she should proceed. In fact, the sun barely penetrated the dense thicket of stunted piñon pines that had somehow bullied themselves up to whatever growth they could manage in the deeper shadows of the live oaks that dotted the dusty terrain.

She stopped, took a deep breath, and listened.

"Ben!" She called. "Brian? Rich?" There was no response. "Taw-nee! *Here,* Tawny!"

Well, she thought. I'm not that far from civilization. Unless I walk north. To the north is a national forest, a wilderness area. In any other direction, there will be something.

She squinted up at the sun. In the summer, she vaguely remembered, the sun was more to the north. Or was it the south?

You are losing your mind, Theresa told herself.

Realizing that she was close to losing something else, she looked around for an ad hoc privy. There were definite disadvantages to being of the female persuasion when one was out in the wilds, or out on a boat. A partly fallen tree promised to serve the purpose, complete with handgrips in the form of broken-off limbs. She managed to do the job without messing up her shoes, feeling thankful that at least she did not need to worry about being observed. Or did she?

After what felt like an hour of random trudging through decidedly prickly and hostile terrain—actually it was only fifteen minutes, by her watch—Theresa began to realize that the microenvironment was changing. The piñons were thinning out and getting smaller. The oaks were farther apart. The grass and weeds underfoot were getting thicker; foxtails and burrs were beginning to cling to her socks. The pungent smell of sage brought on an attack of sneezing. Theresa groped into her pocket, hoping that a tissue or two remained. As she did so, she caught a glimpse of something not contrived by Mother Nature: an artifact.

At first, she wasn't sure what she had seen. She took a closer look.

Barbed wire.

A barbed-wire fence.

Which meant a ranch. Which meant a house. Which probably meant a telephone.

She followed the fence downhill, away from the sun. At first, she saw no evidence of occupancy by man or beast. But then she heard a plaintive *mroooOOOOmmm*.

A cow, Theresa thought. My kingdom for a cow!

She tracked along the fence, almost running in her relief. The going was easier now to some extent, but rocks increasingly protruded from the soil. The fence did an abrupt zigzag as it traversed a winter creek. Theresa stumbled down into the gully and found herself using her hands to scrabble up a surprisingly long and steep incline. When she reached the top, panting, she elbowed her way through a dense stand of chaparral and stopped to catch her breath. She was close to the brink of a bluff, she realized. She could see open sky, scudding clouds, soaring birds.

Theresa forced herself to trudge up to the top of the slope, and then she looked down onto an open valley populated by an odd assortment of buildings.

Okay, Theresa told herself. I'm okay now.

She took her time, making her way toward what seemed to be the main house. No point in giving herself a stroke. There must be a gate somewhere in this fence, she thought. People have to get in and out. The ground leveled off as she approached what looked to be a graveled driveway and parking area. There was a gate. It appeared to be locked. What now?

Theresa's blood turned to ice when she heard the deep-throated growling. That, she knew, was the sound of a dog that meant business, a dog that didn't bother with barking or other canine amenities. She very much hoped that the beast was on the other side of the fence. She held herself very still and tried not to exude the smell of fear. How on earth, she wondered, does one do that? She felt sincere empathy for postal carriers.

A human voice rumbled in the distance, and the dog sound subsided. A man appeared from an outbuilding. He waved at Theresa.

"Come on in!" she heard faintly. "Gate's not locked. I've got the dog chained up."

Feeling giddy with relief, Theresa let herself in through the gate. She realized, suddenly, that she was very close to passing out.

Then she looked at the ranch, from the new perspective of the gate, and experienced a rush of déjà vu. She looked at the man, who was rapidly approaching her. He began to look all too familiar.

Oh...My...God, Theresa thought. Options ran through her head in fast forward. Passing out was not an option.

She had, somehow, literally stumbled upon Lloyd Fulton's ranch. Would he recognize her as the DA's investigator who had interviewed him some three months ago?

Would he connect her with whatever heat he might now be feeling?

The man was coming closer, and faster. He was near enough so that Theresa could make out an expression of concern on his face. Maybe he thought she was, in fact, about to pass out.

Well, Theresa thought, I can't outrun him—or his dog. I can barely walk. I'll just have to bluff it out and hope that he doesn't remember me.

"Hey, whoa, lady, are you all right?"

Theresa felt a firm supporting arm under her elbow. "Yes and no," she said truthfully. "I was hiking, and I sort of got lost. I could do with a drink of water, and I need to use your telephone."

She tried not to look at Fulton, but she could feel his eyes raking over her. Did he remember her? Was he wondering whether she remembered him?

He helped her toward the ramshackle dwelling that appeared to be his home. She remembered that when she had talked to him at the ranch before, they had remained outdoors—that somehow she had assumed he'd lived in the impressive main house.

"Water, I can manage," Fulton said. "The well hasn't failed yet. Telephone—well, that depends on what sort of mischief the squirrels have been up to. When we finally got a line out here, it didn't come with maintenance guarantees. Most of it's underground, but we have our problems. Of course, we don't have much use for a phone."

We? Theresa thought. He *doesn't* remember me. Or else he's playing a double bluff. "If I could just sit down for a while," she said weakly.

Fulton deposited her gently on a rump-sprung wicker sofa. "I'll bring you some water."

What's my best plan? Theresa asked herself. She realized that she was in no shape to, had no time to, design any sort of sophisticated strategy. Whom would she call? What would she say in front of Fulton—even if the telephone proved to be operative? Keep it simple, she told herself. Don't threaten him.

When Fulton reappeared with a glass of ice water, Theresa was thrashing and gasping on the faded chintz cushions. "Call nine-one-one," she croaked. "I think . . . having . . . heart attack."

THIRTY-NINE

AFTER THEY HAD REVIEWED the options for retrieving Theresa and agreed that, whatever else might pend, they were all in drastic need of lunch, Bernadette and Rich decided that their best strategy was to head down to civilization and call for reinforcements. Given that a couple of the nuns were already occupying the backseat of Wing's truck, fussing over the dog, Brian climbed in the front seat of the van next to Sister Bernadette. He felt dazed, unable to function. Where was Theresa? Why hadn't he taken care of her?

"Fasten your seat belt," Bernadette reminded him.

"Huh?"

"Your *seat belt*. Fasten it!"

"Oh. Oh yes. I'm sorry, Sister."

"Not as sorry as I'd be if I had to scrape you off the pavement. I'm a paramedic, remember?"

Jolted into a reunion with reality, Brian looked anxiously at the nun. For some reason, it seemed important that she not be upset with him. But she gave him a reassuring smile and squeezed his knee, a seemingly innocent gesture that had rather alarming results in terms of Brian's reflexes. He affected a sneezing fit and doubled over in an attempt to disguise what had rapidly become a highly embarrassing state of affairs.

"Oh, dear. God bless you! You'll find a box of tissues in the glove compartment."

God bless me indeed, Brian thought, groping thankfully into the glove compartment. This is a *nun*, for God's sake. What is happening to me?

"It's a bad time of the year for allergies," Sister Bernadette said consolingly as she turned right, onto the paved highway that led to Oak Canyon. Feeling momentarily back in control of himself, Brian looked over his shoulder and

was relieved to see that Wing's truck was following close
behind. Thus he was not prepared for the sharp braking of
the van as it pulled over onto the graveled shoulder to make
way for what appeared to be an ancient army field ambulance—repainted in Paloma County lemon and azure and
sporting a couple of jury-rigged crisis lights—which was
barreling along in the opposite direction.

Bernadette frowned as she gently nursed the van off the
sloping sandy shoulder and back onto the pavement. "That
looked like Casey," she said to herself.

"Casey?"

"Casey's a paramedic," Sister Bernadette explained.
"He's a volunteer fireman, actually. He was my first EMT
teacher. That's his own rig; he fitted it out himself. They
don't have public ambulances up here."

"Is he on an emergency call?" Brian's adrenaline went
into overdrive. "Doesn't he have a siren?"

"No siren. It just upsets people, gets them freaked out.
The lights are enough. And everybody knows Casey."

Brian fidgeted. "I can't help wondering whether that call
has something to do with Theresa. I mean, maybe she fell
and knocked herself out, and some hikers found her. Or
maybe she had a . . . some sort of seizure."

Bernadette maneuvered around a pothole. "It's certainly
possible. And it's obvious that you're worried. I'm worried, too. And I'm sure that Rich is wondering what is happening."

"So what do you think we should do?"

"I think we should stop at the first sign of a phone. You
call in and check with the county communications center."

"Good plan." Brian set his teeth and concentrated on not
throwing up.

THE RANCH HOUSE BEHIND the roadside produce stand was
peeling and flaking, but the telephone was working. Somehow Brian managed to cut through several layers of part-
time petty bureaucrats by invoking the name of the
esteemed Norman Paloma Bascombe. Maybe he even pretended to *be* the illustrious Norman of county attorney
fame. At any rate, he finally got through to a dispatcher

who informed him that a 911 call had been logged in from an Oak Canyon number, and that the East Canyon fire station had responded.

"What was the nature of the call?" Brian asked.

"Possible heart attack."

"What was the disposition?"

"I'm sorry; you'll have to hold." He was abruptly cut off.

Brian looked at Sister Bernadette, who was discreetly hovering while sipping from a cup of local lemonade. The Wings and nuns were similarly sipping and asking for seconds. Sister Rosella seemed to have revived herself, and was negotiating for a case of lemon preserves. Tawny was making friends with the family mutt. This was all too laid-back, Brian decided. Everyone seemed to have forgotten that a crisis loomed. Theresa was missing!

"Theresa is missing!" he shouted at Sister Bernadette.

"I beg your pardon?"

"If that was Theresa, if she had a heart attack and the paramedics were called, where would she be taken?"

"Paloma County General. Unless they decided to airlift her to civilization."

"Do you know the best way to get to there from here?"

Bernadette nodded.

"Let's go." Brian bowed and scraped to the bewildered farm family. "Someday," he promised them, "I'll tell you what this is about. When I figure it out myself."

FORTUNATELY, the emergency room at Paloma County General Hospital was having a slow day when the ill-assorted caravan invaded its territory. Sister Bernadette seemed to be in charge, to the collective relief of the personnel thereof. To their puzzlement, no one seemed in need of medical attention—until the venerable former army ambulance pulled into the drive-up area.

A man and a woman, visibly arguing, emerged from the front seat.

Brian and Bernadette exited the glass doors simultaneously.

"Theresa!" Brian yelled.

"Casey?" Bernadette ventured tentatively.

The man was large and red-faced, and sweating heavily. He wore a Paloma County Fire Department uniform. "Who is this broad?" he asked Bernadette. "Heart attack, my ass. I'm a helluva lot closer to having a heart attack than she is."

Bernadette gave Casey a substantial hug. "I don't know what happened. It's all pretty complicated. We'll sort it out later. But meanwhile, we're just glad she's safe."

FORTY

HAVING AGREED THAT THEY were all famished, Brian, Theresa, Casey, and the Wings (père et fils) headed as one in the direction of the hospital lunchroom. Tawny, clearly running out of gas, had not objected to being bedded down in the Wings' truck, where she almost immediately fell asleep. Sister Bernadette and her compatriots had departed in their van with apologies, pleading other commitments.

For a traumatized kid, Ben ate surprisingly well, demolishing a brace of hot dogs, an order of fries, and a chocolate milk shake that looked to Brian like sewer sludge in an advanced state of decomposition. Theresa toyed with a chef's salad and iced tea. Casey ate so fast that it was not possible to determine what he had eaten, short of performing an autopsy. Rich Wing seemed to inhale a barbecued-something sandwich. Brian had trouble remembering what he had ordered. A cheeseburger, hold the fries? Whatever, he appeared to have cleaned his plate.

He shook himself awake from a semitrance. Theresa seemed to be explaining to Casey why she had feigned a heart attack. He half-listened, and then jerked awake. What?

"What?" Brian screamed. Heads swiveled throughout the lunchroom. "You ended up at *Fulton*'s ranch? In his *house*?"

Theresa sighed. "I didn't realize where I was until it was too late. I had to improvise. And Brian, Fulton *did* call nine-one-one. Maybe we're on the wrong track here."

Brian shook his head. "You just shocked him. He acted on instinct." He leaned toward Theresa, realizing that Ben was closely attending. "You don't know what I found down by the creek. I haven't had a chance to tell you."

Theresa stared at Brian, bewildered.

"I found Jessie's gravestone. I'm sure of it. We need to go back up there. Are you game?"

Casey stood up. "I'm still on call," he said. "I've got to go." He crumpled his napkin into a ball and shifted his weight from foot to foot. "For what it's worth," he said, "I've been called up to that ranch before. Once I had an unconscious female who was barely breathing. I had to do CPR on her. The man who phoned it in said she'd had a stroke or OD'd on something. Same guy as this call." He looked at Theresa. "By the time I got her to the ER, the bruises were beginning to show up on her throat. He'd done a good job of trying to strangle her, but then he must have changed his mind."

"Was the woman Fulton's wife?" Theresa whispered.

"So he said." Casey pulled his cap from his pocket and jammed it on his head. "You're a lucky lady, I think."

THE SECOND TRIP UP to the forensic dog dig found a dispirited crew in the Wing truck. Brian felt sick. Was he doomed to relive all of this? The dog, Tawny, whimpering in his lap, seemed to share his anxiety.

Ben gave her a drink from his canteen (Yuck, Brian thought) and patted her head. "Good girl," he told her. And she *had* been a good girl, Brian reflected—dozing conveniently while matters got sorted out at the hospital, and then perking up when the truck got going.

"Do you think we can find that rock?" Ben asked.

"Eventually," Brian said. He pondered. "It was right next to the creek. I pretty much went straight downhill from where we found the bones. If we can get back to that place, it will just be a matter of going up and down the creek."

"Tawny will take us back to the bone place," Ben reassured him, attaching the dog's leash to her collar. "Then we'll give her a sniff of your shirt—like under the arm—and she'll probably track where you went. Unless she gets distracted."

"Distracted?" Brian felt unhappy. "What we have here is not exactly a hound, is it? We're not out here on a bleeping duck hunt. This is a retrieving dog, not a tracking dog."

"Please!" Theresa appealed to Brian. "Let's give it a try."

Tawny was more than eager to lead them to the bone depository. The dog was less than eager to follow Brian's meandering odyssey down into the ravine. At one point, Brian took off his shirt and let the dog get a good smell. She sniffed at it and nuzzled at Ben, who gave her another slurp from his canteen. The dog looked at the shirt, snuffled at it again, and then took off.

But somehow, Ben had let go of her leash. Tawny plunged, untended, into the dense underbrush.

"Tawny!" Ben called, close to tears.

The ill-assorted posse stopped, and listened. A sporadic sort of canine whining met their ears. They followed the sound, sliding and skittering down the steep slope that led to the creek.

Ben was the first to find the dog, who was frantically pawing at a damp depression in the ground. Brian slid down the last few feet on his behind. Theresa followed suit. Rich Wing stayed at the top of the declivity, apparently in the belief that at least one of the party ought to remain intact.

Ben grabbed the dog's leash. "Is this the place?"

Brian took a good look around. "This is the place," he said with certainty.

Theresa was shaking. "What about the stone? You told me you thought you'd found Jessie's gravestone."

Brian looked at the shallow, damp concavity. "It's gone. The stone is gone."

"You're sure it was here."

"It was here. I'm sure."

"But who could have moved it?"

"The same person who rolled a rock down the hill at me, and fired a shotgun at me," Brian said wearily. "I'll give you three guesses, and the first two don't count."

FORTY-ONE

"WHAT *IS* THE MATTER with you, Jo?" Gretchen's exasperated voice crashed into Joanna's distracted internal musings. Jo felt instantly guilty. They were working late, preparing to cater an "Authentic English Tea" that the Crystal Cove Chamber Music Society had scheduled as a fund-raiser. Dainty finger sandwiches made of cucumber and watercress, that sort of thing. And scones, of course. Not that anyone in Crystal Cove knew scones from skittles, but once supplied with plenty of marmalade and sweet butter and fresh-brewed Earl Grey tea in antique eggshell china cups, nobody was likely to complain.

"I'm sorry, Gretch."

"Jo, I'm concerned about you. You look terrible."

"I haven't been sleeping well," Jo muttered, dipping her chef's knife into a bowl of ice water. "Nightmares."

"Well, what's going on?"

"I wish I knew."

"Come on, you must have *some* idea. Or have we stopped communicating?"

"It's about Sam," Jo confessed. "I'm just—scared."

"Shit," Gretchen said, with feeling. "This has to do with that phone call you had from Sadie's son, doesn't it?"

Joanna nodded, miserable.

"Have you heard from Sam since then?"

Joanna shook her head.

"So what kind of scenario are you cooking up?" Gretchen retrieved a tray of rising dough from one of the deep cupboards in the kitchen of Blue Cottage and proceeded to knead strenuously. "I think you need to come to some kind of closure here."

"I think you're right," Jo said. "I need to talk to Brian again."

"Brian?"

"Sadie's son. I'll need to call her to get his phone number."

"HI, JO HONEY!" Sadie, as almost always lately, sounded perky.

"Am I calling at a bad time?"

"No, couldn't be better. I just finished watching 'The Golden Girls.' Do you know that show?"

"Um, I've heard of it."

"You don't *watch* it? Sweetie, it's the best thing on TV. The lines those ladies get away with!" Sadie chortled. "I haven't laughed so hard since that Jack Benny bit. You know, the mugger says, 'Your money or your life,' and Jack doesn't say anything. The audience laughed for two minutes. A record. And that was *radio*!"

Joanna felt disoriented. "Sadie..."

"Oh, I'm sorry. You're too young to remember radio. Or Jack Benny, for that matter. And why would you watch 'The Golden Girls'?" Sadie seemed to audibly deflate.

"I've heard that 'The Golden Girls' is a really good show," Jo ventured. "But the reason I'm calling is..."

"Oh, honey, I'm feeling ashamed. I should have told you how much we all enjoyed that life-drawing session. Such a revelation! I do feel sort of liberated. I mean, the whole experience was a bit of a shock to some of us, particularly the admiral: He's been keeping close to quarters for the past few days. Hank is looking a bit frazzled—who knows why? I haven't asked, of course, but it's occurred to me that Tiddy might have had a delayed reaction. You know." Sadie giggled. "He might be storming the beachheads or battalions or whatever it is that navy men attack. And that Luke! What a hunk! I've been sketching him on the sly as he goes about his work. I don't think he minds—he winks at me from time to time."

"Er, Sadie." Joanna managed to get a phrase in edgewise. "Thank you and all that, but the main reason I'm calling is to get Brian's phone number."

There was a pause and a stifled gulp. "You want Brian's phone number?"

"Yes. His home phone number."

Sadie obliged. "You'll probably get his answering machine," she warned, "but if he's home, he'll pick up the phone. Unless Mabel hangs up on you."

Mabel?

Jo poured herself a glass of chardonnay and dialed.

FORTY-TWO

DAMN! WHY HAD HE SET THE alarm clock? Brian reached out blindly to punch the Off button and realized that he was not in bed, that he had conked out fully dressed on what passed for his sofa, and that what in fact was ringing was his telephone.

He rolled off the sofa and collided with his coffee table, dislodging a precarious pile of papers. He looked at his watch, which seemed to be telling him that it was 9:40 A.M. or P.M.? Thoroughly disoriented, he had no idea. But it seemed to be dark outside, which would appear to indicate P.M., unless the unclear winter had descended during his unaccountable nap. What day was it? What month? What on earth was happening?

Brian groaned as he suddenly remembered what day it was—Saturday—and how he had spent it. He had barely made it home after collecting his Hyundai, briefcase, and glasses from Rich Wing's ranch. He wasn't sure where he had parked—probably not in his own personally designated place.

The telephone continued to ring until the answering machine clicked in. Beep. "Hello, Brian?" The voice was tentative. "This is Joanna Starrett. Sadie gave me your number. I need to talk to you. Please call..."

Brian pressed the manual override button. "Jo? I'm here. I'm just not in the best of condition..."

"I have to know about Sam, Brian."

"Sam?" Brian realized that he was starving, that he had come home and flopped without even a halfhearted attempt to feed himself—or, good God, Mabel.

"Sam Fox. My writer, er, friend who lives up your way. You called me, remember? You told me that I might be in danger from him..."

He sensed that the lady was retreating.

"Oh, *that* Sam Fox. Well, actually, things have been happening pretty fast up here. We haven't had much chance to figure out whether Lloyd Fulton and Sam Fox are the same person, but we think we're closing in on Fulton." If he doesn't close in on me first, Brian thought.

"I need to come up there."

"What?" Brian carefully uncoiled the long phone cord and liberated a long-necked Beck's from the refrigerator. Quick carbohydrates, he told himself. Jump-start the old brain cells.

"I want to come up there and find out for myself who Sam Fox is."

Brian opened the freezer compartment and unearthed a microwavable pizza. "Why do you need to do that?" He quickly read the directions on the package and punched the buttons on the microwave oven. Where was Mabel? A corner of his mind began to worry.

"Just because I need to. I'm not sleeping well these days."

Well, neither am I, Brian thought. "I'm sorry," he said.

"So you're telling me that it doesn't matter whether Sam Fox is the same person that you're closing in on."

"Technically, at this point, no." Brian relented. "But I get your message: It *does* matter to you. And I can see why."

"I'm going to drive up tomorrow, after Blue Cottage closes," Jo told him. "I'll get a cheap motel room, and then I'm going to stake out the Oak Canyon post office."

"The post office?"

"I'm going to see who picks up mail from box two-five-oh-one," Jo said. "You might want to join me"

Brian was about to reply when the connection was abruptly severed by a feline paw.

"Where the hell have you been?" Brian asked Mabel, who did not deign to reply.

LOU ESPINOZA'S MOOD, when Brian called him on Sunday morning, could be described only as surly. "What the hell are you doing, Kayne? Have you finally gone over the edge?"

"Look, Lou . . ."

"The sheriff's office called me yesterday afternoon, paged me out of a wedding reception—Flora's niece; ye gods, everyone had given up hope; she's pushing thirty and ugly as a cake of homemade soap—to ask me whether I, personally, thought you were compos mentis."

"Lou, I..."

"You know what kind of dingaling story they told me? That somebody had called in a nine-one-one, a possible heart attack, and it turned out to be Mother Theresa. And the call was a phony. So the respondent takes the complainant to Paloma General and what he finds there is a bunch of nuns and a dog. Nuns! What were you thinking of, Kayne? You don't mess with nuns."

"I wasn't *messing* with..." Brian began to feel queasy. Had he finally pushed it too far with Lou?

Lou took a deep breath and hissed it out slowly. "So may I ask why you are calling me this morning, when I am in the middle of the sports section and haven't finished my coffee?"

"Coffee? I thought you were off coffee. Doctor's orders and all that."

There was an ominous silence.

"I asked for a scene-of-the-crime unit. Did the department tell you that?"

"They did." Lou seemed to be having trouble with his eruption level. "I got some complaints about that, too."

"But Lou, I found a rock. Somebody had chiseled some words into it. I didn't have my glasses, but I could make out 'Jess.' I think—I'm sure—that it was a makeshift gravestone. And then somebody rolled a boulder down the hill at me, and shot at me."

"So where is this alleged gravestone?"

"I don't know. When we went back, it had disappeared."

"Why are you calling me?"

"We need a search warrant for the ranch where Fulton lives," Brian said desperately. "We need to drag Lake Chumash for Carole Fulton's car."

"Brian," Lou said with admirable restraint, "we don't have any more grounds for doing that today than we did a week ago."

"But what about all the other bones that the dog dug up? Deputy Wing took them in to be processed. Did he tell you that?"

"Yeah," Lou said. "But you know that's going to take a while. A couple of weeks, at best—maybe a month, depending on the backlog in the state forensic lab. And anything they come up with will only be speculative, in the absence of a skull." There was a pause and a slurping sound. "You didn't find a skull, did you?"

"Not yet." Brian's adrenaline was ebbing fast.

"And then there's this matter of a false nine-one-one call."

"Lou!" Brian slammed down his own coffee mug. "That was Theresa's only hope of getting out of there! It was a damned smart move, I think!" He looked dejectedly at the spatters of coffee that now decorated the walls and ceiling of his so-called kitchen. "You don't believe me, do you? You don't believe any of this! You don't believe that I found Jessie's homemade gravestone, that Lloyd Fulton shot at me. Well, damn it, I have witnesses!"

"A dog?" Lou suggested wryly.

"Both Theresa and Rich heard the shotgun blast, Lou." Brian tried hard to remain calm.

"That could have been anything, anyone. People go up there and shoot, especially on weekends. You know that, Brian. Which brings up a good question: What the hell were *you* doing up there?"

Brian had to think for a moment. "Theresa got a phone call Friday night, from some kid who wouldn't give her name. Apparently she's a friend of the Jurgenson girl. Anyway, she told Theresa she saw Fulton with Jason Banks under the bleachers, *after* the wild discus throw that was supposed to have cracked his skull."

"Well, well," Lou said thoughtfully. "And exactly what did this alleged witness observe them doing?"

"She said it looked as though Fulton had sent Jason to find the discus and bring it back, but then the coach followed him and sort of dragged him behind the refreshment stand. That's all she saw. At that point she got scared and took off out of there.''

"If she was telling the truth, this looks bad for Fulton," Lou admitted. "But I can't ask for a warrant on the basis of an anonymous tip, and besides, this business about the Banks kid has nothing to do with the missing-person cases."

"I'm not so sure of that," Brian said grimly. He took a deep breath. "Listen, Lou, I know in my gut that Fulton is a killer, and I'm going to nail him. On my own time, whatever it takes, I'm going to get the bastard."

FORTY-THREE

WHAT AM I DOING? Joanna asked herself as she defensively threaded her way through the eighteen-wheelers and motor homes and pickup trucks and general crazies who seemed determined to make a demolition derby out of the interstate.

She hadn't driven up this way for almost twenty years, and the terrain was unrecognizable. Gretchen had warned her that on a summer Sunday evening it would be at least a four-hour drive up to Paloma—more like five, probably. She hadn't believed Gretch. What was there between here and there, after all? A hell of a lot, Jo was discovering. Where had all this come from?

She almost lost it when the interstate split. Expecting to bear to the left, she saw the overhead sign almost too late. Jo wrenched the steering wheel to the right and skidded laterally across the broad, tapering median that apparently had been designed for such fools as she. A huge truck blared at her from her rear bumper. Jo began to shake. What the hell was she doing?

Finally, she merged herself into the number-two lane and got her knees back into working order. For a half hour or so, the traffic flowed freely, but then it began to clog up again. Small trucks and vans towing boats—some of which seemed enormous—began to dominate the pavement. Jo realized how far she had to go yet, and reflected that Gretchen had been right: five hours, at least.

I must be mad, Jo thought. Why am I doing this?

Sam.

I have to know who Sam is. Who he might be in another life. Who he is to me.

Flashing red and blue lights signaled trouble. Cars in her lane were moving over, cautiously. Jo clicked on her right-turn blinker and looked over her shoulder, on the alert for a Good Samaritan. There was just enough natural light left for her to see that a middle-aged lady in an elderly station wagon was waving at her, giving her permission to cut in. Bless you, lady, she thought, waving back a thank-you message.

The lady acknowledged Jo's gratitude with a gesture that seemed to explain, in a surprisingly articulate fashion, that she had spent her life letting other people cut in. And that, really, she wouldn't have had it any other way.

I am reading too much into this, Jo told herself.

The sporadically moving traffic lane into which she had insinuated herself took her directly past the accident scene. Jo didn't really want to look but couldn't avoid doing so. The two left lanes of the freeway were occupied by emergency vehicles of various sorts. There was an upside-down car, crushed against the median barrier. Apparently someone—dead or alive—was still inside. Jo fleetingly recognized the Jaws of Life apparatus, and noticed that a paramedic ambulance was standing by. She averted her eyes. Her knees began to shake again. Dear Lord, what was she doing?

I need to find out about Sam, she told herself.

Why? asked Jiminy Cricket.

Because I have let myself become obsessed with him, Jo admitted to herself. She heard Gretchen, in her head: "...he's ruined you for all other men. *Real* men."

Sam's real.

Yes, Sam's real.

But who is he?

And *what* is he?

An unexpected progression of mirror-windowed high-rise office buildings, flanking the freeway on both sides, made Joanna gasp. Ye gods, what had been going on here during the years since she'd been gone?

She groped in her purse and found the Snickers bar that she had stashed for an emergency. The candy was more than a bit hard, but it gave her something else to chew on. Helpful, but not enough.

What am I going to do? Jo asked herself. What if Sam really turns out to be this suspected mass murderer or whatever?

She crunched down decisively on a mouthful of peanuts. Go back to square one, she told herself. Go out and play on the freeway.

FORTY-FOUR

BRIAN WAS ACTUALLY enjoying himself when the phone rang, scarfing up a bag of Orville's salt-free microwave popcorn, butter flavor (well, he had cheated and added a little salt), while he watched *The Brother from Another Planet* on an obscure cable-TV channel for which he was not entirely sure he was being billed. He monitored his answering machine with half an ear.

"Brian? I know you're there. Turn off that stupid machine. You want a machine to talk to your mother?"

Oh, shit. Sadie. Brian looked wistfully at the TV screen and punched the manual override button on the machine.

"Hi, Ma."

"So what is this, your Bruce Weitz impersonation?"

"Mom, the guy's a hell of an actor; he's done other roles besides 'Hill Street Blues.'"

"You don't seem entirely thrilled that I'm calling," Sadie observed. "Am I interrupting something?"

Brian sighed. "Just a movie on TV. But it happens to be a good movie. It's very funny."

"Not the Marx brothers? W. C. Fields? No, don't answer. I don't know from movies, these days."

"So what's happening, Mom?"

"'So what's happening?' my son has the nerve to ask me? Like I'm some floozy he met in a bar!"

Sheesh! Brian carefully uncoiled the phone cord and headed for the refrigerator. With any luck, there was a Corona left—or at least one of the Bud Lights that he had stocked in case Lou dropped in.

"Mom. I'm sorry. We don't seem to communicate so well over the phone." He found a pop-top Bud can and eyed it dubiously. Could he open the sucker without severing a major artery?

"Joanna called me," Sadie said with an edge of smugness. "She wanted your home phone number."

"I know." Brian carefully attempted to apply just the right degree of leverage to the magic ring that stood between himself and the can of brew. "We talked, briefly, last night. She seems to be planning to come up here."

"She is? Oh, Brian, I'm so happy. She's such a lovely young woman, you know. I'm so glad that all of this seems to be—"

"Shit!" Brian screamed into the phone, dodging eruptions of Bud foam. "Oh, shit, I'm sorry, Mom."

There was a guilt-impregnated silence.

"Mom, this beer can just exploded on me!" Brian looked up at his kitchen ceiling and observed that yellowish splashes had joined with the dark brown coffee spatters to produce a not-altogether-unpleasing surrealistic effect. "I've got a mess here."

Mabel minced into the room and began to systematically lick up the beer that had puddled on the floor.

Sadie huffed and pouted. "You never listened to your father, did you? Sid must have said it a thousand times; I can hear him to this day: 'Never drink beer from the can, kid. Show some class.'"

FORTY-FIVE

How LONG COULD ONE unobtrusively loiter in the box lobby of a post office? Joanna asked herself. Not long, she figured, if the lobby was approximately the size of a postage stamp.

She had been there since the lobby opened at 8 A.M.—more than two hours ago—having arrived half-asleep and unshowered after spending the night at a motel whose amenities did not include wake-up calls. Nobody had yet shown signs of approaching a post-office box. And of course she didn't know who she was on the lookout for. Whom, she mentally amended.

How shall I limn thee, Sam? Jo asked herself. Let me count the ways: Six feet two, with eyes of blue? Five feet nine, with reek of wine? Gaunt and slender? Plump and tender? Bald as an eagle or fuzzy as a bear? Spaced-out punk with purple hair? Freak or monster, I don't care. Just let me get a look at you, you bleeping bastard.

Jo realized that she needed to pee in the worst sort of way, and that she was starving.

I need a plan, she told herself. What would Kinsey Millhone do?

She shut her eyes and let her right brain construct a scenario. Well, it might work.

Jo took a deep breath and let herself into the main part of the Oak Canyon post office. Only one of the pair of windows was manned, so to speak—by a lad who looked as though he had yet to apply a razor to his chubby cheeks.

"I have a serious problem. I think I need to see the postmaster."

The kid grinned. "You've got him."

"You're the postmaster?"

"Acting postmaster. It's a long story. See, my mom's *really* the postmaster, but she's in the hospital and—" The kid stopped himself short. A natural shortstop, obviously. He attempted to reclaim some dignity. "How can I help you?"

Jo crossed her fingers behind her back. "I desperately need to contact my ex-husband. Our child is very ill, you see, and I don't know how to reach Sam except through his post-office box number. I've been waiting since the lobby opened, but he hasn't shown up. And I can't wait much longer." At least that was the truth, Jo told herself. "I drove all day yesterday to get here."

The boy frowned. "I'm not sure what you want me to do."

"He has mail in his box; I can see it. Take out the mail and put a message in his box, telling him to ask for his mail. And when he comes to the window, call me at my motel room and stall him somehow." Joanna scribbled down a phone number.

"Oh, ma'am!" The kid looked shocked. "I couldn't do that! I have a sacred responsibility to safeguard the mail!"

Jo sensed movement in the box lobby, out of the corner of her left eye. She squinted through the reflections on the glass door that separated the lobby from the main part of the post office. A man, slightly built and wearing a battered hat, was bent toward a box that seemed to be in the right place for number 2501. She grabbed her purse and reentered the box lobby in what she hoped was a casual but purposeful fashion. She took out her key ring and pretended to fumble for her box key. The metal door of the man's box was open wide, but too low for the number to be readable. Jo dropped her keys. "Damn, she muttered. Bending down to pick them up, she made out 2501 on the door of the post-office box just as the man slammed it shut and relocked it. He paid no attention to her.

Jo tried not to stare at him. This man couldn't be Sam Fox. But who else would have the key to Sam's post-office box? She felt alternately hot and cold and decidedly faint.

Follow him, Jo told herself.

Realizing that she was damned close to panicking, Jo decided to compromise: She would follow the man to his vehicle and get the description and license number. Then she would find a ladies' room, if she wasn't too late.

She hurried out of the post office. The man was approaching a beat-up pickup truck, shuffling through his mail en route. He carelessly tossed away a couple of envelopes, which fluttered to the pavement of the post-office parking lot. From what Jo could see of the guy, he had longish, dirty-looking hair.

Jo gathered her courage and picked up the discarded items. She stole a quick glance at the addresses. One envelope, bearing the imprint of a prestigious women's college, was addressed to a Carole McKee Fulton. The other—oh, shit, the guy was opening the door of his truck. Abandoning caution and sanity, Jo took a deep breath and ran toward him. "Excuse me, sir! I think you dropped some of your mail," she said, panting.

The man turned and gave her a hard look. Now Jo could see that he wore wire-rimmed glasses, that his mouth was hidden behind an untrimmed mustache that somehow resembled a litter of small forest creatures. He looked, she thought, like a freeze-dried hippie.

Then the man gave her a smile that was like sun breaking through a dense fog.

"You caught me red-handed, lady," he said in that melted-chocolate voice that she knew so well. "Littering."

Joanna grinned in spite of herself. "You can get anything you want..." she sang in a quavering contralto.

"...at Alice's Restaurant," Sam finished in a strong and tuneful baritone. He reached out and took the offending junk mail from her hand. Their two hands touched, ever so fleetingly. Jo felt a shiver run through her body. "Glad you caught me before the dep-you-tees did," Sam said. "Maybe I'll buy you a beer someday."

Jo was afraid to say anything more. If she had recognized *his* voice, wouldn't he be sure to recognize *hers*? She smiled and nodded, struggling to control the spasms that were threatening to overwhelm her, and turned away. But as Sam revved up the truck, she managed to get a good look at the license number.

BACK AT HER MOTEL, having relieved her bladder and had herself a good cry, Jo attempted to reach Brian. This endeavor was handicapped by her inability to remember exactly what Brian's job was, and by the absence of the relevant pages in the phone book supplied by the motel. Finally, after several false starts and wild-goose chases, she found herself talking to a person—an actual person, and one who confessed that she actually knew a guy who called himself Brian Kayne and that, yes, he actually worked in her office. Beyond that, the person (who was, of course, Marge Hedstrom, in the middle of a world-class snit) was not terribly forthcoming.

"This is urgent," Jo attempted to impress upon the alleged actual person.

"He's in court."

"Can you have him paged?"

"Out of *court*?" Shock waves transmitted themselves through the telephone lines.

"Is there somebody else I can talk to? Or can I leave a message?" Jo felt herself starting to lose control.

"Hold on." There was a long pause—too long. Jo was on the verge of hanging up when a motherly sort of voice came on the line.

"Theresa Scanlon here. You say you have an urgent message for Brian?"

"This is Joanna Starrett. I don't know whether Brian has told you about me."

"You're the lady from down in Crystal Cove, right? Where all of this Lloyd Fulton business got started."

"Yes. I came up here to see for myself who and what Sam Fox is. And I came, and I saw. And I have a license number for you. The license number of Sam's pickup truck. And I can give you a description..." Jo had to stop; it was all getting to be too much.

"Honey," Theresa said, "calm down. Give me the license number of the vehicle, okay? And a description of the man and the vehicle."

Choking back sobs, Joanna obliged.

"Brian didn't have a chance to tell me much, but he did say that you were intending to stake out your friend Sam's post-office box up in Oak Canyon. Are you sure the guy you saw is the man you know as Sam Fox?"

"I'm sure he's Sam. I'd know his voice anywhere. As to whether he's this Fulton person . . ." Jo took a deep breath. "I have no way of knowing. But there was a letter in his post-office box addressed to a Carole Fulton."

"*Carole* Fulton?"

"Yes. He threw it away in the parking lot, and I picked it up."

"Joanna," Theresa began. There was a pause. "You've never met this Sam Fox face-to-face, right? Never before, anyway."

"Right."

"Does he have any pictures of you?"

"No. I don't think so. I've never sent him one."

"But you recognized him from his voice."

Jo shuddered. "Yes."

"Do you think he recognized *your* voice?"

"I don't know. I hope not."

Theresa sighed. "What are you going to do now, Joanna?"

Jo stared at the telephone, feeling like a zombie. "I don't know. Go home, I guess."

"I think that's a good plan. And I want you to stay in touch and not do anything silly. Especially, don't try to make any kind of contact with Fulton. Or Sam, or whoever he is."

Jo took a deep breath. "I promise. Okay?" She depressed the receiver and gave in to grief.

FORTY-SIX

THERESA WAS FEELING reasonably pleased with herself as she unlocked her kitchen door, cradling a fresh bottle of gin in what seemed a precariously flimsy paper bag. Pleading a need for some personal time, she had persuaded Lou Espinoza to let her take the afternoon off. It had been a productive afternoon.

First, she *had* taken some personal time—to touch base with Patrick and Beth. Young Terry, it seemed, was doing fine, gaining weight even faster than the doctor had optimistically expected and showing nary a sign of lung problems. The hospital, fortunately a progressive one, allowed Beth to suit herself up and spend a lot of time with the baby in the preemie nursery—both Beth and Pat were worried about bonding.

Second, Theresa was relieved that she had finally made contact with Amy Jurgenson and Kerry Perez. Both kids had basically confirmed what they had told Brian about Fulton's general weirdness, and Kerry had guardedly described what Jason Banks had told him about the man's sexual abuse of his stepdaughter. Hearsay evidence, of course, not admissible in court. But Amy had opened up a bit further.

"Jess asked me how you know whether you're pregnant," Amy had told Theresa, obviously struggling with embarrassment. "I gave her a little book that my mom had bought for me. Jessie called me later and told me that she hadn't been menstruating long enough to know what her schedule was, that she was really unpredictable. But she said she was feeling really strange—hungry and sleepy all the time. I didn't know what to tell her. I knew she couldn't go to her mother, because she wouldn't want her mother to know. And her father—stepfather, I mean—would have *killed* her. Or at least thrown her out of the house. And maybe killed Jason—that is, I guess it must have been Jason; he was the only boyfriend Jessie ever had that I know of. Mr. Fulton had violent opinions about—sin. He was always talking about furnicaters and how the Lord would punish them.''

''Furnicaters?'' Theresa briefly considered and then discarded images of furnaces and furniture.

''You know, people who do it when they're not married. To each other.''

''Oh, yes, of course.''

''I told her she should go to a doctor, that doctors don't always tell your parents. I'd heard of a clinic down in Paloma—I said I could probably find somebody to drive her down there. She said she'd have to think about it.'' Amy had choked off a sob. ''That's the last time I ever talked to Jess.''

Poor kid, Theresa reflected as she liberated a Stouffer's entrée from the freezer and administered a couple of sharp raps to the chronically jammed ice maker. Poor kids. Mother of God, she thought, here we have one eighth grader turning to another eighth grader for sex education. She turned on the oven and wished for the umpty-ninth time that, good Catholic as she believed herself to be, she could take the Pope by the hand and give him a guided tour of the *real world*.

Frozen entrée in the oven, Theresa allowed herself a healthy swig of a Gibson on the rocks and lit the fourth of her daily ration of six cigarettes. As usual, she almost passed out.

I should quit smoking, she told herself. I should just *quit*. She shredded some limestone lettuce into a chilled bowl and sprinkled it delicately with Newman's Own salad dressing. She took a couple of deep breaths and tried to let the day roll off her back.

But something was clinging to her shoulders, bugging her.

I miss Archie, Theresa told herself. I miss the damned dumb dog. I miss having him drool all over my feet when I let myself in the door at night; I miss having him shed all over the furniture and jump up on the bed when he thought I was asleep and practically push me out of bed, snoring like a son of a gun. I miss how warm Archie was, how he radi-

ated heat on chilly winter nights. I even miss his awful
breath. And I haven't even thought about the stupid dog for
a long time.

The Wing kid's dog, Theresa thought. The golden Lab.
What was her name? Tawny. That's what had done it.
Tawny had reactivated her need for loving and being loved.
Tawny had made her miss Archie.

Do I still miss Joe? Theresa asked herself.

Not really, she decided. Joe had been gone for so many
years that he no longer seemed real to her. He existed in a
series of photographs, preserved in albums and—fading
slowly—in her head.

Theresa set the table for her dinner: a table for one, a
separate table.

I miss—having someone, something, she mused. I like
being alone, usually. But sometimes being alone is damned
lonely.

All my kids are gone, she thought. They're not kids anymore. They have their own lives. They have their own kids.

Theresa flashed back on Rich Wing and his son Ben and
almost doubled up from the pain that came from what she
suddenly, unexpectedly, let herself experience that she was
missing.

Theresa took a final drag from her neglected cigarette and
stubbed it out.

I need to have something to love, she told herself. Something that loves me back. I'm not particular about species
or gender.

Good God, she reflected, even *Brian* has Mabel. Obnox-
ious as she was, Mabel loved Brian, and Brian loved—

Brian!

That's what had been bugging her, Theresa realized—she
hadn't been able to get through to Brian. She needed to tell
Brian about Joanna's visit to the Oak Canyon post office;
she needed to tell him that Jo's description of Sam Fox
seemed to fit exactly the person that Theresa and Brian
knew as Lloyd Fulton, and that Joanna had picked up a
discarded envelope addressed to Carole Fulton. Not that any
of this was material to the case they were trying to build

against the guy, but it all might be extremely important to Jo—especially if Fulton had recognized her.

She had tried to warn Joanna, but she wasn't sure that the woman had taken her seriously. And, Theresa realized, she hadn't shared with Jo any of the recent developments in the case—developments that made Fulton seem to be dangerous indeed, a far more sinister character than the mild-mannered persona that he affected.

Theresa opened the oven and poked a knife around in her TV dinner. Another ten minutes, she estimated. She sweetened her drink and headed for the phone. She knew Brian's home number by heart, but she fully expected to encounter his answering machine, complete with the cutesy message-of-the-month.

Theresa dialed.

"Hi," she heard, "This is Brian. I am otherwise occupied at the moment, but if my astrologist says the stars are properly aligned, I will get back to you as soon as possible if you will leave your name and number after the—"

There was a definitive click and a prolonged hum.

"God damn that cat!" Theresa exclaimed.

FORTY-SEVEN

LACKING A TAPE DECK in her little Honda, Jo ran a series of head tapes during the long drive back down to Crystal Cove. Her traumatic encounter with Sam had put her in mind of Arlo, so she started with him—offering up a silent prayer that Woody's kid was still doing okay. She sang out loud those lyrics of the "Alice's Restaurant Massacree" that she remembered, and chuckled silently at the parts she only half-remembered. And as she crested and swooped over the series of roller-coaster hills that presaged what she privately thought of as the Valley of Death, Jo wondered why she was feeling so suddenly nostalgic about a time, and a movement, from which she had deliberately distanced herself.

My God, she thought. Arlo isn't a kid anymore. He must be as old as I am. He's bleeping middle-aged.

An improbably tall gas-station sign, rearing up from a cloverleaf interchange looming ahead, prompted her to check her gauge. Better fill up. She swung off the freeway, wondering whether she had the right sort of plastic card—or enough cash.

Accustomed as she was to self-service/no service, Joanna was surprised when an eager-looking young man trotted up to her car window. She was even more surprised when she recognized the music that was emanating from the portable tape player parked on the service island: Seals and Crofts.

"You want me to fill 'er up, lady?"

Jo made a hasty reconnaissance of her wallet. "Ten dollars' worth. Unleaded."

"Check under the hood?"

"Why not?" Jo knew that she had a long way to go. On the other hand, she had come a long way. Why did she feel so sorry for herself?

"Lady," the kid told her. "This air filter has had it." He showed her the filthy cylinder. He was right. "And you're overdue for an oil change. I can give you a new air filter for seven ninety-five.''

Jo surveyed her wallet again. "Will you take a check?"

"In-state?"

Jo nodded.

"Can I see your driver's license?" This kid was nobody's fool. Jo obliged.

"I guess you're into oldie music," she ventured. "Seals and Crofts, I mean. You can't possibly remember them."

"Ah, but I do." The kid grinned. "From the womb." He winked at Jo. "Back in a jiff with your new filter."

Jo felt a hundred years old.

"Summer Breeze" wafted its way into her ears. She closed her eyes and remembered a beach on Martha's Vineyard, a solitary beach on the south coast of the island. "Summer breeze . . . makes me feel fine." Actually, she had been feeling scratchy and itchy from the dune grass, but not about to admit it—not while in the middle of a world-class orgasm.

With whom?

Ah, there Jo's memory deserted her.

She settled up with the kid and tackled the freeway again, properly gassed up and refiltered.

During the seemingly endless trek through the city and its depressing, rotting outskirts, Joanna comforted herself with Simon and Garfunkel, no apples being near to hand. Tears were running freely down her cheeks. "I know I'm fakin' it," she sang to herself. "I'm not really makin' it." She cried for herself, barely able to see where she was going. "In the corner stands a boxer . . ."

She snuffled up her tears and trucked on.

"So here's to you, Ms. Joanna. Gretchen loves you more than you deserve."

A tractor-trailer cut in ahead of her, forcing Jo to change lanes abruptly.

"Swerve swerve swerve," she sang, her mood unaccountably lightened in spite of the close call. "God help me please, if you care at all. I don't have a life that's worth a damn—but I love Sam."

Realizing that she was beginning to sob out loud, that she was imperiling both herself and other drivers, Jo looked for the next off ramp and exited. Maybe a little food in the system would help.

AFTER A COKE AND a quarter-pounder with cheese at a handy McDonald's, Jo had felt fit to go on the road again. She knew that she was grieving, that she would grieve for some time. She vowed to forswear head tapes and just drive home.

The daylight was fading when Jo finally pulled her Honda into the gravel driveway that led to her garage/studio.

Gretchen poked her head out of the back door of Blue Cottage. "Are you okay?"

"Yeah. I think I need a nap. I'll talk to you later, all right?"

"Have you eaten?"

"Yes, after a fashion."

"Do you want me to come upstairs?"

"No, hon, but thanks anyway. I'll crash for awhile, and then I need to go out to the studio. I have a lot of work to do."

"So do I," Gretch said. "I'll catch you later, when I see your lights on out back. Talk to you then."

Jo let herself out of her car and locked it. She looked up at the sky. Wisps of night fog were beginning to drift in from the coast. She took in a deep breath of eucalyptus, star jasmine, a hint of roses. She closed her eyes and listened to the sounds of silence.

FORTY-EIGHT

BELCHING STRENUOUSLY in a reflexive attempt to exude some of the lingering effects of the ill-advised and hastily consumed Reuben sandwich that he'd ordered in the Government Center lunchroom, Brian let himself into his apartment and scooped up the loudly protesting Mabel. Was it a microwave night or a can-opener night? Too pooped to check out the situation, he extricated a new can of cat food from the cupboard and clamped it into the electric can opener.

It had been a bitch of a day, Brian thought. He'd spent most of it cooling his heels in the lobby outside a courtroom, waiting to testify. Judge Munoz was adamant about not letting prospective witnesses observe the proceedings, even when such witnesses happened to be DA's investigators. And Brian had known all along that the case was a loser, that the DA didn't have enough evidence to prosecute. A waste of everybody's time, and money, and energy. And, possibly, the ruination of a person's life—a person unjustly accused and brought to trial without any kind of hard evidence to support the prosecution's case.

District Attorney Norman Bascombe, Brian thought—not for the first time—was an anal orifice. He further reflected that Lou Espinoza, hanging in there for his pension and much-needed medical benefits, had little choice but to pretend that the esteemed DA's ass was an ice-cream cone.

The whole business was depressing.

Brian cracked a Corona and risked a glance at his answering machine, which was winking at him with a malevolently crimson eye. He switched on the playback and heard a series of cryptically interrupted messages.

He glared at Mabel, who was cleaning her ears smugly.

I need a dog, Brian told himself. Cats are too devious. And this particular cat is doing a thorough job of screwing up my life.

Not that he needed any help.

He replayed the aborted messages and managed to identify at least one voice: Theresa's. Time to give Mother a call.

"BRIAN, JOANNA WAS UP here today," Theresa told him. "She hung around the Oak Canyon post office until a man came to collect the mail from the box that Sam Fox rents. Her description of the guy tells me that he has to be Fulton. She got a license number from the guy's old pickup truck, and it checks out—it's Fulton's truck, all right. She found a letter addressed to Carole Fulton. What's more, she says she talked to the man—enough to recognize his voice, anyway. And he may have recognized hers."

"Theresa, all this is really immaterial now. I mean, suppose Fulton *is* the same person that Jo knows as Sam Fox. It has nothing to do with the case."

"Brian, you're not computing. How did you get hooked on this business in the first place?"

"Well, it was sort of an accident."

"Lloyd Fulton is not likely to see it that way."

Brian sighed. "I guess you're right."

"Brian, I'm seriously worried about Joanna."

"Is she still around?"

"She said she was going back home. That was, oh, around noon, just before I left the office. But I didn't think to ask for her phone number in Crystal Cove. Can you give her a call?"

"Why?"

"Just to make sure she got home okay. And, maybe, warn her."

"About what?"

"That Fulton might come after her. Brian, I've got a funny feeling. Actually, it's not funny at all. But I think Fulton knows we're closing in on him. I'm sure he recognized me the other day when I stumbled onto, or into, his ranch. Somebody moved the rock; somebody shot at you. After a point, babe, I don't believe in coincidences."

Brian stretched out his phone cord and groped in the freezer. "But why would he go after Jo? How can she be a threat?" Without really looking at the label on the frozen dinner, he punched up the microwave and shoved it in. He drained the Corona and reached for another. "Okay, I was worried about Joanna for awhile. But if Fulton is going to go after anybody, isn't it more likely that he'd go after you? Or me? Or one of those kids who talked to us? Why would he drive all the way down to Crystal Cove? Jo can't bring anything to the case we're trying to build against Fulton."

"Because he *blames* her." Theresa took a deep breath. Brian heard the chunk of ice cubes. To each his or her own, he thought.

"I know people, Brian. I have good instincts. Fulton is an actor. He can charm people, disarm them, confuse them. He plays whatever role fits the situation—unsophisticated hick, sensitive poet, lay preacher, you name it. But at bottom, he has both a contempt for and a fear of women—emotionally, intellectually, and physically. As long as he feels in command, everything is groovy. But when his control is threatened . . ." Theresa paused and obviously took a swig. "I think he kills, Brian.

"Look, everything was going fine for Fulton until you went down to Crystal Cove to visit Sadie, and got involved with Joanna. Nobody really suspected him of anything—or at least we didn't have enough grounds to warrant a serious investigation. But now we're breathing down his neck, and he's got to be feeling the pressure."

Brian's microwave beeped at him. "Theresa, we still don't have any *evidence* against the guy. You know how the system works as well as I do. Even with all the new stuff we've unearthed, the interviews with the kids and all that, we still can't get Bascombe to push for any warrants." Grabbing a pair of pot holders, he levered the instant dinner onto a waiting plate and carefully peeled off the cover. Surprise! What the hell was it?

"Brian, have you got a pencil? I want you to write down the description and plate number of Fulton's truck. Just so you can keep your eyes open. Do the old gal a favor, okay?"

Brian set down his plate and scrounged for something to write on. He ended up using the flap of the envelope from his utility bill. Dutifully, he copied down the plate number but balked at the description: "A *1954* Ford pickup? Theresa, that can't be right."

"I double-checked with the DMV. It's right. Don't ask me how come it's still on the road. Maybe the guy's a wizard mechanic."

Brian groped for a fork and poked tentatively at the unidentifiable microwaved dinner. It smelled vaguely like refried beans. He offered Mabel a whiff and she turned her back and made burying motions. Desperate, he ventured a bite and seared his tongue on the hidden melted cheese. Gargling quickly with a mouthful of cold beer, he struggled to regroup. "Theresa, as of now we can't touch Fulton, and you know it."

Theresa took another audible sip, and sighed. "Yes. But does *he* know it?"

FORTY-NINE

VOWING THAT HE WOULD never again purchase a frozen Mexican combination dinner, Brian consoled himself by enjoying the miniview from his minideck. For once, he could see something, and it was spectacular. The sun was sliding lazily toward the Pacific through a succession of gauzy wisps of clouds, each layer tinted a subtly different shade of pink or mauve. The scene reminded him of something that he couldn't quite identify. He closed his eyes, and immediately saw a painting. No, not a painting, a—he heard Sadie's impatient voice—a collage. He had admired it, at Jo's tearoom or art gallery or whatever. It had been the one piece of work on display that he could imagine hanging in his apartment.

Oh my God. Jo. He needed to call her. He didn't think it would do any good, but he had promised Theresa.

Brian groped in his jacket pocket for his dog-eared reminder book. Oh, shit, the jacket was in awful shape, he realized, probably beyond salvation. He would be embarrassed to take it in to the dry cleaner. Would the Salvation Army want it?

You are digressing, Brian told himself. He found a scrawled number that he hoped was Joanna's apartment and dialed it. No answer. Well, there was another number, which might be the tearoom. He squinted: Blue something. But which was which? The disorganized state of his memo book motivated him to try the other number. Surely the tearoom would be closed for the day; no one would answer the phone. On the other hand, if Jo had left Paloma shortly after noon, she should have been home long ago. Brian dialed the second number.

He let the phone ring eight times. He had, of course, no way of knowing that he had reached the Blue Cottage number and that Gretchen was there by herself, working various piles of dough and quick-freezing the last of the wild black raspberries that overran the back of the lot, climbing over the fence like desperate prison escapees and trailing their runners wherever they could find a purchase in the sandy soil. Brian could not have guessed that Gretchen had no intention of answering the phone, that she was feeling basically pissed off at those people who were likely to call at that hour—such persons being those whom she knew and loved best, and who seemed to have deserted her en masse. He could not see the tears that dripped into a mound of supposedly salt-free dough, as Gretchen kneaded—and needed. Of course, he could not see Gretchen swallow hard and set her jaw as the echoes of the ringing phone filled the steamy kitchen.

Brian put down the phone. Oh, shit, he thought.

What could he do?

Well, why did he need to do anything?

Guilt, of course—an ethnicity of guilt, an eternity of guilt.

He sank back onto the sofa and pondered. Mabel jumped into his lap and began to make bread on his trousers. At first, it felt good, and then the cat began to unsheathe her claws a bit in her ecstasy. Brian realized that his pants were in peril, and that Mabel's kneading was beginning to smart.

"Mabel," Brian told her. "Stop kneading."

Stop kneading, he told himself. Stop needing.

"No!" Brian said loudly. He stood and dumped the cat off his lap. Ignoring Mabel's vocal protests, he dialed Fulton's number. There was no answer. He dialed again and gave it a dozen rings. No answer.

Oh no, poor doggy! Please, save the little doggy!

Brian pulled his windbreaker out of the closet and headed for the Hyundai.

FIFTY

HALFWAY UP THE DARK, twisting road that led to Oak Canyon, Brian began to seriously ask himself what the hell he was doing, what he hoped to accomplish. He'd had some sort of half-assed idea about conducting an unofficial search of Fulton's ranch, given that the guy seemed to be gone. But what if he *wasn't* gone? Maybe he had just decided not to answer the phone. Or maybe he was in the shower, or out on the grounds someplace.

Besides, Brian told himself, the ranch doesn't seem to have electricity. Had he brought his torch? He groped under the dash on the passenger side at the risk of running off the road. The long, heavy-duty flashlight was clamped in its place. Were the batteries okay?

This is crazy, Brian thought. I could lose my job. I could get myself killed. The guy has a shotgun; he already tried to kill me once, or at least scare me away. If it was him.

The flicker of headlights glancing off trees signaled the approach of another vehicle, headed downhill. Brian paid attention to staying strictly in his own lane. As he absorbed the sound of the oncoming traffic—engine running rough, maybe missing a cylinder—he reflected upon the nature of the most profitable local agricultural crop and the kinds of people likely to be employed therein. He looked for a wide spot in the graveled shoulder, found one, and pulled over, killing his own lights.

Whoops, Brian thought as the vehicle careened around the curve up ahead. A single headlight. Motorcycle? As the vehicle roared past him, there was just enough lingering twilight to reveal that it was an ancient one-eyed Ford pickup truck.

Fulton, Brian thought. Had to be Fulton.

Without really thinking, he backed and filled until he had the Hyundai turned around on the narrow road.

Sadie perched on his shoulder, tut-tutting. "What are you doing, Brian?" she kvetched. "He's gone now; you can search the ranch."

"For what, Mom?" Brian rejoined logically, and audibly. "What am I going to find there? Bodies?"

Realizing that he had been speaking aloud to a person who was not in his presence, Brian shuddered and concentrated on keeping the pickup in sight. What was it they said about the rate that brain cells die off after the age of nineteen? Was he drinking too much beer, hastening the process?

And why, in fact, *was* he following Fulton instead of scoping out the ranch?

As the road leveled off, dipping down into the seaward plain, Brian had no more trouble keeping up with the old truck, which seemed to rely on gravity as a major source of propulsion. Rather, he found himself needing to drop back, to cut his lights from time to time.

Where was Fulton headed?

As the road transformed itself into a semifreeway and overhead lights illuminated the exits, Brian chanced pulling up close enough to get a look at the license plate on the truck. Bingo. This was Fulton, for sure. But where was he going?

The interchange for the major north/south freeway was fast approaching. As traffic thickened, Brian felt more confident about sticking close to Fulton's old truck. When Fulton turned off onto the southbound on ramp, a tickle of ice ran up Brian's spine.

Theresa was right, he thought.

The sucker's going after Joanna.

I should call and get help, get reinforcements.

But what if he isn't going after Jo?

I'll look like a goddamn fool.

And what has the guy done, anyway? He hasn't broken a law. He's just taking a spin on the freeway.

Brian gritted his teeth and concentrated on keeping the pickup in sight amid the always-clogged traffic that coursed in and out of Paloma. Semitrailers, moving into and out of the right-hand lane, obstructed his vision. He kept losing sight of the pickup, which seemed able to do no better than fifty mph except on downgrades—and this was flat-assed-flat terrain. Somewhere in the middle of Green Valley, he realized that he had lost Fulton's truck, that he hadn't seen it for at least five minutes. Had he overshot it? Or had Fulton taken an off ramp?

Cursing, Brian maneuvered himself into the right lane and exited the freeway on the fringes of Carrillo—a mysterious collection of housing tracts that had always defeated him, geographically: There appeared to be no way to get from one part of it to the other. But he seemed to remember a sort of frontage road—which turned out to exist, for awhile. But—too late—he remembered that the road didn't connect with anything, that it sort of meandered out into the Green Valley croplands. Brian consulted his mental road map and aimed himself back toward the freeway. One more shot, he thought. He'd give it one more shot.

Once back on the freeway, Brian moved into the left-hand lane and floored the accelerator. Traffic had thinned out considerably by now, and he was easily able to survey his fellow vehicles. No ancient pickup truck was visible. He looked at his watch and estimated that he'd used up fifteen or twenty minutes getting lost. The Carrillo grade, leading up from the Green Valley Plain to the higher inland valley, was a long and steep one, sure to present a stiff challenge to Fulton's old truck. If Fulton was still on the freeway, Brian thought, his best chance of catching up to him was on the grade. And if he didn't get Fulton there, he'd go home. Maybe Mrs. Otani would be up for a wild game of gin rummy.

FIFTY-ONE

JOANNA AWOKE FROM a restless doze, wondering why she was awake and where she was. Not in bed; it didn't feel like bed. And she seemed to be fully dressed. Yet it was deep-night dark in her tiny apartment in the attic of Blue Cottage.

Gradually, she oriented herself. She had flopped down on the sofa, after the drive down from Paloma, without bothering to turn on any lights.

"Hello, darkness, my old friend..."

Jo sat up and gingerly groped for the lamp on the end table. Yes, she was going to paint tonight. She needed to work, if only in order to exorcise demons.

"You caught me red-handed, lady. Littering."

Jo tried to shut out the voices in her head—one voice in particular. I have been royally had, she told herself. I have been manipulated, conned, seduced, and screwed. Well, no. Not screwed, but not for lack of wanting to be.

She slipped on her shoes and headed for her tiny kitchen, where a half-consumed bottle of Phelps chardonnay reposed in the refrigerator. Grabbing up the bottle and her key ring, Jo headed down the stairs that led to her semiprivate entrance, which doubled as a back door for Blue Cottage. She peeked into the kitchen of the tearoom and noticed that Gretchen was dozing over her rising dough. Should she wake her?

I ought to feel guilty, Jo thought. I just took off and left Gretch to do all the work. And she never complains. Well, hardly ever.

Tonight, Jo told herself, she was not going to spend her energy on feeling guilty. She was going to paint!

A surge of adrenaline propelled her down the gravel drive that led to her studio. She let herself in, turned on the lights, and opened the windows and skylight. No watercolors or collages tonight. For the first time in ages, she felt in the mood to work with oils. Fortunately, a couple of pieces of canvas were at hand, stretched and primed and waiting for the urge to strike.

Jo peeled off her outer clothes and hung them on the reasonably venerable brass coat tree that she had found at a local estate auction. As she scrummaged around for one of the grungy model's smocks that she customarily wore while engaged in projects that were likely to prove messy, she had a crazy idea: What would it feel like to paint without any clothes on? Not that nude paintings represented an innovation, of course. But generally, the model, not the artist, was au naturel.

She took a deep draught of the chardonnay. Well, why not? She unhooked her bra and let her panties drop. A heavy load seemed to slide off her back. Dutifully hanging up her undies, she kicked off her sandals and danced around the room, moving to music in her head.

"See the curtains, hangin' in the window..."

Her skin tingled as tiny hairs responded to the moist, balmy breeze that filtered in from the ocean. Suddenly, Seals and Crofts gave way to Tchaikovsky's Sixth Symphony, the *Pathetique*. Joanna soared and leaped, sending an easel crashing to the floor.

What the hell am I doing? she asked herself. I came here to work.

She opened one of her hopelessly disordered storage cupboards and unearthed the tackle box in which she kept her tubes of oils. My, what a mess. Most of the tubes were cracked and bent, their contents probably dried up beyond salvaging. Well, she wouldn't need many colors tonight. Black, she thought. And blood red.

Joanna closed her eyes and saw a woman kneeling, her forehead pressed to the ground in despair. The figure was in deep shadow, almost silhouetted against a dying red glow in the background, and surrounded by a pool of deeper, brighter red. She shuddered, feeling the woman's wordless pain, and selected a brush.

FIFTY-TWO

As HE AIMED HIS HYUNDAI up the gracefully undulating concrete ribbon that was locally known as the Carrillo Grade, Brian considered his strategy. Given the state of Fulton's ancient pickup, the guy would certainly have to stay in the truck lane in low gear—which meant that he might easily be concealed between a couple of the heavily loaded semis that were laboriously crawling up the long and steep hill even at this hour. He decided that his best bet was to stay in the lane to the immediate left of the truck lane, keeping a sharp eye out for the deadheading behemoths that periodically swung out to pass their burdened brothers. If he held it to forty or so, he wouldn't miss Fulton—if Fulton was still on the road.

Brian was close to the top of the grade and ready to call it quits when feathery white flakes began to flutter down in the beam of his headlights. What? No, impossible. It had been known to snow here, but never in August, for Christ's sake. Not even for Christ's sake, notwithstanding the zeal of some of the local born-agains. He blinked and wondered whether he was hallucinating. The sound of an air horn and a blinking left-turn signal ahead motivated him to let up on the accelerator as what looked like a moving van pulled out to pass an invisible slower vehicle. Suddenly, Brian's vision was almost obscured by a blizzard of whirling white feathers, some of which adhered to his windshield.

Jesus, Brian implored fervently. Oh, Bro, what's going on here? He groped for the spritzer button and activated the wiper, realizing that he had automatically braked and that his car was in immediate danger of stalling on the steep uphill grade. A strong and unpleasant odor suddenly pervaded the Hyundai, almost causing him to retch. As he frantically floored the accelerator, praying for the mythical (he suspected) overdrive to take over, he glanced to his right and saw that he was passing an open truck loaded to the gunwales with chickens. Live chickens—supposedly live. Row after row, tier upon tier, of metal cages stuffed with chickens. Heads and feet poked out indiscriminately, here and there, through the mesh. Feathers flew. The stench was indescribable.

Brian fought with all his will to keep from gagging. I will never be able to eat chicken again, he thought.

Something in the car—he had never understood how this car worked, or any car for that matter—finally kicked in, and the Hyundai shot past the chicken truck.

In his eagerness to leave the doomed and wretched hens behind him, Brian almost missed the little red pickup that was wheezing and hiccuping its way up the hill, barely in front of the chickens and snugly behind an obviously over-loaded move-it-yourself van.

Oh, shit, Brian thought. He eased up on the gas and cruised, thinking hard. Both of the large trucks would have to pull off at the weigh station at the top of the grade—if the station was open. Would it be open at this hour? At any rate, Fulton was stuck on the freeway until the next off ramp—Tammy Drive in Canterbury Park, if he remembered correctly. At least two more miles, maybe three.

Brian decided to drive on in a normal fashion and pull over onto the shoulder just before the Tammy Drive exit. Fulton would have no way of recognizing his vehicle—no reason to expect a tail, he told himself, realizing that he was internally lapsing into law-officer lingo.

But what am I doing? he asked himself.

Following Fulton, of course.

Why?

Because my suspicions have been confirmed, that's why. Fulton *has* to be going after Joanna.

Brian wondered whether he had gone totally bonkers. Talking to yourself, they said, was a serious symptom.

As he gradually slowed down and moved off onto the paved shoulder of the freeway, he heard Lou Espinoza's voice in his head: "What makes you so sure that Fulton's going after Jo? Maybe he just wants to cruise the Valley, pick up a girl. Or head down to the West Side to catch a first-run flick? You're overreacting, Kayne."

I just know, Brian thought stubbornly. Did Hispanics have a word for *kvetch*?

"So what are you going to do, be a hero?" Sadie chimed in. "Some hero. You don't even have a gun."

Theresa put in her two cents' worth: "Brian, if you're seriously worried, call down to Crystal Cove and ask the local law to keep a lookout. Give them a make on the vehicle and a description of Fulton. Then turn around and go back home."

Brian took a deep breath and longed for a cold beer. He felt a desperate need for the sense of security that he somehow derived from holding an icy, sweating bottle in his hand. Talking to yourself was one thing. Hearing other people talk to you, when they were not in your immediate vicinity, was quite another. He seriously considered doubling back and checking himself into the Carrillo State Hospital for the Criminally Insane—providing that he could find it. He had never been able to find anything in Carrillo.

Brian pounded on the steering wheel. "Okay, you're right, all of you!" he said aloud. "This whole idea is stupid. I am acting stupid all right?"

The reflection of a single headlight made itself apparent in Brian's rearview mirror. A motorcycle? No, it was approaching too slowly to be a bike. He watched numbly as the old red pickup chugged past. The engine of the Hyundai seemed to start itself.

Okay, Lloyd, Brian thought. Whither thou goest, so go I.

The die had been cast.

FOLLOWING FULTON unobtrusively, Brian soon found, was not easy even on relative straightaways. Before the traffic thickened, he resorted to the Highway Patrol trick of exiting at an off ramp and reentering at the next on ramp—always assuming, of course, that there was one. He abandoned that strategy when the stream of eastbound vehicles was abruptly dammed by a "freeway improvement" project, largely carried on at night, which bottlenecked everybody down to one lane. He panicked, having totally lost track of Fulton's old heap. Well, if he couldn't go any-place, neither could Fulton.

Finally, the dam dislodged its resentful contents, and ve-hicles spread at will over several lanes. Brian kept to the right, ever-watchful of large trucks, and drove as slowly as he dared. Ah, an old red pickup. And luck, he thought, was with him for a change, for immediately behind Fulton's truck was an even more ancient foreign vehicle of the small persuasion, driven by what seemed to be a nearsighted nonagenarian. Perfect. He tucked himself in behind the senior citizen and turned on the car radio. The last thing he needed was to fall asleep at the wheel.

Whatever lingering doubts Brian might have harbored about Fulton's intended destination were dispelled when the old pickup bore to the right as the junction with the inter-state loomed ahead. He's going south, Brian thought. This is going to be a long trip. Amid the crisscrossing chains of merging vehicles, the little truck seemed to disappear, then reappear. Angrily honking horns brought Brian to the re-alization that he'd better pay attention to his own driving. The automotive chorus line reassembled itself for the trek over the next pass—another hefty grade, not as long as Carrillo but maybe steeper.

Where was Fulton? Brian looked around, his adrenaline surging. Ah, there, a bit to the rear. Brian slacked off on the accelerator and was shocked by the blast of an air horn from behind. He looked in his rearview mirror and saw that the radiator of a tanker truck appeared to be on the verge of eating his nice little car. Oh, shit. Shades of *Duel*.

He switched on his right-turn signal and motioned help-lessly at the truck. He had no business on the freeway. He knew it. What the hell was he doing?

As the tanker pulled around to pass, Brian glanced into his right-side mirror and saw that steam was rising from the hood of Fulton's pickup. Oh, thank you God, he thought. He'll never make it over the pass. I can go home.

But such was not to be.

FIFTY-THREE

DOGGEDLY ATTEMPTING TO sing along with the Top Forty hits on whatever misbegotten radio station he seemed to have tuned in to, Brian once again asked himself what he was doing and why.

He'd been on and off the road for more than four hours.

How Fulton had managed to revive his old truck was a mystery. Brian had pulled off the freeway near the top of the pass, taken a leak behind some handy chaparral, and watched the road for fifteen minutes just in case. Bingo. The ancient red pickup had come chugging along, crowning the pass with a sort of triumphant smugness. Tailing a vehicle, Brian thought exhaustedly, was not as easy as it was made out to be on "Hunter" or "Spenser." Especially when the tailee had the torque of a tortoise.

The process was tougher now that the sprawling metroplex was well behind them. Traffic had thinned, and what traffic existed was moving at a steady seventy or seventy-five mph. So as not to be obvious, Brian had reverted to the old Smokey off-and-on trick, but the exits were less frequent now and would soon be even farther apart. How would he manage during that long stretch through the Marine base?

Pondering, he happened to glance at his gas gauge. Oh, ye gods. The needle was wavering well below *E*. A lighted overhead sign loomed ahead: GOLONDRINA HWY, 1 MI. Well, he had no choice. Brian aimed his car at the off ramp and prayed that he would make it up the hill to the nearest service station.

While the attendant was filling up his tank, Brian used the pay phone to try to call Joanna again. Still no answer. Feeling desperate, he dug into his pocket for change and dialed Directory Assistance, hoping to get the number of whatever passed for law enforcement in Crystal Cove.

"I'm sorry. We have no such number in our computer."

"Well, can you tell me what police or sheriff's department has jurisdiction in Crystal Cove?"

The voice became frosty. "This is a telephone company. We do not have that information. You will have to call elsewhere for that information."

"Elsewhere? Where?"

"You will have to consult your own personal telephone directory, sir." Was it Brian's imagination, or was this lady beginning to sound exactly like Ernestine?

Brian felt desperate. "Look, Lily—and let me take this opportunity to tell you how much I've always admired your work—I'm calling from a public phone booth, and the book is missing."

"To what long-distance service do you subscribe, sir?"

"Shit," Brian said. "I don't know."

"You will have to call your own long-distance service for any further information sir." There was a click and a humming sound.

Brian considered tearing the phone from its mountings, but managed to restrain himself. He glanced out through the glass door of the booth and noticed that the gas station attendant was signaling to him. He was puzzled and somewhat alarmed to notice that the hood of the Hyundai was still open.

The attendant seemed agitated. "You gotta problem, mister."

"A problem?" How could that be?

"You don't take care of your car, ya know? I put in a quart of oil and topped off your battery and changed your air filter, which was the worst I've ever seen, but I can't do nuttin' about this radiator hose."

"Hose?"

"Look." The attendant grabbed his arm and dragged him over to the exposed engine. Brian tried not to recoil. "See this hose here?" He pointed with a grubby finger. "See this crack? The sucker's about to rupture on you. Drivin' on the freeway like you've been doin', I'm surprised it hasn't blown up on you already."

Brian forbore to explain that he had been driving at something less than maximum freeway speed. "Well, can't you fix it?"

"Fix it? I'd have to replace it, and I can't get a new hose until tomorrow. Maybe tomorrow afternoon, if I'm lucky."

His head swimming, Brian took refuge in pompousness: "Look, my good man, I am an accredited law-enforcement officer, engaged in pursuing a major investigation—"

"I don't care if you're the fucking Pope—"

"I can show you my credentials—"

"Credentials? Look, buddy, you don't seem to understand. I don't have the part. Read my lips, okay? *I don't have the part.* If I had a replacement hose, I could fix your car in maybe fifteen, twenty minutes. But *I don't have one.*" The attendant slammed down the hood of Brian's Hyundai. "So you're dead in the water, buddy." He sneered unpleasantly. "Maybe you'd like to call a cab. We could probably get one here inside a couple of hours."

"No, no. That won't do. This is an emergency." Brian closed his eyes and attempted to shift his brain into overdrive. "Okay, you say there's a crack in the radiator hose. Can you patch it somehow? Just a temporary quick fix, so to speak?" He aimed a hapless grin at the gas-station attendant, who at this point seemed his only hope. "With some sort of tape, maybe?" He dug into his pocket for his wallet. "I would certainly reward your ingenuity if you could keep me on the road for a while longer, say"—he did some quick mental calculations—"another hour."

"Another hour, huh?" The attendant looked around nervously. "How much money are we talking about? In terms of reward, I mean?"

Brian consulted his wallet. "I don't suppose you'd take a personal check." He chuckled nervously. "No, I didn't think so. Well, the most I can give you is fifty bucks."

The attendant pondered, and nodded. "Electrical tape ought to do it for an hour, if you keep it under the double nickel. Any speed over that and the sucker could blow on you. And it could blow up at any time; there are no guarantees, got it?"

"Got it." Brian pulled two twenties and a ten out of his wallet and pressed the bills into the gas station attendant's grubby fist. "Do it, will you? And hurry." He looked at his watch and reflected that the problem of how to unobtrusively tail Fulton through the largely deserted stretch of interstate that bisected the Marine base had now been resolved. He'd be lucky to get to Blue Cottage before Fulton did, if that's where Fulton was headed. Was there any question about it? Where else could the guy be going?

As he watched the attendant raise the hood of the Hyundai and do mysterious things to his engine, Brian decided to try one more time to raise Joanna. He headed for the phone booth, and then realized that it was occupied by a largish woman wearing a sort of Hawaiian tent. She seemed settled in for a leisurely conversation. Sweating heavily, Brian paced back to his car and tried not to hover over the attendant.

"This is as good as I can do, mister," he said, closing the hood. "Remember, no guarantees. And take it easy on the upgrades."

"Thanks," Brian said fervently, levering himself into the driver's seat.

"For what? I didn't do nothing. You put that tape on yourself, didn't you? I mean, I don't wanna get sued."

"Yeah," Brian said, gingerly revving up the engine. "I did it all by myself."

FIFTY-FOUR

JOANNA WAS CONTEMPLATING her painting from afar—or at least from as far away as she could get, within the narrow confines of her studio—and trying to decide whether she was finished with it when a rap on the door startled her out of her reverie. "Gretch? Mercy, are you still here?"

"Jo..." Gretchen's voice sounded odd. "You have a visitor."

Visitor? Ye Gods, and here she was, starkers. "Just a minute," she said, frantically groping for a smock.

"Please don't cover yourself, Joanna. The view is quite spectacular. And after all, I've never seen you in the flesh, so to speak."

Jo froze. She forced herself to turn around.

Gretchen was looking nervous and entirely bewildered. "This man says he's Sam Fox, Jo. Were you expecting him?"

Sam smiled at Jo, gave her a gentle, sweet grin. But his eyes were cold behind the wire-rimmed glasses. He wore a faded blue work shirt with the sleeves rolled up; the strap of what looked like a canvas golf bag was slung over one shoulder. He smiled at Gretchen. "I told you she'd be glad to see me, Alice."

"Alice?" Gretchen rubbed her eyes.

"Isn't this Alice's restaurant?" Sam slid the bag down from his shoulder and unzipped it. Joanna felt paralyzed.

"Jo, do you want me to stay? Is everything okay? I mean, do you *know* this man?" Gretchen's indignation level was audibly rising, but her face was alarmingly pale.

"Um, yes." Jo cleared her throat and forced a smile. "Of course, this is Sam. I recognize his voice. Sam, I'm sorry; it's just that you startled me so, I couldn't react." She frantically tried to send a mental message to Gretchen, wishing desperately that she had filled her in on the day's events before rushing upstairs to crash. "Gretch, you'd better go on home—goodness, it must be late." Maybe too late. "Sam, I really would be more comfortable with some clothes on, so if you'll please..."

"No, Gretch," Sam mocked, "I think you'd better stay." He closed the door to the studio and stood with his back against it. The gun that he seemed to hold negligently, crooked over one arm, looked very large to Jo. "I have a story to tell you both. Joanna knows that I'm a wonderful storyteller, don't you, my lovely?" Sam smiled again and nodded toward Jo. "This story is about treachery and betrayal—classic themes, of course. But then Joanna could probably tell it better than I."

Jo felt dizzy. "Look, can I sit down?" she croaked. "I feel like I'm about to pass out. And can't I put some clothes on? I'm freezing."

"Why don't you both sit down? Make yourself comfortable. Against that wall over there, if you will. But Joanna, I prefer you just the way you are at the moment—beautifully naked, baring your body to me if not your soul."

As Sam's eyes surveyed her, almost clinical in their inspection, Joanna felt hideously violated. Foolish, half-remembered fantasies rose in her throat like bile. I did this to myself, she thought. I daydreamed about this moment; I wanted Sam to find me desirable. Now I hope he finds me ugly. Middle-aged, with sagging breasts and...

"Don't worry, my muse. I promise that you won't feel cold for long."

Sam seemed suddenly to notice the painting on the easel, its colors still glistening wet, and a change came over his face. "What's that?"

"It's a painting," Jo gulped. "I just did it tonight. I'm not sure whether it's finished yet."

"No," Sam said impatiently. "I mean what *is* it? What is it supposed to mean?"

There was a charged silence. Jo summoned up all her theatrical skills and took a deep breath.

"It's for our show, Sam. 'The Phoenix Garden.' I had a new idea; I haven't had a chance to tell you about it. You see," she babbled, "I want to do a series of oils, companion pieces to the watercolors—symbolic, rather than representation. I mean, instead of depicting the flowers, these would reflect the original myths. Demeter and Persephone, that sort of thing. I've done a little research ..." she trailed off, lamely.

"You have indeed," Sam said, too quietly. "You did some today, didn't you? Up at the Oak Canyon post office. Quite a drive just to do a little research."

Jo stole a glance at Gretchen. Her normal color seemed to have returned, and she was gazing calmly at Sam with what seemed to be intense concentration. Maybe the old "Go and Fetch" combo could figure a way out of this one yet. Maybe.

"Sam, I can explain that. I'm really embarrassed ..." Jo covered her face with her hands and attempted a nervous giggle. "Look, that gun is freaking me out. Can't you put it down so we can talk?"

Sam slid down the door until his backside was resting on the floor. He looked totally relaxed. "I can talk the way we are now. So can you, as far as I can see. The gun will have a chance to talk later. Meanwhile, I'm waiting to hear your explanation." The voice was as silky as ever, almost caressing in its affect.

"Well, it's just that ... I've been so upset. I was terribly disappointed that you didn't come down for the opening of the show, and then I thought that I had ruined our relationship by probing into your life. I just felt devastated about that. I was—grieving, really grieving. Ask Gretchen. She'll tell you."

Sam glanced at Gretchen, who nodded solemnly and leaned forward, making eye contact with the man.

"Jo feels very deeply about you," Gretch said. Sincerity seemed to ooze out of her pores like custard from a napoleon pastry. "You and I—I think that we're the only people who are really important to her."

Something peculiar seemed to happen to Sam's chin.

"I just had to *see* you," Jo continued, gathering steam. "I wanted to know what you *looked like*. Oh, I know it was a stupid, childish thing to do, lurking in the post office until you came to pick up your mail, but it was the only plan I could think of. And then when you showed up—I guess I lost my nerve. I didn't want you to remember me as a silly person. I was afraid to let you know who I was. I don't know what I thought I was going to do if you..." Joanna trailed off again.

Sam seemed to be staring at the painting, to be in a sort of trance. Jo chanced a sideways look at Gretch. Could they make a grab for the gun? No, Sam was across the studio, too far away. And Gretchen was staring fixedly at Sam.

"That painting..." Sam said in a strange sort of high, singsongy voice. "It's for *Poppy*, isn't it? Yes—Demeter, mourning her lost daughter."

Joanna took a cautious breath. "Somehow, tonight, I could feel her pain. I mixed my paints with her tears, and some of my own."

"Turn all pain into paint, right?" Sam turned his head slowly and looked into Jo's eyes. "Just add a *t* for tears."

"You know that's how I work," Jo said softly, realizing that tears were, in fact, running down Sam's cheeks—and down her own. The moment seemed as fragile as a snowflake. She felt Gretch's hand squeeze hers, briefly.

"You loved her very much, didn't you?" Gretchen's voice came out as calm and sweet as a lullaby. How could she know?

"I loved them both!" Sam stood up abruptly. "I never meant for...Jessie was so beautiful, so pure. She made my poetry! She gave me my poems!" He began to pace agitatedly. "She was barely walking when I first saw her, toddling on the sand. A cherub, so innocent. I knew immediately that it was my mission to protect her." He was almost whispering now. "Carole was sympathetic, supportive. She was a good person, a good mother. And she never knew, not for a long time. I don't think she ever suspected that *Jessie* was the one I yearned for, not Carole, even though I could never..."

Gretchen leaned toward Sam. "You were never able to make love to Carole?" she suggested gently.

"I tried. God knows, I tried! And I tried not to touch Jessie. But as she grew up and I could see that she would soon become a woman, desirable to other men, I could not help myself. I am but flesh, and the flesh is weak." Sam ran his free hand through his hair in a parody of agony. "I wanted to introduce her to love. Pure love. I wanted her to love me forever. Not anyone else, only me. Yes, I was being selfish. Egotistical, if you will. But I was beyond the point of restraint."

"How old was Jessie then?" Gretchen asked in a matter-of-fact way.

Sam looked around distractedly. "Oh, maybe nine."

You filthy, perverted bastard, Jo thought. "And you kept it up until you got her pregnant," she blurted. Gretch's elbow jammed itself into her ribs. But Sam didn't seem to have heard her outburst.

"I tried to protect Jess, to keep her away from those terrible *boys*. I know those boys. I try to teach them proper English usage; I coach them in their silly games. Barbarians, all. But I usually fail with them, and I failed with Jess. She became close with a *boy*. She told him her secrets. *Our* secrets. The boy came to me; he had the nerve to *threaten* me. He was going to expose me, destroy my career and my reputation!" Sam seemed manic now, pacing in circles and waving the shotgun. "And then Jessie turned against me—and finally Carole did." Sam began to sob audibly. "My world was crashing down around me. I *had* to do it. There was no other way."

"So you killed them all," Jo whispered to herself.

And then the roof fell in.

FIFTY-FIVE

WINDING DOWN THE HILL into Crystal Cove, Brian prayed a sort of prayer that he would remember how to find Blue Cottage. By the time he had finally ransomed his Hyundai from the gas station at the Golondrina Highway interchange, he had known that Fulton must be far ahead of him; it had been a struggle to stay under fifty-five mph on the largely deserted freeway. "Better late than never" might not apply in this case, he thought.

He scoped the scene, feeling disoriented in the dark, and headed down through the state university campus, which was mostly deserted at this time of year. Once he had cleared the campus, illuminated overhead street signs—none of which meant much to him—began to appear at major intersections. Blue Cottage was near the center of town, Brian seemed to recall. On a little side street just off one of the main drags. But which one? And where was the center of town?

He came to what seemed to be a five-way intersection and slowed to a near stop, even though he had a green light. A low-riding old sedan, coming up fast on his rear end, screeched its brakes and honked, then peeled out to pass him just as the light turned yellow. Assorted fingers, thrust out through open windows, pointed toward the heavens and exhorted him to pray—or so he charitably assumed. The creeps and punks seemed to be everywhere, perhaps cloning themselves.

I'm not a bleeping speed reader, Brian thought resentfully. He looked up at the bewilderness of lighted signs and found one that read TOWN CENTER. Aha. As the light turned green again, he aimed the Hyundai in that direction, and was disturbed to notice that the engine seemed sluggish in responding.

Was he running out of luck?

He cruised cautiously, coasting on the downgrades and looking for familiar landmarks, until a profusion of lights ahead indicated that he was at last approaching the surprisingly extensive and prosperous-looking shopping core of Crystal Cove. Lots of money here, Brian thought. Upscale retail businesses. Plenty of wealthy retired people looking for ways to spend their children's inheritances—well, more power to them. Not to mention tourists in search of art and culture and local color. Blue Cottage, he thought, might make out very well indeed.

If he could find it.

He slowed down, as the terrain began to look right. What the hell was the name of the street? Some sort of flower or plant, he was sure. But then all the little side streets seemed to be named after flowers. Forsythia? No, but close. Fuchsia? That didn't sound right. Geranium? No, no.

A stuttering sound came from the front of the car, along with a couple of muffled pops. Brian let up on the accelerator and allowed the car to coast gently along what was fortunately a slight downslope, meanwhile continuing to squint at the street signs. Hibiscus? Hydrangea?

Wisps of steam began to emerge from under the hood of the Hyundai, mingling with the tentatively exploring tendrils of fog that drifted in from the ocean. Jasmine?

Jasmine!

Brian braked hard just as his radiator core blew, spewing a blinding, steaming shower of sludge over his windshield. Half in shock, having no idea of what had just happened to his car, he realized that scalding goo was dripping from under the dashboard onto his shoes.

He went out the door, fast. This sucker's going to blow up on me, he thought. He heard his father's plaintive voice: "If you can't buy American, can't you at least buy Japanese?"

Standing well clear of the fuming Hyundai, Brian willed his heart to stop pounding. He took a couple of slow, deep breaths. The car seemed to be settling down, stabilizing itself—no longer an immediate threat, but probably comatose and terminal. He took stock of his situation. Jasmine Way. Yes, that's where Blue Cottage was.

Save the poor doggy!

Summoning up all the resolve he could muster, Brian forced himself back to the car and retrieved his heavy long-handled flashlight from under the dashboard. It felt a bit sticky, but it seemed to work. He walked back to the intersection and looked down the short block that was Jasmine Way. Most of the buildings were dark; a light shone here and there. Feeling like Gary Cooper—or was it John Wayne?—in a remake of *High Midnight*, Brian strode purposefully down the middle of the dark street.

A few lights were burning in the house that he recognized as being Blue Cottage. A shaded, subtle light shone from an upstairs window—Jo's apartment, he thought. A brighter glow emanated from what he surmised must be the kitchen that served the tearoom. But an outbuilding, to the rear, was the most brightly illuminated; light poured from side windows and, improbably, from the roof.

Brian surveyed the scene. I need to get closer, he thought. I need to look in windows, that sort of stuff.

As he started up the graveled driveway, he realized that a vehicle was parked there; an old pickup truck, Lloyd Fulton's truck.

Oh, shit, Brian thought.

He tried to tread without sound on the loose gravel, but his goop-filled sneakers were squishing and squeaking and, worse, sticking to his socks. He stooped and slipped off his shoes and took a few steps. Not much of an improvement; now his gooped-up socks were collecting minibits of sharp stones. But it was better than walking barefoot on the killer aggregate, Brian told himself.

He flashed back onto a beach, to hot sand burning his feet. He heard his parents, *saw* them: "The doctor said he should walk barefoot on sand, Sadie! He's got flat feet!" "But Sid, it's hurting him, can't you see? The sand is too hot! You've got sandals; I've got sandals; *we* don't go barefoot on the sand!" "Sadie, you should listen to the doctor; so what are we paying him for already? Since when do you know from feet?"

Brian shivered and tiptoed, in an uncomfortable sort of crouch, across the gravel to the kitchen window. Cautiously, he stood up and risked a peek. Nobody was in sight.

The sound of a voice, raised agitatedly, came from the outbuilding to the rear. A garage? Brian crept closer and saw that the wall where the original garage door must have been had been covered over with siding and that a couple of strategically situated casement windows, now wide open, had been added. He dimly remembered Jo's description of how her partner's husband had converted what was once the garage of Blue Cottage into a studio by putting in windows, some plumbing, a skylight—an old-fashioned skylight that could be cranked open and closed.

Keeping to the skimpy grass that bordered the gravel driveway, Brian cautiously reconnoitered. The functional door seemed to be on the side of the building, around to his left. He circled the former garage, treading carefully. Windows had been punched in on two sides; all seemed to be screened.

The agitated voice was louder now. Brian could not make out what was being said, but the timbre and tone seemed to change periodically, as though it originated from more than one person. And yet, somehow, Brian didn't think so.

Clutching his torch in a death grip, Brian crept close enough to look in a window.

The man he recognized as Lloyd Fulton was pacing around the studio, waving a shotgun and gesturing theatrically. Brian heard snatches of words and phrases. My God, Brian thought, what a ham. The scene struck him as being oddly comical, as though he was watching a TV soap opera with the sound turned off.

But he's not in there alone, Brian reminded himself.

He ducked under the window and peered in from the other side. Joanna and the woman he remembered as being her partner—Kristin? No, Gretchen—were sitting side by side against the far wall, holding hands. They both looked surprisingly calm, considering the circumstances. But something seemed bizarre.

Brian blinked and did a double take. No, his eyes were not playing tricks on him. Whereas Gretchen was clad in cutoff denims, a faded T-shirt, and funny-looking leather sandals, Joanna wore only a bemused expression.

She's not really all that skinny, he thought, somewhat surprised.

He forced his mind back to the problem at hand and reviewed his options.

Don't be stupid, he told himself. Fulton has a gun, and you don't. Fulton is crazy and you aren't. Yet.

Go back to Blue Cottage, he heard Theresa telling him. Call the cops. You're local now; just dial 911—or the operator, if 911 doesn't work.

Brian heard his heart pounding. But what if . . . ?

What if the door to Blue Cottage is locked? What if Fulton decides to shoot them while I'm working on being sensible?

Just *do* it, Theresa insisted. If you persist in acting like a total idiot, I'm going to change the channel.

His knees quivering uncontrollably, Brian proceeded to mind Mother.

FIFTY-SIX

BRIAN HUNG UP THE telephone quickly, having said as little as possible—only that an armed and apparently deranged man was holding two women hostage in an outbuilding behind the Blue Cottage tearoom on Jasmine Way. Situation urgent.

Wincing as tiny sharp stones dug into his feet through his saturated socks, he tiptoed down the splintery wooden steps that descended from the kitchen entrance to Blue Cottage, having carefully eased the door into its jamb.

He took a deep breath and listened. Everything seemed quiet now; even the fitful breeze was momentarily calm. But as he picked his way back toward the garage/studio, Brian thought he heard someone sobbing. A man? Had Fulton killed them? Surely he would have heard a shot!

I need a strategy, Brian told himself. I need some way of surprising Fulton, disarming him before he knows what's going on.

He knew what Lou would say about that: Kayne, you've been watching too many TV shows. You don't go unarmed against a guy with a shotgun. And even if you're armed, you don't go alone.

"I am not a wimp!" Brian whispered out loud.

He looked at the building and thought hard. Light was streaming from the windows—and from the skylight. An old-fashioned skylight, Jo had said. Not one of those sealed synthetic domes, but a flat glass-paned skylight, one that could be opened—one that *was* open, if his eyes were not deceiving him. I need to figure out how to get up onto the roof, he thought; that's my only chance of surprising Fulton.

As Brian inched his way around the studio—to the right, this time—a poignantly familiar odor suddenly made him feel dizzied by déjà vu. He realized that the air was saturated with the scent of roses—rambling roses. Climbing roses. The kind that his father had loved best, had nurtured along the back fence and up the side of the house. "Rambling rose..." He could hear Sid's cracked tenor, singing along with his old Nat Cole records.

Rambling roses needed something to climb on, he remembered. A support of some sort: a fence—or, lacking that, a trellis.

Afraid to chance using his flashlight, Brian groped along the side of the building. There were no windows set into this wall, only a couple of vents, obviously newly installed, which he suspected were associated with the retrofitted plumbing. The scent of roses was stronger now, almost overpowering. He bit back a yelp as his exploring hand encountered the sharp corner of what seemed to be a trellis and an even sharper thorn.

Wishing mightily that he had a pair of stout gloves, Brian took a calculated risk and flicked on his torch for a moment. Yes, the trellis went all the way up to the shallowly pitched shingled roof. Toward the top, it seemed sparsely populated by roses and their concomitant thorns. On the other hand, it looked old and insubstantial and was probably rotten.

"I tried! God knows, I tried!" The voice roared out of the skylight and then faded to an indecipherable moan.

This man is crazy, Brian told himself. I can't afford to be sensible anymore. There's not enough time. I don't hear any sirens. Nobody's going to come and rescue us. There's only me. There's nobody here but me, Chicken. Chicken Little, that is. And the sky's about to fall.

He shoved his flashlight into the waistband of his trousers and used both hands to propel himself up the trellis, trying as best he could to remain silent and testing each flimsy slat before he trusted it with his altogether-too-full weight. Thorns snagged his clothing and raked his skin; his socks stuck to the lathing until he finally freed his hands, one at a time and very cautiously, and ripped them off.

After what seemed an hour of climbing, Brian realized that he had run out of trellis. Now what? The half-open skylight—gaping in the wrong direction, as had now become apparent—was just a few feet away. But there were no handholds on the sloping roof; there was nothing to hang on to. The shingles seemed ancient, no doubt infected with dry rot. Brian felt suddenly light headed, remembering that acrophobia ranked high on the list of his many weakness.

The voice from below rose again in a crescendo, ranting uncontrollably. Not really thinking, Brian began to worm himself up over the unreliable shingles, scrabbling with his fingertips for a purchase. Really, it wasn't that difficult once he had a little momentum. Just keep going, he urged himself.

Brian somehow made it to the spine of the roof and hooked his arm over the ridge, panting with relief. From this vantage point, he could see down through the skylight easily. Fulton was pacing again, emoting and waving his uncomfortably large gun but apparently unaware of any activity overhead. Brian couldn't see Jo or Gretchen, but he assumed that they were still sitting with their backs to the wall. Sweating, he carefully maneuvered himself into an attack position.

A sudden tension in Fulton's posture sent a chill up Brian's spine, and he retrieved the heavy torch from its uncomfortable resting place inside the waistband of his pants. As he inched himself back down toward the skylight, he could see that Fulton was raising the shotgun, pointing it in the direction—he supposed—of Jo and Gretch. He looked down through the skylight at the top of Fulton's head and noticed that in spite of his long hair, the guy was going bald, from the top down.

Why am I paying attention to the guy's hair? Brian asked himself. I've got to do something! Now!

"Hold it right there!" Brian barked, pointing the butt of his torch down through the skylight. "Freeze, buster! Put down the gun, nice and—" Suddenly, he realized that he was sliding headfirst down the roof, that his toes had lost their tentative grip on the ridgepole. He seemed, dispassionately, to watch himself as he fell into brilliant light; he saw Fulton's startled face looking up into his own, heard the shatter of glass as his flailing flashlight crashed through a pane of the skylight, felt himself collide with bone and flesh and, finally, with unforgiving floor. And then the lights went out.

FIFTY-SEVEN

TO JOANNA, THE NEXT FEW moments passed in a kaleido-scopic blur of sensory impressions. The disembodied voice that was emanating from the skylight, sounding like a segment from a "Cagney and Lacey" rerun, had barely registered in her head when the body that presumably belonged to the voice did a kamikaze dive down into the studio, landing smack on top of Sam. Scraps and shards of glass rained onto the floor from overhead. There was a brief and probably reflexive scuffle of bodies; then, aside from a muffled groan that emerged from the tangled heap of arms and legs, everything was still.

As she took a careful breath, convinced that all of this must be a dream, Jo realized that Gretchen was on her feet, moving toward Sam and the as-yet-unidentifiable surprise guest. She watched numbly as Gretch slid the shotgun out from under Sam's unresisting form.

What a strange movie this is, Jo thought, suddenly aware that she was trembling all over.

"Jo!" Gretchen's voice was sharp. "Get up. Go into the kitchen and call the police. *Now*."

Joanna rubbed her eyes and felt a sharp sting. She looked at her hand and saw blood.

"It's only a sliver, Jo. Get up! Go call for help! *Hurry!* Gretchen had backed herself into the corner by the door and was holding the gun as though she knew how to use it—and was prepared to do so.

Oh, God, Jo thought. This isn't a dream. This isn't a movie.

She got up fast, too fast, and felt as though she had climbed into a Tilt-A-Whirl. Various mutters and stirrings arose from the mingled mound of fallen warriors. Move! she told herself.

She staggered across the studio and lunged out the door, her eyes fixed on the soft glow that shone from the kitchen of the main house. Tiny sharp stones pierced her feet; her body felt extremely strange. Cold. Something was wrong. Something was most peculiar. Surely she was dreaming, dreaming that she was lurching, hopping, limping down a gravel driveway in the middle of the night without any clothes on.

Wake up, stupid! she told herself.

Suddenly, her arms were firmly gripped by persons unseen and, certainly, unknown. Then a beefy, sweaty hand clamped itself over her mouth—a hand that smelled strongly of raw onions.

I'm not dreaming, Jo realized. I've dreamt in Technicolor, but never in Smell-O-Vision.

This is it, she thought. I've had it. Well, at least I'll get to see my life pass before my eyes. That ought to take a long time. On the other hand, it might not take very long at all. It depends on who's doing the editing, and on what parts they leave out....

She realized to her surprise that she was being gently deposited on the by-now-dew-drenched grass that bordered the gravel driveway.

"Lady," a voice was saying to her. "Lady, we need to know what's going on in there. We got a report about a maniac with a gun, holding some people hostage."

Jo cautiously opened her eyes. The faint light emanating from the kitchen window enabled her to see that the man who was talking to her was a uniformed police officer.

"Oh." She sat up and took a breath. "Oh, my God. I was going to call you. Who called you?"

The policeman shook her, not quite roughly. "Look, lady, that doesn't matter. Just tell me what's happening, okay?"

"There's a crazy man in there, all right," Joanna acknowledged, finally—to herself as well as to the cop. "But he doesn't have the gun anymore. At least, I don't think so. My partner, Gretchen, had the gun last time I looked. And there's another man who sort of fell in through the skylight, but I'm pretty sure he was trying to rescue us. He's out cold, I think. And so is Sam. The crazy man, that is. But they won't be unconscious for very long."

The cop gave her a strange look.

"I know I'm babbling, but it's all been such a..." Joanna's cheeks felt wet. She swiped a finger through the wetness and licked it. Her finger tasted salty and metallic. She heard sirens approaching, saw uniformed men moving around purposefully. Blue and red lights swirled around her head. People seemed to be talking at her, over her, around her. Their voices sounded froglike, as though all of this were happening underwater.

"We'd better get a blanket to wrap her..."

Something dabbed at her face, her head.

"Did you call the..."

A maelstrom of voices gurgled and boiled around her.

I can't breathe, Jo thought. I am drowning. Well, okay. Let it be. "Let it be, let it be." Playing her internal Beatles tape, she unclenched her teeth and uncurled her toes and let go of her precarious hold on consciousness.

FIFTY-EIGHT

TECHNICALLY CONSCIOUS BUT not really functioning, Brian took in the teeming scene around him (in what he vaguely recognized as being a tiny attic apartment) much as he might have half-dozed, dispassionate and uninvolved, through a boring TV sitcom. People, many of them in uniform, were hustling and bustling here and there, apparently busy in mysterious ways.

He himself seemed to be semireclining in a semicomfortable chair, with some sort of box propping up his feet. From his fuzzy perspective, he could see across the room to where Joanna, swooning on a sofa in full recline, appeared to be doing a creditable impression of Mimi in *La Bohème*. He halfway expected that she would burst into song at any moment.

Brian realized that someone was holding his hand—well, actually, his wrist—and that it felt rather pleasant. He looked down at his wrist and at the hand that held it. The hand seemed to be feminine in conformation, which was something of a relief. Feeling almost euphoric except for a lurking headache that threatened to overwhelm him once he *really* woke up, Brian let his eyes drift upward from the hand that was holding his wrist, up along a delicately tanned arm to the short sleeve of a navy blue garment. Optically ascending, hanging a left at an aesthetically sloped shoulder, he encountered a stubborn tendril of not-quite-black hair that had managed to escape from a haphazard ponytail.

He closed his eyes, flashing back to a dusty mountain trail. Sister Bernadette. Could it be? Surely not.

He opened his eyes, searching for a face. "Sister?"

The face was turned away, at the moment, intent on a notepad attached to a clipboard. Brian's wrist felt suddenly naked and unprotected.

Well, of course, he thought. She's been taking my pulse.

"You really should be in the hospital overnight, Mr. Kayne. Your vital signs are in the normal range, but you *were* unconscious, and I suspect that you have a slight concussion."

The voice was soft and caressing. The face that went with the voice did not belong to Sister Bernadette, of the Order of the Immaculate Conception, but it was equally enchanting. Heart-shaped, actually, with dimples to die for, maybe even kill for, and a smile that lit up the room.

Brian let his eyes glide discreetly downward from the face to nether regions and noticed that an official-looking name tag was attached to the nearer of a pair of gloriously rolling foothills. S. BRODKIN, the name tag proclaimed. Sharon? Sheila? Sandy? Surely not Shelley! Shirley? He let his eyelids drift shut and abandoned himself to biblical fantasies. "'Thy two breasts are like two young roes that are twins, which feed among the lilies,'" he sang along with Solomon.

He gazed up into the twinkling blue eyes of S. Brodkin, Certified Paramedic. Oh, mercy. Here, surely or Shirley, was a Nice Jewish Girl. Sadie would have an orgasm, if he didn't beat her to it. Certainly he was experiencing some peculiar physical sensations.

Brian closed his eyes again, wondering whether perhaps, after all, he wouldn't be better off in a hospital.

"'Stay me with flagons, comfort me with apples...'" he sang silently. "'For I am sick...'"

Brian sat up so abruptly that his traumatized but still relatively unyielding skull made violent contact with the chin of the unfortunately unsuspecting S. Brodkin.

"Sick," he gasped. "I'm going...to be..."

FIFTY-NINE

DURING THE LONG DRIVE back to Paloma on Wednesday afternoon, Brian had plenty of leisure to reflect upon the events of the last two days. Had it been only two days? Somehow it seemed as though half a lifetime had transpired since he had followed Fulton's old truck down to Crystal Cove.

After having thoroughly disgraced himself by throwing up on what he later learned was Joanna's heirloom Oriental rug (and by doing so somehow evening a vague sort of score with her, but never mind that), he had given into the entreaties of the entrancing S. Brodkin and let himself be checked into the local hospital for an overnight stay. Fulton/Fox, he had been assured by the San Miguel County authorities, was in custody and would remain in that condition pending psychiatric evaluation. Brian had talked to Lou, who had promised to call Theresa and fill in the estimable DA on the course of events. Finally, unfamiliarly bedded down in his hospital room, he had crashed with a vengeance.

Tuesday had been devoted to getting the Hyundai fitted with a new radiator core and hoses, not a simple matter as it had turned out. Tuesday night—ah, Tuesday night, Sadie had fed him and fussed over him. Fed him too fully, too fondly. He really hadn't felt much like eating. And then there had been the bathroom anxieties: Shake yourself thoroughly but not violently, and *examine your zipper*. Sadie had insisted upon bringing him warm milk before bedtime and even tucking him in, for Christ's sake—all the while making him feel guilty, of course.

Well, Sadie didn't realize that she was making him feel guilty, he reflected. She was just being a mother.

Oh, shit, Brian thought. There was simply no way of working through all this stuff. It was just *there*, and it would be there until long after everybody was dead. There was no cure for this disease called guilt.

Turning off the freeway at his exit, rolling down the car windows and trying to persuade himself that his head did not ache persistently and ominously, Brian felt a surge of panic, borne on a wave of *something important forgotten*—a seed of a nightmare.

Mabel.

He had left her, as usual, on Monday morning—expecting to return, as usual, on Monday evening. Now it was Wednesday afternoon, late. He envisioned his poor cat starving to death, expiring of dehydration. Or, worse, trashing his apartment—peeing all over the furniture, shredding the drapes. After all, she *had* mastered drinking out of the toilet. (If only he could persuade her to use that appliance for its normal purpose.)

I am being silly, Brian told himself; cats have survived for weeks when accidentally imprisoned or whatever. And the odds are ten to one that I left the toilet seat up.

Still, a combination of guilt and anxiety propelled him as he recklessly aimed his Hyundai toward home.

The apartment smelled stuffy and musty and sounded strangely silent as Brian turned the key in the door to let himself in. There was no sign of Mabel. His stomach lurched, and tears rose in his throat.

Oh, Mabel! he thought, grieving already. He steeled himself to search the apartment for her poor stiff body.

"Blian!" Mrs. Otani was suddenly at his door, in an especially agitated condition.

Brian felt a surge of relief. "Mrs. O! Say, look, I can explain. Something happened that I didn't anticipate..."

"Oh, Blian...I so ashame. When you not come home, Mabel make lossa noise; she need food. So I go get her. Use key."

Mrs. Otani brandished the key that Brian had left her for use in emergencies. Her English, Brian noticed, was fading fast.

"Then, yesserday, she ack so funny. All time, she wanna go out. Funny sounds, she make. I sink, sis cat, see not been spaded; see want"—a deep blush suffused Mrs. Otani's still-doll-like face—"see wan make love wid boy cat. An tis af-fernoon, when I get mail, see get out. See no come back, Blian!" Mrs. Otani began to wail.

"Oh, please, Mrs Otani!" Brian felt a mixture of relief and a new anxiety. And, of course, guilt; he should have had Mabel spayed months ago. But surely Mrs O. could be per-suaded to take at least one of the kittens.

"I'm sure that Mabel will come home when she's, er, through. You did the best you could, and I appreciate it. Now, you go back home and have your dinner, okay?"

Much later, after he had picked at a microwaved frozen pizza and opened the door that led to his so-called deck (just in case Mabel decided to come home) and crashed deci-sively into his very own bed, Brian half-heard a crescendo of primal yowls that seemed to exemplify ultimate pain or ultimate ecstasy or some combination thereof.

Have a ball, Mabel, he hoped as he fell off the cliff of consciousness.

SIXTY

SADIE WAS TENDING SID'S rose garden, nipping off dead-heads and pruning back leggy stalks, when Joanna pulled her Honda into the visitor's parking area. Immersed in her task, Sadie appeared not to notice Jo's arrival. The Widow Kayne, Jo thought, presented an engaging if eccentric spectacle in her orange and purple muumuu—no doubt a comfortable and entirely sensible outfit, given the late-summer heat wave that was affecting even the coastal areas. A floppy straw hat, tied rakishly under Sadie's chin with what seemed to be a swath of lime-green chiffon, completed the general effect, which was that of a rather long-in-the-tooth Kate Greenaway child.

I could sit here and watch Sadie all day, Jo thought. But that's not what I came here to do.

She maneuvered her long legs out of the door of the little car and took a deep breath. Sadie turned as the car door slammed, and carefully laid down her pruning shears. "Oh, Jo," she said. "Jo, honey!" Sadie peeled off her gardening gloves and gave Jo a violent hug somewhere in the vicinity of the latter's navel.

"Ooooff," Jo said involuntarily. "Look, Sadiebelle, I apologize for just dropping in on you like this..."

"No, not at all; I'm delighted to see you. I've been meaning to give you a call. Anyway, it's too hot to work outside. I was just thinking about going in and having a glass of lemonade; I've got some in the Frigidaire."

Jo let herself be gently nudged up the steps leading to the porch of Sadie's mobile home, feeling ridiculously as though she were the Q.E.II being guided to berth by a tiny but tenacious tugboat.

"Can you believe this weather? I've actually had the air conditioner running for the last two days. Just a little window unit, but such a difference it makes! Sid insisted on installing one; I said who needs it in this climate, but he said, "Sadie, a mobile home, it's like a microwave oven, just a little window unit, you'll be sorry if we don't..."

Jo found herself being steered toward and deposited onto a pouffy-looking sofa as Sadie bustled and dithered, talking nonstop, into what presumably was the kitchen.

"So of course Sid was right, as it turned out, which he usually was, but not always, for example, the time he..."

Jo began to feel unaccountably dozy. She let her head loll back against plump cushions as the sound of ice cubes chunking into glasses interrupted Sadie's monologue.

"And so I said to Sid, 'No, that didn't happen in *1971*, because my niece Rochelle had twins that year; it must have been the year before or maybe the year after, because I remember Rochelle at the seder, big as a house she was, and...'"

Realizing that her eyelids were drooping, Jo made a concerted effort to open them wide and found herself looking up at what appeared to be a carnivorous plant. An overwhelming sensation of déjà vu made her gasp; she sat up abruptly, feeling dizzy and disoriented.

"Well, Sid never could remember dates." Sadie reentered, bearing a pair of tall glasses. "I always had to remind him." She set the glasses down on the coffee table and looked at Jo with concern. "Are you okay, honey? You look a little pale. It's from the heat, maybe?"

"Maybe." Jo steadied herself and took a sip from her glass. "Or maybe a lingering aftereffect."

"Oh, sweetie!" Sadie's forehead puckered into a sort of plaid pattern—of which particular tartan, Joanna was unsure. "What a terrible experience that must have been for you and Gretchen! And for my Brian, of course. But thank God nobody was seriously hurt, and that Brian arrived in time to save you!"

Jo bit her tongue. "Yes, well, Sadie..."

"But as I always say every cloud has a silver lining, and I'm sure that this awful thing has brought you and Brian closer together." Sadie looked at Joanna hopefully.

"Er, look, Sadie." Jo suddenly felt a surge of sympathy for Brian. "Those things happen in TV shows. And silly mystery novels. I mean, just because ..." She took another deep breath and started over. "Your son is a fine person; he's a good man and you have every reason to be proud of him. But Brian and I—well, some things just aren't meant to be. That's all," she finished lamely. "So I don't want you to keep hoping that ... hey, *we*'re friends, you and I. Isn't that enough?"

Sadie chugged the last of her lemonade. "Sure," she said gamely. Muscles trembled at the corners of her mouth.

"Sadie ..." This isn't working, Jo thought. "I'd love to have you for a mother-in-law." Okay, that's a white lie. So I'll burn in hell. "I'd love to give you a grandchild. I'd love to have a child myself. But Sadie, this just isn't *right*, and it's never going to *be* right. Trust me."

"So, I'm easy," Sadie said brightly. "How about some more lemonade?"

"No, thanks; I've really got to be going."

"You know," Sadie confided, "that life-drawing class really got some blood circulating around here, if you know what I mean. Do you think you might talk Luke into ...?"

"Um, I think he's going back to school this week." Jo suddenly felt a desperate need to escape. "Maybe during semester break; we'll see. Or I could find a different model. How about you?"

"Me?" Sadie shot to her feet, giving Joanna a plausible excuse to do the same. "Well, sweetie, I guess I'll see you at Dancercize. Come again, soon, okay?"

"I'll do that," Jo assured Sadie as the Little Tugboat That Could escorted her fussily back to her Honda. "And keep up the good work with the roses. They're looking gorgeous!"

Which they in fact were, Jo reflected as she put the little hatchback into reverse gear. There was, indeed, something to be said for organic gardening.

SIXTY-ONE

FROM THE PERSPECTIVE of Theresa's redwood deck, which was cantilevered over the west-facing hillside, the ropy ridges of clouds appeared to be on fire. A coppery glow suffused the ocean below, which seemed glassily, almost eerily, still. Relaxing back into the cracked plastic cushions of what passed for a chaise lounge, Brian took a long swig from his bottle of Molson's Golden and half-wondered what it was, suddenly, that he was hearing—or, rather, not hearing.

Abruptly, the clatter and chatter of birds had been replaced by an ominous silence.

I know what this means, Brian thought without thinking, as his receptors shifted automatically into Full Red Alert. He jumped up and charged through the open sliding door that led from the deck into the kitchen, where Theresa was in the process of retrieving a crab salad from the refrigerator. "Downstairs!" he yelled, shoving the salad back into the cold and slamming the door of the fridge.

"Huh?" Then Theresa began to feel it through the soles of her sandals. "Oh. Oh!"

By the time Brian had propelled them both down the stairs that led to the lower, bedroom level of Theresa's house, which had been built halfway into the slope, they were struggling to maintain their various equilibria.

"Do you think this is *the big one*?" Theresa gasped.

"It's big enough," Brian answered grimly, wondering whether he had remembered to close his kitchen cupboard doors. Clutching each other, they waited until the nauseatingly rolling motion subsided.

"I didn't hear anything break, did you?" Theresa said hopefully.

"No, but there could be another one coming. A major aftershock. Or maybe a bigger quake. I think we should stay down here for awhile."

"Nonsense. Look, the power didn't even go off. This was just a baby, maybe five points max. Besides, I'm hungry, and we have lots of things to talk about."

"Well, you're the expert," Brian conceded. After all, Theresa had lived her whole life in Southern California, whereas he had been in residence for barely ten years. And he was feeling fairly ravenous himself.

They cautiously ascended the stairs and reconnoitered. Pictures on the walls were hanging askew, objects on countertops had skidded dangerously near to edges, but there seemed to be no damage.

"No harm, no foul," Brian observed, pulling a fresh Molson's from Theresa's refrigerator.

Theresa sighed. "I guess you could say that. Do you still want to eat outside?"

Brian stepped out the door and scoped out the scene. The wisps of cloud had thickened and darkened; the surf had quickened. Tiny lines of froth were marching in formation toward an invisible beach far below. Dogs were howling in the distance; birds had tentatively resumed their evening concert. "It seems very pleasant out here, actually."

"Light the candle, then. I'll be right out with the salad and rolls and wine."

Theresa seemed subdued, Brian thought. Whereas he felt almost giddy with relief. Saved, once again. How long could this go on? "I'll pour the wine," he offered gallantly, fetching a couple of goblets from Theresa's china cabinet. "Of course I'm hopeless with a corkscrew."

"The bottle is open," Theresa said. "Breathing."

Ah, yes.

"WELL," BRIAN VENTURED as Theresa leaned back and fired up her Salem Ultra-Light 100, "we survived."

"Some of us did."

"Come on, Theresa! When all of this started, we didn't even know what we were dealing with."

Theresa sighed. "That's true. And we did accomplish something. We got Fulton off the street, anyway."

"So I understand. But I haven't really been following all of this for the last few weeks. You know that I've been totally wrapped up in the Duran retrial. You remember, the first one didn't add up, didn't make sense. The jurors didn't think so, and they hung themselves on second degree. I don't blame them. Now, as it turns out..."

"Do you want to hear about the Fulton case?" Theresa leaned forward and pointed her cigarette at him. "Stop babbling, will you?"

Brian tipped the last of the wine into his glass. "Sorry."

"Well, as you remember, San Miguel County agreed to hold Fulton in custody pending psychiatric examination. They already had him cold on several serious charges based on his behavior in Crystal Cove, but they agreed to cooperate with us."

"Yeah, I know that." Brian tried to repress his impatience.

"We sent a psychiatrist from Carrillo State Hospital down to examine Fulton...Dr. Terry Haig. He got really excited about Fulton—says he's a unique borderline case, somewhere between a genuine multiple personality and a sophisticated sociopath. Haig obviously sees a book in the case; he's practically drooling. But I think he knows what he's doing. At least he got Fulton to open up to him."

"That's how you found the rest of Jessie—and her backpack."

Theresa paused and clutched the table. "I think we're having a little aftershock here. I hope. I mean, I hope it's a little one."

"I need a beer," Brian declared, heading into the kitchen. Theresa followed, looking pale.

"Maybe a tad of brandy?" Brian suggested.

Theresa nodded. "Throw a few ice cubes into it, will you?"

"I'm sorry, Theresa. I know this is a tough one for you."

"They're all tough."

"I mean, a young girl was killed...by her stepfather, who had been sexually abusing her for at least five years."

Theresa settled in a deck chair with her brandy. "Fulton confessed to that, at least. He seemed contrite. He led the deputies to where he had buried her body and her back-pack. Of course, he didn't bury the body deep enough, so almost everything but the head was dug up by animals." Theresa's voice began to sound remote, as though she were distancing herself from the grisly story she was telling. "The head was too heavy for the animals to carry away, so it was still pretty much intact."

Oh, God, Brian thought. "Where I found the stone."

"Yes. It *was* a grave, and Fulton had carved a crude sort of marker. The backpack was found nearby." Theresa took a long sip of brandy. "Brian, it's so pathetic. He really did love the kid, in the only way that he was able to love any-one."

"Perverted," Brian said. "Sick."

"Yes, perverted and sick. The guy's a nut case. But this wasn't a crazy, out-of-control crime. Fulton planned it all cleverly. He put the sort of stuff into Jessie's backpack that she would have taken if she had run away on her own. He buried the backpack some distance away from where he had put her body. Later, after he learned that Boy Scouts and other people were planning to search the area intensively, he started a brushfire—hoping, of course, to destroy any evi-dence that might remain."

"He told all of this to Dr.—who?"

"Haig. Terry Haig. But that's all Fulton would say."

"But Carole's body was found. He didn't confess to that?"

"No. We finally got a court order to drag Lake Chu-mash. Not the whole lake, of course, just the area under 'Lovers' Lookout.' It's the only high bluff that you can drive a car up to, and the water below it is deep. They found Car-ole's car down there, and what remained of Carole."

Brian sighed and swallowed. The bottle felt sweaty and substantial in his hand. "No evidence, of course."

"None. There wasn't much left of Carole. No way to do tox tests—barely enough left to establish who she was. The car held up a lot better than she did."

Both Brian and Theresa were silent for a time, perhaps reflecting on the fact that Lake Chumash supported a hungry population of largemouth bass, crappies, catfish, and ferocious turtles.

"What about the boy?" Brian asked. "I mean the other kid, Jason. The boy who was killed at track practice. Fulton did it; I know it! Jason was about to blow the whistle on the sainted track coach, wasn't he? I'll bet he threatened to go to the school board if Fulton didn't leave Jessica alone. The guy's teaching job would have gone down the tubes, at the very least. And other kids would have come out of the woodwork and told tales."

Theresa shrugged. "We've got nothing on that. And we never will have. Let it go, hon."

Brian took a swig from his bottle and emitted an inadvertent belch. "Theresa, the guy's whole facade would have crumbled if that story had come out—or rather facades, because everybody seemed to perceive Fulton differently. Look at how he conned Joanna—for years—into seeing him as a brilliant, sensitive writer and scholar. And maybe he is that. He's also a religious fanatic, to some. A tyrant, apparently, to his family. An unsophisticated ranch hand, to unexpected callers. I think Haig's probably right; Fulton may be a multiple personality. For sure, he's wacko. Did he tell Haig *why* he killed Jessica?"

Theresa shook her head. "Maybe he will, eventually."

"Well, my guess is that Jessie suspected that Jason's death was not an accident, and that she confronted her stepfather with her suspicions. And maybe threatened to go public herself. And Carole Fulton had to know that something was going on. She was not a dumb woman, by all accounts. Fulton knew he had to get rid of everybody who knew too much about him. He never cared about anyone except himself; he only pretended to care when doing so suited his purposes."

Theresa sighed and topped up her brandy glass. "This is Antioch, cum laude in sociology, speaking, right?"

"Okay, okay, but do you think I'm wrong?"

"No, not really. But Brian there's no evidence to connect Fulton with Carole's death, or Jason's. The girl who called me that night—the one who said she saw Fulton grab Jason behind the refreshment stand—never did come forward; we have no way of tracing her. And even if we could find her, and if she agreed to testify, she didn't actually see Fulton attack the kid."

Theresa sounded unutterably depressed. Brian realized that she was a little bit drunk. Well, maybe he was, too. Okay, so he could always bunk here, in a pinch. And Theresa was already home.

"Theresa—" Brian reached over, found her hand, and gave it a squeeze. "Look, we've got Fulton for Jessica; that's better than nothing, isn't it? And this doctor is never going to let Fulton loose, not while he sees him as a prize guinea pig. He'll be in the state hospital forever. Nobody's ever going to believe Fulton again. He won't be able to pull any more con jobs."

Brian gave Theresa's hand another squeeze. She squeezed back, weakly. He felt suddenly woozy. "Erm, Theresa . . ."

"Can you steer me to bed, Brian? Suddenly I think I'm about to fade." Theresa groped for her brandy glass and knocked it off the table.

"Gosh, I hope I'm up to it." Brian stood up shakily. "Are we having another aftershock?"

"I think so," Theresa said hazily. "Of a sort."

Brian planted his feet firmly, got a good grip on the sturdy redwood table, and picked up the brandy glass. "It didn't break," he marveled.

"Some things don't break easily," Theresa managed to enunciate. "I think you brether stay overnight."

"My sediments essackly." Brian grabbed for her arm and maneuvered them both into an upright position. "Good thing it's Sayerday night. No work tomorrow."

He aimed Theresa toward the kitchen and lurched around the deck, picking up dishes and glasses. Drunk was drunk, but it was important to remain orderly. He managed to deposit everything breakable onto the kitchen counter and turned on the faucets in the sink, preparing to scrape and rinse the plates. Sadie perched invisibly on his shoulder, tut-tutting.

"Take coupla asprins, Theresa," Brian mumbled as the garbage disposal gargled and gurgled. He realized that he was losing it, fast. "Where are asperns?" Oh, I'll be sorry tomorrow, he thought with whatever brain cells were still functioning. I will be so very sorry tomorry.

"You sleep in Jonny's room," Theresa said decisively. "Clean sheets. Assiprin in barthoom."

Brian made a conscious effort to focus his eyes on the dishwasher buttons, and pushed Start. He prepared to unload. It had been a long day. A long month. A long year. He was entitled. Wasn't he? But first he had better make sure that Theresa made it to bed okay.

Something nagged at the fringes of whatever consciousness remained to him—a subject he had meant to bring up with Theresa.

As he steered the lady carefully down the stairs, it came to him.

Mabel. Mabel *enceinte,* as the vet had confirmed.

"Tresa?" he ventured.

Although Theresa was technically still on her feet, she seemed to be snoring lightly.

"How wouldja like a coupla kittens?"

DEADSTICK
Terence Faherty

First Time in Paperback

AN OWEN KEANE MYSTERY

Why would a millionaire in his sixties, with no accusers to answer to or social ambitions to protect, move to reopen a forty-year-old scandal?

That's what ex-seminarian Owen Keane, an introspective, introverted, often idiosyncratic law-firm researcher is being paid to find out.

The firm has been discreetly retained by Robert Carteret, seeking answers to the mystery surrounding the plane crash that killed his brother and socialite fiancée. Now the archives are buttoned up tight, and Owen has to fall back on the gossip.

Following a cold trail of the dead, he finds something alive and almost forgotten—and threatening—as he winds his way backward to the players in the mystery: the murderer, the victim and the crime.

"Plenty of intellectual guts."—*New York Times Book Review*

Available in May at your favorite retail stores.

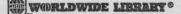

WORLDWIDE LIBRARY®

DEADSTICK

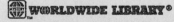